RED
HOT
Liar

Also by Noire

The Misadventures of Mink LaRue Series
Natural Born Liar
Sexy Little Liar
Dirty Rotten Liar

Lifestyles of the Rich and Shameless (with Kiki Swinson)

Maneater (with Mary B. Morrison)

Published by Kensington Publishing Corp.

RED HOT Liar

The Misadventures of Mink LaRue

NOIRE

Dafina BOOKS

KENSINGTON PUBLISHING CORP.
www.kensingtonbooks.com

DAFINA BOOKS are published by

Kensington Publishing Corp.
119 West 40th Street
New York, NY 10018

All Kensington titles, imprints, and distributed lines are available at special quantity discounts for bulk purchases for sales promotion, premiums, fund-raising, and educational or institutional use.

Special book excerpts or customized printings can also be created to fit specific needs. For details, write or phone the office of the Kensington Special Sales Manager: Kensington Publishing Corp., 119 West 40th Street, New York, NY 10018. Attn. Special Sales Department. Phone: 1-800-221-2647.

DAFINA and the Dafina logo Reg. U.S. Pat. & TM Off.

ISBN-13: 978-1-61773-491-5
ISBN-10: 1-61773-491-8
First Kensington Trade Paperback Printing: January 2015

eISBN-13: 978-1-61773-865-4
eISBN-10: 1-61773-865-4
First Kensington Electronic Edition: January 2015

10 9 8 7 6 5 4 3 2 1

Printed in the United States of America

This work is dedicated to my boo and my mini-boo! Belonging to you has taught me what true love is, and shown me that life really is worth living.

Acknowledgments

Thanks going up to the Father above for blessing me with a mind that allows me to write from my own creative pen. I'm sending big ups to my entire team! Thanks for keeping me in the space I need to be in and for looking out for me 24/7. Nisaa, Kelly, Black, Reem, Man, Ree, Missy, Jay, and all the rest, I see you and love you for everything you do.

To my loyal readers and friends in The Urban Erotic Tales Book Club on FB, I'm sending crazy lub to you guys for holding me down while I was off doing that thang. I have the best damn readers in the world and I'm gonna keep on saying it because it's true! Keep riding the train every time it pulls into the station because there are many more Flirty Dirties yet to come!

To Reem Raw, I see you with that New York State of Mine! Your pen is hot and your flow is beast. Thank you for mixing ink with me!

Lub y'all,
Noire

WARNING!

This here ain't no romance it's an urban erotic tale
Rival cliques and conniving tricks are sure to be unveiled!
Scandals, secrets, scams and leeches all begin to surface,
Pilar, Ruddman, and Selah's husband have reasons
to be nervous!
Mink and Bunni are living lovely but now they face
dilemmas . . .
Barron's blinded and Suge is forced to set his own agendas!
The Dominion clique is once again in sudden imminent
danger,
By faces known and close to home and even from
total strangers.
So welcome back and brace yourself and watch us
set this fire,
Because this *thot* is red and hot, but of course she's
still a LIAR!

CHAPTER 1

Started in the projects now I'm here! Now I'm here!

Yeah, the hard-knock hood life might take a Harlem girl down, but if she was slick with the lips and smooth with her groove, it damn sure couldn't knock her out!

Me and my rowdy Bowlegged Bunni Baines had come a long way from the run-down tenements of New York City, and if it was up to us we wasn't never going back! For a gritty con-mami turned club stripper who had spent her life swinging off poles and yappin victims for illicit loot, I was finally saying good-bye to my beloved con game and upgrading to the life of an heiress to a multi-billion-dollar fortune.

All those long days and nights of hustling, scheming, and conniving were over forever. With about nine hunnerd grand in my bank account and more pouring in every day, the whole world was at my fingertips and I had enough yardage to do whatever the hell rocked my boat!

It felt like a dream. A minute ago I was just a regular old Harlem girl. A broke-ass Club Wood headliner: crotch-polishing them golden poles and luring horny niggahs with my slinky slides and my notorious double-hump lap dances.

But then Bunni came home from the corner store with a carton of milk that was sporting my six-year-old face on the back, and suddenly my luck—and my life—straight up changed forever.

You see, Selah Dominion, the mama-bear in the stupid-rich Dominion Oil family of Texas, had gotten tipsy while on vacation in the Big Apple and lost her three-year-old daughter Sable outside of a Duane Reade drugstore. Eighteen years later she was still looking for the kid, and for Sable's twenty-first birthday Selah had offered a fat-ass bundle of reward money to anyone who could help find her.

Bunni had been hyped as hell when she spotted my age-progressed picture on the back of the milk carton, and some kinda way I let her convince me to catch a flight down to Dallas so we could hustle the Texas oil family out of Sable's inheritance and the reward money too.

"This lil mama is *you*, Mink!" my ghetto day one chick had sworn up and down as we eyeballed the pictures of the missing girl on the back of the carton. "I swear this chick is so you!"

"*Me*?" I had bucked on her real quick. "Heffah, *please!*" Me and Bunni went way, way back. She knew damn well I wasn't no missing heiress to no shit-load of money way down in no Texas! Hell, I was Harlem born and Harlem bred. From my rooter to my tooter I was a con-mami, a pole dancer, and if shit wasn't nailed down I could also be a big-ass thief.

Bunni had called the number on the milk carton and we almost checked out when they told her in order to get the money I'd have to take a DNA test and the results would have to match what was on file for little Sable Dominion.

"Forget about it," I had told Bunni. "It's a wrap, boo. The only damn DNA I got in me is from those lying-ass LaRues!"

But the lure of fifty grand in birthday cash was more duckets than us two broke bandits could possibly resist. Me and Bunni's ratchet little minds got to clicking and calculating like computers as we tried to come up with a ruse to swindle those mofos outta that dough. Bunni had back-rent due out the ass on her and Peaches's apartment, and I had some real major playas hounding me for some real major cash in Harlem's drug game. Getting our hands on a few racks was right up our alley. So, with visions of fitty thousand big ones dancing in our heads, we had flown down to Texas looking to pull a sweet little flimflam on a bunch of uppity rich niggas who were just a-swimming in cream.

We busted up on the scene during a Fourth of July barbeque and damn near set that whole mansion on fire! You shoulda seen the way I performed for them boojie-ass black folks. I was super slick with my con game, and I laid my brilliant make-money scheme down on them with sass and finesse! I didn't give a damn if the sisters and the brothers believed a word I said, with Big Daddy Viceroy laid up in the hospital in a deep coma, all I had to concentrate on was yanking Mama Selah's heartstrings as I lied out the ass and pretended to be her long-lost daughter, Sable.

To top the act off, freaky-butt Bunni hooked up with a pain slut at the DNA lab and got him to write a phony report saying my DNA was a match for the missing girl Sable. I ended up rolling fifty thousand deep in happy birthday heaven, and Bunni ended up getting twenty-five racks as a reward, and a few days later we hauled ass back to New York City with our pockets fat and full.

Well, you ever heard that saying, "Give a hoodrat a hunk of cheese and she'll gobble the whole thing up in one day"? Yeah, yeah, yeah. Easy come and easy the fuck go. By the time me and Bunni shopped our asses off, took us a vacation, got swindled by a slanga named Punchie Collins, and tried our hand at flipping dope, we were broke as hell again and right back where we started from.

We probably coulda handled all that, but when my ex boothang Gutta hit the bricks and came gunning for my throat, I had no choice but to get up outta Dodge, and where in the world was a Harlem hoodrat like me supposed to hide? Damn right. It was back to Texas time, where me and Bunni made plans to dig our grimy little fingers even deeper into the Dominion family pie.

It looked like this time everything was gonna go smooth and according to plan. Viceroy was about to kick the bucket, Mama Selah was hanging off my loose bra strap, and the rest of the family was practically eating outta the palm of my hand. I was *this close* to getting hold of a sweet three-hundred-grand annual payday when big brother Barron pulled a slick move and dragged some stink-ass Philly 'rilla named Dy-Nasty down to the mansion to toss her nasty weave up in my game.

Dy-Nasty turned out to be a ratchet-looking extra-gutter version of me, and to say that trick was a natural born liar wouldn't hardly be saying enough! Between the two of us thirsty heffas we got to scratching and biting and kicking and slapping, and doing whatever it took to get our hands on the Dominions' pot of gold. But when it was all said and done Dy-Nasty messed around and dipped her chips in the wrong damn bowl and ended up on lockdown, while me and Bunni claimed us a prime suite in the Dominion mansion and got ready to live La Vida Loca for the rest of our days!

Oh, what a joy it was to be a paid-out-the-ass chick like me! Rich, black, and beautiful! Damn right, I had it *made*, baybee!

CHAPTER 2

Viceroy Dominion was on a big one. The slick and ruthless Big Daddy of the Dominion Oil family was straight wildin' out in his plush corner office as he stared at the colorful image glaring at him from the large computer screen. The virtual box of Gurkha Black Dragon cigars were stacked like a pyramid, with three on each side and one sticking up prominently in the middle like it was screaming *fuck you, chump!*

But it was what was slid down on that "finger" that had him ready to reach in his desk drawer and grab his tool. It had him ready to jump in his whip and haul ass to the Omni Hotel and bust a cap in Rodney Ruddman's monkey-ass grill!

But first he was gonna handle his muthafuckin' wife. How in the *fuck* did that bastard get a hold of Selah's million-dollar engagement ring? Oh, Selah was about to explain that shit. She was gonna tell him how her precious ring, the one she claimed she had lost eighteen years ago, had ended up in his arch enemy's fuckin' hand!

A graphic vision of Ruddman ramming his black meat up in Selah as he held her pretty legs high in the air flashed through Viceroy's mind and he had to grip the desk to keep from passing the fuck out.

Enraged, he swung his arm in a wide arc and knocked the forty-inch monitor off his desk along with almost every damn thing else that was up there. Foaming at the mouth, he stomped his foot and crunched the hell outta their framed wedding photo that bore her smiling, deceitful face.

"That dirty rotten *liar!*" Viceroy screamed. He *knew* it. He knew that shit all down in his bones. While he was laid up in a coma for all those months Selah had been out there fucking that frog-faced bastard! Now that he was back on his feet and ready to roll she didn't wanna give *him* no pussy, but she'd been steady sucking Ruddman's dick and licking his balls!

Whirling around, he snatched a jewel-crusted photo from their Mediterranean vacation off the wall and hurled that shit across the room like it was a boomerang. It hit the far wall and exploded, and countless glass shards rained down on the floor.

"I'ma murder her ass!" Viceroy fumed as he kicked over a fifty-thousand-dollar Chinese vase and started snatching wooden plaques and awards off his shelf and flinging them at the tinted glass window. "I swear to God I'm gonna kill that bitch!"

There were rushing sounds of footsteps in the hallway and then his door belched open as several of his staff members burst into his office and swarmed around him, their frowning faces red with concern.

"Mr. Dominion!" His chief contractor and long-time friend Bob Easton grabbed him by the shoulders and held him firm. "What's going on in here? What's the problem, sir?"

"It must be his head injury," his elderly secretary cried out. "It has to be his head!"

"I'ma kill her!" Viceroy shrieked as he stared down at his toppled computer screen where the seven cigars were still screaming "fuck you" and mocking the shit outta him. "Y'all better hold me back," he hollered, "'cause when I get my hands on that grimy bitch I'm gonna fuckin' *kill* her!"

"Mr. Dominion!" His secretary trembled as she grabbed

hold of his arm. "Please sir, you'll be fine. Just don't say such things!"

"Get the hell off me!" He jerked his arm away so hard old Miss Ginny lost her balance and stumbled forward, then yelped as she landed hard on her brittle knees.

Ignoring her cries, Viceroy looked around wildly, searching for something else to throw. But when his staff fanned out around him so they could protect him from himself, Viceroy drew his hand back and threw a short, hard jab at the wall. Every bone in his knuckles screamed. The impact split his skin and a mist of bright blood sprayed from his hand in a wide arc.

"Oh, shit . . ." Viceroy moaned, ignoring the staff members who were pulling out handkerchiefs and rushing to his rescue as he damn near crumpled to his knees from the pain.

"That lying bitch!" he groaned and gasped. "Look at what she did. Just look at what the fuck she did!"

"Rise and shine!" It was the crack of dawn on a Monday morning and Bunni busted her tail up in my luxurious suite making all kinds of crazy noise.

"Hey now!" She plopped down on my bed, disturbing my groove. "You gonna be on TV today, Miss Rich-ass Domino! Wipe summa that slobber off the side of your lip and let's roll!"

Squinching my eyes tight, I raised my arms and stretched out in my luxurious Egyptian sheets ignoring Bunni as I fought back a satisfied smile.

Ever since I hit the once-missing-but-now-found jackpot I woke up in the mornings feeling like a real shady crook. Like I had just ganked somebody for their whole damn life. For *Sable's* life! Every night old broke-ass Mink from the projects went to bed just a' praying like hell that the super-turnt-up mansion, the shiny whips, the jewels, and especially the ocean-deep moolah wasn't some sorta crazy hallucination. And when the sun came up in the sky and I opened my eyes again—still rich and surrounded by all the luxury and finery a hood chick could ask for, I couldn't help feeling like a straight-up thief!

"I got a taste for some grits and bacon this morning," Bunni blurted in my ear. "And maybe some panny-cakes too. You want me to call the cook and tell her to bring Okrah's ace boon coon some grub, or are you gonna get up off ya royal ass and go downstairs and get it yourself?"

The news of my return to the Dominion family fold had been blowing up the airwaves. I mean that shit had made big-time headlines everywhere. It was the best rags-to-riches ghetto princess story in decades and the media ate that shit up. The word FOUND stamped over my smiling face was in every Internet news feed, not to mention all the newspapers and magazines between New York and Texas, and my name was ringing major bells.

The National Centers for Missing and Exploited Children had gotten a big boost in donations after that special milk carton campaign, and they quickly arranged for me, Selah, and Viceroy to go on a whirlwind media tour. We had already done some radio and a few television spots, and now they were calling for us to appear on *Good Morning America*, TLC, and *The View*, but first we had to get past Okrah Sinfree, who was coming to D-Town to blow up the spot live from the mansion.

Okrah was a white, southern-fried ratings diva who billed herself as a cross between Wendy Williams and Paula Deen. She was the queen of the south and had a real hot talk show and a nasty cooking show that white people amped out about, and with Viceroy's permission she was bringing a film crew to our crib to shoot a live segment about my miraculous return to the fold. The attention I was getting was real exciting and all that, but Bunni was ten times more hyped over that shit than I was.

"Get up, Mink!" she hollered, jumping all over my plush king-sized bed like she was two damn years old. "They're film-ing live, you know. Whatever comes outta your mouth is going straight into America's ear. So come on now. You only got a couple of hours to shake some of that ugly off ya face before all them cameras roll up in here."

"Owww!" I shrieked as Bunni jumped high in the air and landed hard on my shin-bone. "Sit your ass down, Bunni! Stop acting so damn ill! We ain't back in the projects no more, you know."

She snatched my pillow from under my head and cackled.

"You goddamn right we ain't! 'Cause if we was in the projects wouldn't nobody on the Oh-So-Sinful Network wanna hear shit you had to say! Now get up, Mink! You snooze you lose, boo, and you got a date with the Queen of the Dirty South today!"

I igged Bunni and rolled over on my stomach. I had gone to sleep with a big smile on my face after receiving a real sweet good-night sex-text message from my boo-baby, Suge. We had started out playing our roles with him as my so-called uncle and me fronting like I was his missing-from-a-long-time-ago niece. Suge was big and fine and powerful as hell. His massive build and his gangster swag put you in the mind of a cool, calm, and calculating killer. He was the enforcer in the family. The big homey behind the Dominion fortune. Whether shit needed busting up or burying deep, Suge was the nigga everybody called when the crack of their ass got hooked on a fence.

A flaming hot spark had flared up between us the very first time we met, and it wasn't long before we were deading all that "Uncle" shit and getting our undercover smash on. Hell, the Dominions had adopted their missing daughter Sable anyway, so even if I *was* her—like I had been tryna fool everybody into thinking—me and Suge still wouldn'ta been related by blood.

The real deal was, I had come down to Texas looking to gank the Dominions out of as much dough as possible. Falling on Suge and all that good ol' country sausage he was packin' just happened to be the icing on top of a thick hunk of cake.

The text message Suge had sent me late last night had been sexy as fuck and it promised to set the stage for the kind of x-rated showdown we was gonna have the next time we ran a horse race at the OK Corral. I pushed my face deep down in my pillow and squeezed my thighs together as I thought about his big ol' rough cowboy hands and the way he slung his monster pipe up in me like he was roping wild steer. Bunni was right, I thought as I shivered with excitement. I needed to get my horny ass up and get it in gear. For true, for true, I was amped about getting turnt up in front of the cameras with my rowdy Okrah, but on the real tip the best part of my day was gonna pop off tonight when I climbed on that chocolate bronco and got my guts busted open by my favorite black stallion, Big Suge!

CHAPTER 3

Selah Dominion stood in front of her floor-to-ceiling mirror dressed in a six-hundred-dollar bra and matching thong, along with an elegant garter set that had been hand-crafted in white lace. Bending over, she stuck her feet into her thigh-high stockings and then carefully pulled them up over her firm thighs. Pausing right below her crotch, she attached the edges of the stockings to the dangling garters and then stood back to scrutinize her firm, damn-near forty-eight-year-old body.

Not bad, not bad, she thought, turning to peer at her back. Her ass was still damned good, and her legs were holding too. Curvy, with defined muscle tone. She turned back around. Her breasts were high and full, and even after giving birth twice, her tummy was flat and her waist was tightly cinched in a sweet V.

She spritzed a light mist of designer perfume over her body, then carefully stepped into her five-thousand-dollar custom-made Vera Wang scribble lace dress and pulled the straps up over her shoulders.

Today was going to be a very special day. This afternoon she would be opening her home and playing hostess to the beautiful Okrah Sinfree, and not only did Selah want her mansion to look perfect and inviting, she wanted to be at her personal best as well.

With the arrival of Mink LaRue in their lives there had been more drama going down in the mansion than she could shake a stick at. Between Viceroy waking up from his coma with his old gangsta from the hood personality, and Mink's DNA coming back a perfect match to Sable's, not to mention all the drama Dy-Nasty Jenkins had kicked up when she tried to con the family and shake them down for a fortune, it had been a rough couple of months.

Drama! Drama! Drama!

Selah shuddered as she remembered how that Philadelphia gold digger had tried to blackmail her into giving up two million dollars to get her long-lost engagement ring back. And even after Selah had agreed to give her the money, the slick little ghetto troll had tried to double-cross her by leaving her nasty slum toe-ring sitting on her pillow instead of coughing up the real thing!

Selah had been too damn through as she stared at that disgusting piece of moldy green metal stinking up her goddamn pillow. All the Brooklyn had come rushing up out of her, and she had rolled out to the airport and put a grown-woman Bedford-Stuyvesant beat-down on that young girl's ass!

Just the memory of whipping Dy-Nasty's ass had Selah's face flushing hot, and she took a couple of deep breaths and fanned herself with the small square of cardboard that had come in the packet with her silk stockings. She didn't know if her sudden heat storm was from reliving the memory of that beat-down, or from a menopausal hot flash, but she was sure as hell on fire!

Calm yourself, she thought as she sought her inner peace. As a high-class socialite Selah carried herself like an elegant lady at all times. In fact, most people had never seen her when she wasn't poised and dignified, and she typically exuded sophisticated gracefulness with her every word and gesture.

And now, with her long-lost baby back in the fold, life was about to go back to normal around the mansion, and Selah for one, was looking forward to her peaceful reward.

"*Good afternoon, Ms. Sinfree.*"

Selah smiled gracefully and practiced her greeting in the mirror. But should she really call her Ms. Sinfree? Who did that? This was the south, and everyone called Okrah Okrah. Besides, she had just as much money as Okrah did. Probably even more.

"*Welcome to the Dominion Estate, Okrah. Please, make yourself at home.*"

Yes. That sounded much better. She flashed her fake smile in the mirror again and then nodded in approval. It was going to be a splendid afternoon, and Selah couldn't wait to get it started.

"Oooow, shit-shit-*shit!*" Viceroy winced in pain as he cradled his bloody fist in his lap. He had come to the office planning to get a little work done before heading back home to meet with Okrah Sinfree later in the afternoon, but now all that shit was a bust.

"That muthafucka!" He foamed at the mouth as he thought about the slimy tactics of Rodney Ruddman. Everybody knew Okrah would be airing live from his place today, and no doubt Ruddman had wanted to throw some shit up in his flow. "That bitch-ass muthafucka!"

"I know," his chief contractor Bob Easton said as he dabbed his friend's bloody knuckles. "This is the damnest thing but you gotta calm down so you can think clearly, Viceroy. You've got to calm *down.*"

Viceroy had been raging like a crazy bull in his office, smashing pictures, kicking furniture, punching the walls, and full-out tossing the joint up. Bob had rushed in to pluck him from the midst of his stunned and frightened staff, and had just ushered him down the hall to a private conference room that only a handful of executives in the entire building had finger-print access to.

And now, while Viceroy chugged gin straight out the bottle and bitched about his wife's bedroom fuck-outs, cool and steady Bob busied himself slathering antibiotic ointment on his boss's shredded knuckles and wrapping a tan-colored ace bandage around his fist as he spoke in low tones trying to still the beast that raged in Viceroy's chest.

"I swear I'ma kill that bitch, Bob," Viceroy panted and seethed. "So help me God, her black ass is *mine!*"

Bob nodded his understanding. At seventy-two he was an old head in the game of politics and Texas oil. He'd seen wicked women and fine wine take down even the most powerful of men, but he was a shrewd businessman first and foremost, and right now he needed Viceroy to pull his shit together and keep his game tight. He didn't give a damn where Selah had been lifting her skirt or who's dick she had been blowing from her knees, as a chief contractor, political advisor, and major stockholder of Dominion Oil he couldn't have the company's CEO melting down like a love-sick pansy and jumping off a cliff in public.

"I'ma choke her *out!*" Viceroy shrieked hoarsely, clutching his bottle of white lightning to his chest. "I'ma kill her!"

Bob nodded. "Oh, you might have to kill her," he agreed calmly, "but you can't do it on company time, and you definitely can't do it where our stockholders might get wind of it. Remember, son," Bob said, gently taking the bottle from Viceroy's grip and setting it on a low table, "matters like these of a personal nature can be very delicate. They make our stockholders and financiers very nervous so they must be dealt with discreetly and in private."

"Oh, I'ma do her in private," Viceroy fumed. "I'ma drag her ass behind a Dumpster in somebody's back alley and beat her brains the fuck out!"

Bob chuckled, his sagging cheeks bright and rosy. "You'll

do no such thing, Viceroy Dominion. As the richest black man in the oil business I predict you'll settle this matter with your dear wife Selah in the most respectable manner. I'm sure she has a perfectly good explanation that will satisfy all your burning questions. By this time tomorrow your little tiff will have blown over and you two lovebirds will be back in the saddle again."

Bob reached down and hitched up the knees of his expensive gabardine slacks and then sat down next to Viceroy. He crossed his leg and lit an imported Cohiba Behike Cuban cigar, then threw his arm casually over the back of the sofa.

"While we're chatting about stockholders and business, Viceroy, there's something I've been meaning to discuss with you."

Viceroy snatched the bottle from the table and took another swig, then looked up with his eyes flashing darkly. "Yeah, what's that?"

"Well, a couple of the fellas and I were playing the eighth hole down at the country club just the other day. We were discussing the new emission regulations and the downward trend in public opinion as it relates to the oil industry, and of course we were thinking about how we might get in on the inside so we can stop our profits from dwindling and possibly tanking completely out."

"Is that right?"

Bob nodded. "Yes. And ironically, that's when your name came up."

"Oh yeah?" Viceroy swigged again. "In what way?"

"In a way that influences public opinion."

He scowled and waved his hand. "What the hell do I have to do with public opinion, Bob? That pussy playa Rodney Ruddman talked my wife outta her drawers and her engagement ring when I can't even convince Selah to sit on my fuckin' lap! How am I supposed to sway the opinions of a bunch of stiff-ass honkies?"

Bob laughed. "I hate to be the one to tell you this," he drawled in his good-old-boy Texas twang, "but if you wanna stay rich you need those stiff-ass honkies a helluva lot more than you need that fine little wife of yours. Besides, the new drilling legislation is going to have a huge financial impact on the oil industry. That means my pockets and yours too are going to take a hit. Remember, those stiff-ass honkies vote."

"And?"

"And there's a chairmanship position about to come open at the Texas Railroad Commission. David Cooper's illness is terminal and he's stepping down immediately."

"From the Railroad Commission in Austin?"

"Technically yes, but there's no residency requirement so anyone can hold the office. The position oversees the regulatory council for oil, natural gas, and coal, and it guarantees the office holder the top seat on the Public Utility Commission Board and the state regulatory board too."

Viceroy smirked. "Yeah, well too fuckin' bad for Cooper. I'll send him a box of virtual hugs."

"Bad for Cooper, but perhaps good for us. The governor's going to appoint a temporary replacement to fill the rest of his term, and whoever gets it can run for the permanent position in the upcoming election. And that's in three and a half weeks."

Viceroy raised an eyebrow. "And?"

"And," Bob said, "we'd like you to put your name on the ballot and run for office."

"*Sheeit*," Viceroy snorted and picked up his bottle again. "You must be crazy. That old racist Rick Perry ain't gonna give me the nod for nothing big like that."

"He already did," Bob said calmly. "I spoke to him last night. He's willing to ink you into the slot for the next few weeks, and all you have to do is put your name on the ballot, get yourself elected, and become our inside man, Viceroy. We think you're the right person for the job. You can get in there and affect state legislation in favor of our business agenda and ensure we keep our cash flowing like oil, right into our pockets."

"*Me?*" Viceroy laughed and shook his head. "Fool, do I need to pull down my pants so you can see what shade of black my ass is? Nah, I ain't the one. You need a white boy for that."

"Nonsense!" Bob protested smoothly. "You've spent your entire life preparing for a role like this. You've chaired the Regional Power Committee and served on the Gas Committee too. Not to mention that you were nearly killed in an oil rig accident. You survived and spent months in a coma and endured endless rehab and you still bounced back on your feet! You're exactly the man we're looking for, Viceroy. Hell, if you ask me the state of Texas owes you one. The election's going to be tough, but the campaign will be very short. You've got a tear-jerking survival story that's perfect for these bleeding heart liberals, and we need their votes too! Besides, you're the head of the richest black family in Texas. That alone makes for a great public interest story and could help win over the hearts and minds of the specialty voting block."

Viceroy stopped slurping from his bottle and stared at the old man like he was smoking weed.

"Do you know how much crazy shit my family is going through right now, Bob? Didn't you just see me trash my whole damn office? My wife is a fuckin' floozy! My son's banging the shit out of his own cousin, my youngest daughter can't decide if she likes nuts or cooch, I got a crazy New Yorker trying to shoot a reality show in my living room, and a big-dicked cross-dresser named Peaches is flouncing around my house in a little pink skirt!" Viceroy shook his head and swiped his hand down his face. "And if all that don't fuck you up, Okrah Sinfree and her crew are gonna be at my house filming an interview this afternoon."

Bob counted off on his fingers. "Yes to Okrah, no to the reality show, and hell no to the queer guy. In fact, get rid of him right away!" he snapped distastefully. "It sounds like you've got a lot of cleaning up to do at home, but I believe it can be done. Truly, this is the perfect opportunity for a man like you, Viceroy. It's your time. This position is powerful and prestigious and you deserve to hold it. Who knows? It might lead to a federal appointment one day."

Viceroy still couldn't see it. "Man, Bob, I just tore up my whole fuckin' office! I smacked the shit out of an intern and scared the hell outta good ol' Ginny. A couple of leaked emails about that and I can kiss a whole lot of lily white votes good-bye."

"Nonsense!" Bob waved him off. "Remember, you've had a very severe head injury. Everyone expects these type of weird things to happen with you every now and then. Ginny's fine, so don't worry about her, and I'll make sure the intern gets a great job offer and a nice bonus too. All you have to do is agree to do it. Just get your household in order and say you'll run."

"Let me get a few days to think about it."

"We don't have a few days! The election is in three weeks. The deadline to submit your filing documents is in less than seventy-two hours."

"Seventy-two hours?"

"That's right. We need a quick decision here. If you say yes, I can have the necessary forms filed immediately."

Viceroy took a deep breath as his mind flitted over the possibilities. The only way he could truly fuck a big-time oil man like Rodney Ruddman up the ass was from a position of power. Political power. If he was the head of the state regulatory board not only would he have the power to give those in the oil business damn near everything they wanted, he'd have the power to take it all away too.

"Okay." He reached out to shake Bob's hand as he got ready to go home and clean house. "Bet. I'm in. Sign me up. I'll do that shit!"

CHAPTER 4

By the time me and Bunni got dressed and went downstairs for breakfast everybody in the mansion had already left for the morning except Selah, Fallon, and Peaches. Pilar had just showed up and she was standing by the stove looking hungry and waiting for a plate just like she'd been doing almost every morning for the past week.

"Damn! Don't they serve breakfast over at her house?" Bunni smirked and whispered as we rolled our eyes and brushed past her and sashayed into the dining room looking fly as fuck. Bunni had on a sexy little pale peach romper with some slutty high heels in almost the exact same shade. She had pulled her gorgeous dreads up into a big ponytail at the top of her head, and the curly reddish ropes spiraled outta control in all different directions.

I was playing it cute today. Mizz Mink Minaj was flossing big time in some bright red Birthday Cake shorts and a bone-white sleeveless t-shirt with little red kissing lips all over the front. I had washed my hair in the shower and rubbed some gel through the ends, and now I was letting it air-dry into tight little spiral curls.

"Hey now!" Me and Bunni busted up on the scene bringing mad energy into the room with us. The air was already buzzing with excitement and I could tell everybody was amped over Okrah's visit that afternoon, especially Selah.

We asked Mrs. Katie for a bowl of grits and a plate of bacon and eggs, then we sat down at the huge table where Peaches was cuttin' the fool and blabbing to Selah and Fallon about the day he rescued me from a moldy room downtown in New York City's clothing district where my psychopath criminal ex-boyfriend named Gutta had tried to kill my ass.

"Oooh, you shoulda *been there*, Miss Selah!" Peaches cracked up with his long-lashed eyes glinting with excitement. "Gutta is a real booty clencher! That crazy nigga snatched Mink up outta her own mama's funeral! He threw her in the back of a limo and took the hell off! If I hadn't followed them and busted up in that room to save her, ain't no telling what that vicious murderer woulda done to her."

"Really?" Selah exclaimed, staring into his grill like my ass had starred in an episode of Forensic Files.

He rolled his eyes and pursed his glossy lips. "Errrm herrrm. He prolly woulda choked her or stabbed her . . . I know for damn sure we wouldn't be sitting here talking about it right now."

I watched as Selah put her lil petite hand on top of Peaches's big rusty one and smiled. "Well, thank God for you, Peaches. I'm grateful for all you've done for my daughter over the years. Lord knows she probably wouldn't be here without you."

You got that shit right, I sniggled under my breath. Selah just didn't know. Chief Master Grifter Peaches had taught me everything I knew about hustling and ganking. From picking pockets to running con schemes, I owed every inch of my grime game to Peaches Baines, and if it wasn't for his ass then me and Bunni never woulda made it down to Texas to steal Selah's money in the first damn place!

"Yeah, honey," Peaches kept going on and on. He was sitting there in a giant lime-green skirt and batting his false eyelashes as Mrs. Katie walked around serving us our meals. "Mizz Mink done had all *kinds* of close calls and misadventures. Did she ever tell you about the time the cops arrested her in the Bronx on Gun Hill Road and took her down to the station? Man, by the time I got over there to get her Mizz Mink had the whole joint rocking! I mean, she put on a show up in that hizzle! She was standing on a table working her double hump game so hard that even the chief of police was sweating and screaming her name."

Peaches beamed proudly and grinned. "I mean that girl got some real skills about herself. One time she had this old guy from City Hall feening over her *harrrd . . .*" He covered his mouth and giggled. "Mink wouldn't even let him smell it until he agreed to tap into her computer file and delete all of her old warrants and . . ."

I zoned Peaches right on out as him and Selah cracked up at some of the crazy messes I had gotten myself into. At one point in time I woulda felt some kinda way about Peaches busting me out and telling Selah all my bizz, especially with Pilar's floppy ears listening in, but there wasn't no more shame in my game because I'd already peeped Mama Selah's hoe card and she had some bony-ass skeletons in her closet too! Besides, now that I was all up in the family and they couldn't kick me out, who cared what they thought about me? Hell, my moolah was sitting in the *bank* now, and it didn't even matter if the Dominions got their hands on them old videos of me humping on a snake and giving lap dances to them four cockeyed midgets. I was paid out the ass and I was my own damn boss, and there wasn't a damn thing from my grimy past that I had to worry about coming back to haunt me ever again! Nope, thanks to good luck and even better scheming, I was set for life. All I had to do was stay slick, rich, and black, and everything was gonna be everything!

★   ★   ★

Viceroy swigged the last drop out of his miniature bottle of gin as his plush whip rolled up the long, manicured driveway. He had polished off at least six of the little shots since leaving his office, and he was good and tight as his driver stopped right outside the door to his multi-million-dollar mansion.

Rage bubbled just under his skin as he rolled down his window and flung a handful of the empties out. They landed in Selah's precious patch of rose bushes and disappeared as they fell down toward the thorny stems.

"Take that, you ol' tramp!" he slurred, flinging open the door of his limo before the doorman could rush over. He had given his old crony Bob his word that he would run for office, but he hadn't promised a goddamn thing when it came down to putting his foot in Selah's ass.

He fell out of the ride, then pushed past the doorman and busted through the front entrance of the mansion like he was about to pull a kick-door and lay everybody in the joint down.

Stumbling into the foyer, Viceroy heard sounds of female laughter coming from the dining room. He was gonna fix these cutthroat mothafuckas! All of them. They were sitting around his house spending up his damn money and stabbing him in his back at the same damn time. He was gonna show their ungrateful asses who was running shit up in his house, he thought as he jetted toward the voices with his liquor talking to him real loud. He was about to kick some ass and take some fuckin' names!

When he busted up in the dining room Selah, Mink, Pilar, Bunni, and that over-grown monstrosity who called himself Peaches were sitting around the table yakking their jaws. Every eye bucked and every lip paused as the big black demon that was Him filled the doorway and trembled with rage.

"What's the matter, Papa-Doo?" Bunni shouted when she saw the crazy-ass look on his face, but Selah was much quicker and wiser than the young hood rat and she didn't say a god-damn thing.

Instead, her chair scraped backward as she jumped to her feet, just one glance at the sparks shooting from her husband's eyes enough to send her Brooklyn survival instincts kicking into over-drive.

"You dirty *bitch!*" Viceroy cocked back his bandaged fist and roared as everybody at the table got to scrambling out of their seats.

"How'd that muthafucka get your ring?" he bellowed at his wife. "How in the hell did Rodney Ruddman get your muthafuckin' *ring*???"

Selah's mouth fell to the floor as her eyes bucked open wide.

He knew! Dear God up in Heaven, Viceroy knew!

"What in the world are you talking about?" she closed her mouth and played it off real cool, even though her heart had plunged deep down into her bowels. She stared at him with an innocent look on her face and tried her best to sound clueless, but she'd known what time it was the moment she peeped the murderous ghetto look in her husband's eye.

"Your *ring, whore!*" Viceroy screeched. "That black bastard sent me a picture of your old engagement ring today, Selah. So how'd he get it? You must've been damn near in his lap for him to get it off your goddamn finger, huh?"

"That's ridiculous!" she waved him off. "I don't know what the hell you're talking about, Viceroy!" Selah fronted, bluffing for the kids's sake. She pointed her finger at him like a Brooklyn girl. "And don't you call me out of my name either, dammit! Just calm yourself down and get a grip right now!" she said, trying to gain the upper hand. "You and Rodney Ruddman must be playing some real sick pissing games because nobody took my ring off my damn finger!"

"Games my ass! Then how'd he get it, goddammit?" Viceroy demanded, panting hard as he walked up on her with raging bloodshot eyes. "Where'd you say you lost it at again?" he mocked, cupping his hand behind his ear. "What was that? You dropped it in my worst enemy's drawers?"

"Viceroy." Selah sighed and shook her head like he was talking out of his ass. "That doesn't even make any sense, honey! You've been drinking, dear. Come on. Let's go upstairs and talk about this. Maybe you can take a little nap and—"

"Tell the truth! You been fuckin' that ugly black bastard, Selah?" he growled, ignoring her noise and creeping up on her as he got ready to make his move. "I plucked your ass outta the grimy gutters of Brooklyn when you didn't have nothing but two pairs of panties and a raggedy slip to your name, and this is how you do me?"

"No!" Selah shrieked, her cool all gone as she stumbled backward in terror. "I swear to God I've never betrayed you, Viceroy! Never!"

Fallon rushed forward and tried to jump between her parents like a barrier, but Viceroy was hood-slick and he faked right and darted left as he jetted toward Selah. Peaches had already jumped up and was coming at him too, but Viceroy crossed him over and broke his ankles and Peaches went down like a tall tree in those ugly lime green heels he had on.

"Mr. Dominion, please!" Mrs. Katie hollered from the other side of the table where she was still holding a hot pot of grits, but Viceroy didn't even hear her. His mind was locked on getting him a piece of Selah's ass, and nothing and nobody was gonna stop him.

Until he ran smack into Mink and Bunni, that is.

"Put 'em up!" Bunni challenged, jumping in front of Selah and going into a boxer's stance. "First name Bunni, last name Mayweather!" she said, popping her neck twice as her and Mink posted up strong, ready to go toe-to-toe.

"Get the fuck outta my way!" Viceroy screamed and lunged drunkenly, swiping at Selah and missing so bad he almost fell dead on his face.

"Pound for pound, nucka!" Bunni hollered, squaring up

like a champ. "You swing them paws on Mama Selah and we gone hafta go pound for pound!"

The gutter streets of Houston rose up out of Viceroy and he lunged again, falling forward and knocking the hell out of both Bunni and Mink. He heard their Harlem battle cries and felt their blows raining down on his back and head, but getting his hands around Selah's throat was the only thing on his drunken mind.

He rose up and groped for her in the middle of the fighting pile, and he was just about to clamp down on her when Mink jumped on his back and wrapped her arms and legs around him like a little monkey. The four of them went down to the ground again tussling and scrapping, with fists flying everywhere.

Viceroy lunged forward and got his mitts on Selah and managed to twist her around backward and clamp his arm around her throat. She dropped her chin into the V of his elbow and tried to bite him through his shirtsleeve, and he yanked her by the hair then squeezed his arm tight until he was strangling her neck.

A moment later he was jerked violently backward himself and something got tight around his own damn neck. Windmilling in reverse, Viceroy lost his footing and fell on his ass, landing dead in his attacker's lap and taking Selah down with him.

"Get offa her!" Peaches's deep voice boomed in his ear as he choked the shit out of him. "Un-ass her right now, muthafucka! Un-ass her!"

The three of them were laid out on top of each other like a stack of slid pancakes. Peaches was at the bottom of the pile with his skirt hiked up to his waist yoking the shit out of Viceroy, and Viceroy was cradled between the big man's naked thighs yoking the shit outta Selah.

Pilar was watching the fight like she wanted some popcorn. Bunni and Mink were on their knees cursing like guttersnipes and throwing crazy punches at his face and head, and when Viceroy saw a big one coming straight at him, he pushed his ass deeper into Peaches's crotch and yanked Selah up in front of him like a shield.

Pop!

"Owwww!" Selah's knees flew up and she shrieked in pain as Bunni's fist smacked into her eye, dotting that shit.

"Ow! Ow! Ow! That *hurt*, Bunni!"

Even with Peaches choking the shit outta him Viceroy found the strength to open his mouth and laugh, but then he closed it again when another fist came flying at him and this one he couldn't duck.

Splat!

Viceroy shrieked. Suddenly he was stone-cold sober as pain exploded in his bad eye, the one that had been swollen up bigger than an egg after the oil rig blast. He saw bright lights and he saw stars. He saw bursts of lightning and a rocket flare went off deep inside his pupil. The pain was so bad he saw a kaleidoscope of shapes and colors in the brightest and most agonizing images possible.

He saw all that shit and more, but what he heard was the voice of his youngest daughter as she stood over him with her fist cocked back and ready to bust the shit outta him in his other eye.

"Back up, Boy-o! You want another one? Get your god-damn hands off my mother! I hope she *did* mess around on you because you ain't shit, Daddy! You ain't shit!"

"Fallon?" Viceroy said incredulously as he loosened his grip on Selah and came back to his senses. "Baby girl?"

Fallon's twisted lips and the anger in her eyes did something to Viceroy that really messed him up. Pushing Selah out of his lap, he glared at Mrs. Katie and snapped his fingers twice.

"Go get me two servants. Two men! Tell them to grab some big baskets and bring them up to my suite. Now!"

He pushed himself up on his knees with a look on his face

that none of them had ever seen before. His eyes raked over the room and scorched everybody as they swept by.

"*You!*" Viceroy turned and pointed at Peaches with pure disgust shooting out of his pupils. "I want your frilly ass the *fuck* outta my house! You hear me? Walking around here with ya balls dangling and ya dick print showing all through your skirt! I'm giving you one goddamn week, you hear me? One week and your ass better be *gone!*"

"But Papa Doo!" Bunni wailed. "Peaches ain't even do nothing! Selah and Fallon are the ones you mad at! Please, please, please, don't take it out on my *bruvah!*"

Viceroy wasn't even trying to hear it.

"Out!" he yelled, pointing toward the door. "All of y'all! Out!"

"B-b-but what about Okrah?" Selah squeaked, holding her eye. "She'll be here in a couple of hours! They're filming from our garden today!"

"*Fuck Okrah!* She can get the fuck out too!" Viceroy screamed as he stumbled to his feet and cast his hands over the entire lot of them. "Out, out, get the fuck *out!*"

CHAPTER 5

"Please honey, I swear!" Selah pleaded, stumbling behind her husband as Viceroy stormed through her closet stripping all her designer gear off the hangers. Instead of her being the boss bitch up in the joint and pulling all the strings, the tables had suddenly turned and now she was the one caught with her hand in the cookie jar.

"I swear to God I don't know how Rodney Ruddman got my ring! There's got to be some rational explanation for it," she lied, "but I swear on my dead mother's grave I didn't give it to him, baby. He didn't get it from *me!*"

Viceroy moved through their suite like a hurricane with the two male servants following him silently and holding a pair of extra-large baskets in their hands.

"Viceroy, please don't do this!" she cried out as he ripped at her ten-thousand-dollar dresses and flung boxes of her precious jewels around like they were Cracker Jack trinkets. Their fight had been hella nasty. After leaving poor Fallon downstairs crying uncontrollably, Selah had raced up the stairs behind Viceroy as he called for two male servants and stormed up to their bedroom suite.

"Your ass gots to go," he growled as he filled up basket after basket, tossing her shit inside in big heaps. "You gots to get the fuck up outta here!"

For the first time in her married life Selah felt real fear. "W-w-where are you taking all my stuff, Viceroy? Where do you want me to go? Do you want me to move downstairs? Would you like me to put my things in another suite?"

"Hell no!" he spit. "I want you out the *door*! You ain't staying not one more night under my goddamn roof, Selah! Take your ass out there to the pool house!" he demanded. "You can stay out there while I decide if you're *ever* gonna be good enough to crawl up in my bed again!"

"Oh really?" Selah turned down her lip and hit him with a blast from the past. "I didn't pack up your shit when I caught my sister on her knees in your goddamn office! You must've forgotten how that low-down bitch sucked your dick!"

Viceroy's eyes got wide as he thought about the best head he had ever gotten in his life. "Oh I ain't never forgot that shit! I ain't gonna never, *ever* forget that shit!"

"Viceroy!" Selah sobbed, knowing the pain and humiliation of what she was about to face was going to be way too much for her to bear. "But are you seriously putting me *out*, baby? I'm your wife and you're putting me out of our home?"

"You shoulda thought about whose wife you were when you decided to climb your ass in the sack with that grisly bastard Ruddman!"

"I didn't—" Selah started to lie again but then changed her strategy. "What about Fallon? You scared the hell out of her, Viceroy! Her and Jock are supposed to be flying out to their young leaders' camp today and instead she's downstairs crying her eyes out because of you! And what about the rest of the kids?" she wailed. "What are they gonna think when they find out you put their mother out of her home and forced her to go live in some wretched-ass pool house!"

"The kids?" Viceroy whirled around and glared like her tears didn't faze him one damn bit. "The goddamn kids are *grown*, Selah! If they got a problem with what I do in my house then they can carry their asses out to the pool house right along with you! Matter fact," he said with a dark, crazed glint in his eyes. "I'm about to tighten up my will and put the brakes on all these muthafuckas who been up in here milking my nuts! I'm about to cut every damn body off, so the kids better learn how to start scrapping for their *god*damn selves!"

That there shut Selah right the hell up. Viceroy wasn't bullshitting. He had never in his maddest moments threatened to cut all his kids off financially before, and if he could do that to them then Selah knew exactly what he could do to her.

"Baby *please*," she tried one more time. "I understand you're upset and you don't have a lot of faith in me right now. But do you have to go about it like this, Viceroy? Isn't there some other way we can work this out?"

The ice-cold smirk on his face damn near cut her heart in two, and with tears of shame running down her face she hung her head and followed the servants—and all her shit—out to the pool house.

Barron Dominion's muscular ebony body was drenched in sweat. He bench-pressed two hundred seventy pounds of free weights as he tried to quiet his raging mind and burn off some stress. His headphones were blasting a Yo Gotti cut that fueled him to push past the pain in his muscles and embrace the steady burn. Ever since he could remember he had been a thinker and planner. From the time he was a kid he had over-analyzed every detail of every situation from the top to the bottom, and then took it back up to the top again.

In most cases having such a razor-sharp mind was a great thing to possess, and he could remember quite a few times when his ability to think his way out of a box had saved his ass from a burning hot fire. But sometimes all that thinking could put you in a bad spot. It could overload a dude's brain and fuck with all his circuits.

Right now he was thinking that ever since Mink had busted up on the scene funking things up, life in the Dominion Estate had gone to the dogs. She might've been his sister but it was hard to forget about all the grimy lies she'd told and the underhanded schemes she'd pulled trying to get her ass next to that inheritance money. And it was even harder to believe that even after all the low-down con artist shit she'd been running, he had still wanted to bang her sexy lights out from every position possible.

The truth was, he still had some major issues with the girl. Even though he had promised his mother he would be a real brother to her, he just wasn't feeling the ratchet flavor that Mink had added to the Dominion family stew. She was a big shit stain on the smooth, respectable family image that Viceroy had spent his whole life building, and nowadays every which way you looked the Dominion brand was totally out of order. The last few months had stressed his mother out so bad that she had picked up the bottle and started back sipping again, and his father had awakened from his coma and come home acting like a hotheaded thug who was still scrambling for respect on the streets of Houston.

Barron knew he couldn't put the blame on Mink for everything that had gone down, but she was damn sure responsible for a big part of it. He was cool with the fact that she really was his long-lost sister Sable, but he couldn't stand all the drama and disorder that had come down on the entire family and seemed to follow her wherever she went.

He shook his head. The girl was just like a project roach. Them suckers never traveled alone. Thanks to Mink and her entourage they had more hood niggas living under the Dominion roof than a little bit, and if he'd thought Mink's sidekick Bunni was a fooligan, she was a lightweight compared to her flamboyant brother Peaches.

Barron grimaced as he set the bar in the rack and sat up with his entire shirt soaked. He was about fed up with all the bullshit, and if something didn't give in the Dominion household he might just blow his top.

When his father had gotten hurt in that oil rig blast, it was Barron who had taken over as the man of the house, and he had kept things running with an iron fist too. He had stepped into Viceroy's big shoes as the CEO of Dominion Oil and he'd filled those suckers up without missing a beat, if he had to say so himself.

Yeah, Barron thought as he stood up and stretched his hamstrings to get ready for his dead lifts, he could admit that the clout and notoriety that came with such a high-powered position might have swelled his head up a little bit while his father was gone. That type of dominance and authority over a multi-billion-dollar company and its personnel was exactly the type of job Barron had been born to do. But when his father woke up and started bitching about the way he had handled things without giving up any props or even so much as a thank-you for keeping everybody's head out of water, it had left Barron pissed off and more than a little bit offended.

He needed his father to know that stepping into a job like that hadn't been easy. Shit had gotten real tight a couple of times and even now Barron couldn't believe he had messed around and got caught in a sucker move when somebody slipped a tab in his drink at a frat party. It had been one of the worst nights of his whole fucking life, and before it was all over he had driven around town drunk as hell, hit a little kid, crashed into a bunch of cars, and had his mugshot snapped wearing lipstick and a mini-skirt.

If it wasn't for Suge, Barron's nuts could've been crushed in a vise grip for the rest of his miserable fuckin' life, and he thanked God that his uncle was the type of dragon-slaying nigga who could slump the boogey-man and make a nightmare disappear.

"*Grrahhhhh!*"

Barron grunted and exhaled as he bent over and picked up

the heavily weighted bar then straightened his legs and came to an upright stand. He was punishing himself with the weights, but feeling the physical pain was better than feeling the restlessness and the resentment that was weighing heavy on his chest. He didn't deserve all the cheap gut shots Viceroy had been throwing at him, and he damn sure shouldn't have handed over the reigns to Dominion Oil to a man whose head was still fucked up and whose judgment was suspect.

From the outside looking in, Barron knew he looked like the type of dude who had it going on. As a successful black attorney who was a member of one of the most powerful families in Texas, he was living the kind of life that a lot of men would have killed for. But it wasn't the shiny cars, or the hand-tailored clothes, or even the beautiful women that motivated him anymore. None of that came close to the thrill of power he had felt when he was in complete control of his father's empire. And now that he'd gotten himself a nice big bite of that power he missed the shit out of it, and he knew he had to get it back again. Some way, some fuckin' how. He had to get that feeling back again.

Consumed with his desire to guide Viceroy's money-making machine into future glory, Barron grabbed his cell phone and water bottle and went over to the treadmill to get some cardio work in. He returned the nods of a few people who he saw there regularly, knowing none of them recognized him or realized that he was the heir to a multi-billion-dollar throne.

Barron set the treadmill to the steepest uphill incline and dug in and pushed his body as hard as it could go as his legs flew and he imagined himself running to the top of a mountain and screaming, "*I want my spot back! I'm not my goddamn father! I'm my own fucking man! My time is now and I'm going to seize my moment! I'm Barron Dominion, bitches, and I will not be denied!*"

The sight of his cell phone flashing in a distinct pattern brought him tumbling down from the mountaintop with a quickness. He slapped the emergency stop button on the tread-mill panel and snatched it up.

"Ma? What's wrong, Ma?" Barron frowned as he pressed his phone to his sweaty ear. Selah was on the other end crying and babbling so hard that he could barely make out a word she was saying.

"What do you mean Pops put you out? Put you out of where?" Barron's face was pinched as he listened for a few short moments.

"He put you out of the house? Out of *our* house? What are you talking about, Ma? The *pool house*? Are you fuckin' serious? Pops kicked you out of your bedroom and put all your stuff in the pool house? Where is he?" Barron demanded. "Put him on the goddamn phone!"

Barron fell quiet as Selah let loose with another barrage of tears and shrieks. He picked up enough of what she was saying to figure out that Viceroy had already gone back to the main house and that his mother was alone in the pool house crying her heart out.

"It's okay, Mama. Don't cry. Please don't cry. Just hold on, Ma. Let me call Daddy and then I'll call you right back. Don't worry, we'll get this straightened out and I'll get you back inside the house. You know how he's been acting ever since he woke up. The doctors warned us he might get crazy sometimes, remember? It's his head injury," Barron soothed her. "It's not you or anything you did wrong, Mama. It's just his head injury, that's all."

Barron closed his eyes and nodded several times as he listened to Selah babble. "Okay, okay. I understand. Just let me handle it, Ma. I'll have you back in the house in no time, I promise. Just let me handle it."

Muthafucka!

Barron picked up his water bottle and hurled it against the wall. Ignoring the startled looks from the other patrons, he dug down in his sock for his car key and then stormed toward the front door in a rage. He couldn't believe it! That nigga actually put his mother out of her own goddamn house? His father was trippin! He was out of his goddamn mind! That bastard had gone too far this time!

Way too goddamn far!

CHAPTER 6

"Girl, did you see that *bull*shit?" I said as we peeped out the back window and watched Viceroy and the servants drag Selah's shit across the yard toward the pool house. I knew Bunni's eyes had seen the exact same thing that mine had seen, but my eyes just couldn't hardly believe it!

"That muthafucka!" I hissed. "Who the fuck is he to call her a hoe and put her out back in the pool house like that?" I bitched like the ritzy-ass pool house wasn't ten times the size of our old crib back in Harlem.

"Um," Bunni said like shit was real obvious, "he would be the owner of this damn mansion, that's who he is!"

I frowned as I shook my head. "Well, did you see the look in his eyes when he busted up in the dining room accusing Mama Selah of fucking out? Good thing he wasn't packin' no blicky on him 'cause that fool looked like he was on a bang-bang mission for sure."

"Naw! Girl, stop. You really think Daddy-Doo is the type a' maniac who could roll up in the cut and spray a joint?"

"Hell yeah, if his hood ass got mad enough! Bunni please! You from Harlem just like me, girl. We done seen plenty a' harmless-looking niggas get loose with the tool. What kinda dumb-ass question is that?"

Viceroy had truly scared the shit outta me and I'd practically had a flashback when he started wildin' like he was gonna lay the whole house down. I'd been caught up in some deadly dealings with murderous thugs like Moolah, and Punchie Collins, and that cray-cray nigga Gutta too, so I'd seen that look in plenty of dudes' eyes. It was usually right before they wrapped their hands around my throat and started choking the hell outta me.

"Girl, what are we gonna do?" I frowned as I watched Viceroy hurl the last basket of Selah's clothes into the pool house and then storm across the lawn and head back into the mansion. "How in the hell are we gonna convince Viceroy to let Mama Selah sleep in here tonight?"

Bunni cut her eyes at me. "We? What you care about where that old bird lays her head at, Mink? I mean, she *did* have a fuck buddy and she *was* fuckin' out, wasn't she? So why in the ho-ho are you so worried about Selah?" she demanded. "The hustle is over and you got the duckets now, baybee. Why you still all on her tip like that?"

"Who said I was on her tip?" I smirked. "Mama Selah ain't no jump-off, Bunni, he *wifed* her ass! I just don't think he shoulda put her out like that. And what about Peaches? Viceroy said Peaches had to go too."

Bunni poked out her bottom lip and narrowed her eyes. "My bruvah ain't going *nowhere*! Papa Doo can kill all that noise because Peaches ain't leaving this house!"

"And what about *Okrah*?" I said real loud. "I hope Selah can still do the damn interview this afternoon!"

Bunni twisted her lips. "I don't see how with that big old black eye Viceroy made me give her—but I'm down to take her place and get my chat on with Okrah if you need me to. Hell, my ass is dying to be on TV! I want all them old funky-

breath scrippers and hoes down at Club Wood to see us on
they big flashy screens! What good is having a mansion and a
hunnerd thousand whips if you ain't gonna flaunt that shit?
That's why I been on this reality show grind so hard, Mink. So
we can be on TV."

I poo-poo'd that nonsense and waved my hand. "Being on
television ain't everything, Bunni. We didn't creep up on all
this money just to turn into somebody's cable whores! I ain't
wit' it!"

"But why not, Mink? Stunnas like us was born for the camera! Besides, I'm *always* down for your whatevas! Any damn
thing you wanna get into I'm ya roady and I got your back. So
why you don't never wanna be down for me, Mink, huh?"

"It's not like that—"

Bunni cut me off and laughed. "Girl, please, you going on
Okrah, boo! Okrah *Live*! Is you gonna tell her about that time
the toilet overflowed upstairs and we stole an old box of her
thick-ass magazines and used them to soak up all that nasty
water?"

I rolled my eyes. "Bunni, please. Hell no I ain't gonna tell
her none of that! Is you crazy?"

She cracked up. "That was a shitty mess! Remember how
we got mad 'cause every single cover had a picture of Okrah
on the front?"

I nodded and giggled. "And those shits were thick as hell?"

"Like telephone books!" Bunni howled.

"And remember all that nasty-looking white-people food
she cooked on her show the other day?"

Bunni squinched her face up. "*All* her shit be looking nasty!
People be sharing her recipes on Facebook trying to feed her
shit to they farm animals and even the pigs won't eat it!"

"I know that's right!" I screeched.

"See there, Mink?" she said happily. "You about to have your
little shine in the spotlight so why can't I have minez too?"

I sighed. Bunni was right. I could dig what she was saying

and any other time I woulda been flouncing my ass on the national TV tip with her. But I was starting to feel some kinda way about the Dominions, and after all the hustles and the hassles I had been through tryna get on, I was comfortable in my lil spot and I wasn't tryna rock no boats. I'd seen enough of those reality shows to know what kinda fuckery and foolery that grind required, and I wasn't gonna put myself out there and embarrass the family name like that. I just wasn't!

For one thing, Viceroy was never gonna let no film crew get up in his grill and tell all the family bizz, and for another thing I had Suge to think about too. My dude was rich and powerful and he commanded big respect. He coulda had him any type of woman he wanted, but he wanted *me*. Not the old me, but the new me. And I wanted his ass too.

"Yeah, I'll think about it," I lied and turned away so I didn't have to see the hurt look on my girl's face.

Bunni stomped her feet behind me and sucked her teeth. "C'mon now, Mink! What in the hell is there to think about? We from Harlem, baybee! We get it in! This is who we are and what we do, heffa! *Remember?*"

"For real though," I muttered again and waved her off. "I said I'll think about it."

That ugly bastard! Selah sniffled and cupped her swollen eye as she stood in the tiny bedroom of the pool house gripping her cell phone. She had just called Barron and told him what a monster his father had been to her, and now she stabbed at Rodney's number for the tenth time in less than three minutes and listened as once again his phone went straight to voice mail.

Selah cursed under her breath as she clicked off the call and flung the phone down on the dresser. She couldn't believe that bastard had outed her! That he'd had the nerve to send Viceroy a picture of her ring! What in the world could that fool have been thinking? Didn't he know who he was fucking with?

With fresh tears trickling down her cheeks and her lips pinched tightly together, Selah looked around at the junky piles of her personal belongings that were scattered on the floor where Viceroy had tossed them. Deep humiliation washed over her and she bit her lower lip to stop herself from crying out in shame.

Getting put out of her own damn house was a nightmare she could have never imagined in a million years. She felt like a hoodrat. Like a common piece of project trash. All these years she'd spent building herself a prissy-clean image of a classy socialite just to have a bucket of mud slung on her right in her own kitchen. Viceroy had showed his natural black ass in front of her daughters and her trusted staff, and getting marched out the door past her servants and assistants with her ass dragging and her eyes downcast had filled her with the utmost embarrassment.

And all for a piece of revenge dick! she reminded herself.

How could she have been so stupid? Getting back at Viceroy for screwing her younger sister had been the worst idea of her life, Selah had to admit. Especially when she stooped so low as to jump in the sack with his arch-enemy Rodney Ruddman. Damn right they had been fucking like bandits! Little did Viceroy know, but that little frog-faced Ruddman had sucked her toes, pounded her pussy, and licked her slit so good that he had her calling out his name and begging him for more. Rodney Ruddman had a dick on him that was unlike anything Selah had ever seen before. It looked like a foot-long bat, long, thick, and stiff as hell. All Selah had to do was close her eyes and she could relive the memory of the way he had slid that delicious tube of man-meat all up in her guts, and how he knew just where to lick her and how to make her kitty purr.

But she would have traded away all those good feelings Rodney had given her if it meant avoiding this drama with Viceroy. She tried to call up some righteous justification by reminding herself that if she hadn't caught Viceroy getting his dick waxed by her little sister all those years ago then she wouldn't have gotten drunk and lost her baby for almost twenty damn years, and she wouldn't have gone after Ruddman looking to have a revenge affair either. But not even that old rationalization was working for her today.

The truth was, she had fucked around with the wrong man. The fact that she had opened her legs to some outside dick was bad enough, but had it been anyone else but Ruddman then Viceroy's rage wouldn't have been nearly so intense. Deep inside she had expected to get her revenge and feel real satisfied by the look of pain and betrayal she'd seen in her husband's eyes, but instead she was filled with dread and fear. Because Selah knew something today that she hadn't known twenty years ago when her sister was sucking her husband's dick down to the bone.

Standing her ass in that dusty pool house she knew without a doubt that Viceroy held the ultimate power in his hands, and as a man, it didn't matter how doggish and low-down he had been, a woman could never play the fuck-your-homey game and walk away from it without looking like a toilet and smelling like shit.

In her heart of hearts Selah knew Viceroy had seen straight through her tears and her lies of protest. But underneath the finery and the gloss, her blood still ran true to the code of Brooklyn. It didn't matter if Viceroy rented out a mega movie theater and rolled some videotape of her with her ass tooted up to the sky while Ruddman drilled her coochie until oil dripped from her nose, she would never admit to stepping outside of her marriage and having sex with another man. Never.

Clutching her throbbing black eye, Selah took a few aimless paces around the room searching through the mess until she found her makeup kit. Bunni's round-house punch had damn near sent her eyeball flying outta the back of her skull, but the black eye was all Rodney Ruddman's fault, just like everything else that had happened today was. She was too ashamed that her baby Fallon had witnessed the grimy drama going down between her parents, and had heard Viceroy accusing her of whoring around on her knees. That certainly wasn't an impression she wanted her daughter to have of her, Selah thought as she stood at the mirror trying her best to hide the bruise that was darkening under her eye. She had spent her entire life creating a carefully constructed image, and this pile of shit she found herself standing in had the potential to bring her entire life crashing down. She didn't care what she had to do, she was going to make this right with her husband and get back in his good graces. But no matter what, she would never, *ever* cop to being within twenty feet of that fuggly-ass old troll Rodney Ruddman! Never!

Selah dabbed some blemish concealer gingerly under her eye until most of the bruise was hidden, and then she studied her appearance in the chipped mirror hanging on the back of the closet door. Even though her nerves were wrecked and she felt like a hot mess on the inside, beauty was her greatest asset and she looked damn good on the outside. She plastered her public smile on her face and then nodded at her reflection. Black eye or no black eye, she was putting on her designer dress and having her sit-down session with Okrah today!

Selah sighed. Life had been so much easier when Viceroy had been in his coma. Yeah, she had missed him a little bit, but she'd had a peace and freedom that she missed like hell too. Barron had reminded her that the doctors said Viceroy's behavior would be erratic because of his head injury. Well, after the way he had humiliated her today he'd better hope and pray he didn't get knocked in his goddamn head again!

Pilar Ducane had gotten a belly full of crispy bacon at her aunt's mansion and she'd gotten an earful of juicy gossip too. She had been jumping for joy when her uncle Viceroy barged into the dining room drunk and cursing and amping out on everybody in sight. Over the years Pilar had seen a lot at the Dominion mansion. She'd been in and out of their doors practically every day ever since she could remember. Her aunt Selah had even given her a beautiful customized suite to call her own and she was welcome to stay there whenever she felt like it. She had witnessed a lot of shadiness go down with her rich relatives, but she had never, *ever* seen her uncle act the fool and put his paws on her aunt before.

"Yeah," she muttered under her breath as she glanced at the sinking needle on her gas tank. "So the rich and fuckin' famous Dominions are not as perfect as they want the world to believe they are!"

Although Pilar had grown up around the mansion, she'd had the misfortune of being born a Ducane instead of a Dominion. Her father, Digger, was Selah's younger brother, and under most circumstances her aunt had always treated her like a daughter.

But even as a child Pilar had known that she and her father weren't quite as wealthy as the Dominions, but they were still rich by any standard and she had never lacked anything. With her mother dead and gone, her father had spoiled her rotten on a daily basis, and from the time she could open her mouth and say "I want" he had handed her every little thing her heart could desire.

Until he lost his job, that is.

Digger Ducane had once been an employee of Dominion Oil, but when the opportunity arose for him to become a contractor and run his own business, he had jumped at it. He had stayed close to the company though, and his brother-in-law had given him a lucrative transportation contract to move crude oil with his huge fleet of trucks.

But when Viceroy was caught in that rig explosion right around the time that the price of oil skyrocketed and profits dropped, Digger's company had taken a hit. With Viceroy in a coma and his condition touch-and-go, Digger had decided to make a risky move and he jumped ship to go earn a paycheck from his brother-in-law's main competitor, Ruddman Energy.

Pilar glanced at her gas gauge again as she sped down the highway. That baby was damn near sitting on E and she still had miles to go. Money had been super-tight at the Ducane manor, and it pissed her off that while she and her father ate cornflakes for dinner, her rich family members didn't think to so much as throw them a chicken bone outta their table scraps. Things had gotten so tight with their pockets that she'd started eating most of her meals at the Dominion mansion. She'd get with the cook and order up whatever she wanted, and then eat until she was full and take the leftovers home to her father.

Pilar was full of pride and being somebody's charity case was way beneath her. All of her shopping and vacations and dropping a credit card to buy whatever she wanted had come to a screeching halt. She hated using her aunt's mansion like it was a soup kitchen, but with every dime her father brought home going toward the mortgage and keeping the lights on, mooching food from their family members was the least of their worries. It pissed Pilar off that *not one* of those damn Dominions thought to ask if she and her father needed anything. They saw her stepping out looking pressed and perfect every day and assumed her pockets were stuffed just as fat as theirs were, when nothing could be further from the truth.

Deep inside Pilar knew her aunt would come to their rescue and hook her up with some cash if she asked her to, but she shouldn't have to ask! She was family, dammit, and she deserved to have the same damn riches that Fallon and Jock and Barron and Dane, and now even that ghetto bitch Mink had! And to make things worse, Barron knew what kind of financial bind she was in. He *knew* she had big dreams and she was trying to live the high life!

That fucker made her sick. She had tried her best to get his punk-ass to marry her and make her a Dominion. After all the freaky fucking they had gotten down on, and all that spur-of-the-moment dick sucking she had done, she had been *this close* to getting him to put a ring on it. But then, out of nowhere he had stepped up in her house running her some bullshit about how they couldn't be together anymore because his father was out of his coma and might find out that he was banging his own cousin on the sly.

Pilar had gone the fuck off! After all that good pussy she had wiped on him? Barron knew good and goddamn well that they were *not* related! His ass was adopted, and that meant they had no real family ties. So she had trashed his ass. Scratched his face up, beaned him upside his head with whatever she could get her hands on, and straight up cursed his ass out.

And later, after she had calmed down and decided she had played herself just a little bit out of pocket, Pilar had snuck over to the mansion at the break of dawn intending to give Barron some pussy and make nice with him, and that's when she caught him coming out of Mink's room damn near naked with his drawers all caked up with wet cum!

That was it. That was the last fucking straw. Pilar had pulled a bottle of wine out of her sex kit and tried to smash a home run with his head. That nigga was just twisted and nasty! He had tossed her off just so he could bang his so-called sister, Mink, and that shit was unforgiveable. And ever since then she had been on a mission to pay his ass back. To fuck him up in any way she could, and she didn't care how long it took her or what she had to do, Barron was going to get his. Oh, yes the fuck he was!

Pilar's blood pressure had crept up thinking about Barron, and so had her speedometer as she mashed hard on the gas pedal. She forced herself to slow down and take a couple of deep breaths, and she had just gotten the whip under the speed limit when her cell phone rang through her car's speakers.

"Pilar!" a gritty-sounding voice blasted into her car. "Gurl, I need some help."

Pilar frowned. "Hell, I need some help too. Who is this?"

She heard some teeth get sucked. "It's Dy-Nasty!"

Pilar sneered. "Dy-Nasty? Didn't they throw your funky behind in jail? I know damn well you're not calling me collect!"

"No, stupid! Did you accept a collect call? One of the COs let me use his cell phone. Look, shit is getting real funky up in here and I need a favor. Can you bail me out right quick? I promise I'll pay you back as soon as I get on my feet and turn a few dollars."

Laughter exploded out of Pilar's mouth. This bitch had some nerve! This tore-down trick had gotten her funky pussy munched out by *her* man in *her* damn bed! Pilar still hadn't forgiven fat-man Ray for that shit!

"Are you serious? *Me*? Bail *your* ass out? Now why in the world would I want to do that?"

Dy-Nasty sucked her teeth real loud again. "Oh I see how you living! It was all well and good when you needed me to help you get *Bearrun's* ass in a jam, right? We was working together then, but now that I need just a little tiny favor you wanna act brand new!"

Pilar sucked her teeth right back.

"Me and you have never been partners and we're never *ever* going to be friends! Besides, I don't have any money to be giving you for bail! Hell, I'm tryna put some gas in my car! You'd better call Aunt Selah and ask her."

"Stupid she's the one who got me locked up in the first place!"

Pilar laughed. "Well, I guess *somebody's* stuck in the pokey then! No really," she said, getting serious. "You should call her," she advised. "She might be looking for another charity case. Uncle Viceroy just found out that some dude has her old engagement ring and he kicked her ass straight out to the pool house!" Pilar couldn't help giggling. "Maybe she'll bail you out and let you press a bunk out there with her." *Click!*

CHAPTER 7

Barron's tires screeched and burned rubber into the pavement as he slammed on his brakes outside the Dominion Estate. He left his brand-new red Maserati running as he jumped out and sprinted around back and across the grass to the pool house. The pain in his mother's voice had stabbed him deep in his heart and he couldn't believe his father had stooped so damn low.

He had called Viceroy the moment he hung up with Selah but his father's phone had just rang and rang. "Yeah, you better not pick up, muthafucka," Barron had breathed into his cell, mad as fuck and still dripping gym sweat. There was no telling what he would have told that bastard if he had answered the damn phone, but there wouldn't have been an ounce of respect in it.

"Mama!" he called out for Selah even before he hit the pool house door. "Mama, are you in here?"

He strode through the front room and past the small kitchenette and found her sitting on a small stool in the bedroom sipping liquor from a cocktail glass.

"What the hell?" he panted with rage, barely able to control himself as he eyed the baskets of designer clothing that were strewn about the room. "You mean he put your shit out here like this, Mama?" He clenched his fists. "That *mmmm* put all your shit—"

"It's okay, Barron," Selah hushed him. She was on her third drink and had calmed down enough to think a bit more clearly.

"Hell no it's not okay!" Barron barked. He walked over to her and snatched the liquor from her hand and then peered closely at her face.

"What happened to your eye, Mama?" And then a wave of fury washed over him. "Did Daddy hit you?" he roared. "Did that black piece of shit *put his hands on you?*"

Selah stood up quickly, shaking her head. "No, no, no! No, Barron! Your father might talk crazy sometimes but you know he would never, *ever* put his hands on me in anger! Please, son." She reached out and took her drink back. "I'm okay. Everything will work out. It'll all be fine."

"You're damn right it will," Barron said, taking her hand and turning toward the door. "C'mon. I'm taking you back in the house."

"No!" Selah pulled away. "I'm not going back in there."

"Okay, cool," he said. "You don't have to. Daddy's crib ain't the only joint in town. I'll take you to a hotel. The best one in the city. I'll rent you a penthouse suite and I'll even stay there with you."

Selah squeezed her eyes closed and slowly shook her head. "I'm not leaving here, Barron. This pool house is part of my home too, and I'm staying right here. I'll be okay. In fact, I think it'll be good for me. It'll show your father that I'm serious about working on our issues."

"But *you* ain't the one with the issues, Mama! If he's got a problem then let *him* move his stuff out here and you go back inside!"

"I'm staying out here, Barron," Selah said with an air of finality that let him know this thing was settled. "I'm sorry I called you and made you so upset, but I'm going to serve my punishment right out here where he put me, and once I'm done and your father has forgiven me, then maybe he'll let me back into his life."

Even though the mansion was situated practically in the middle of nowhere and there was always at least a couple of staff members patrolling the grounds, Okrah rolled with her own security team and they combed over the joint like the president's Secret Service before they even let her outta the whip.

Mama Selah had selected our interview spot, and it was in an area of the backyard where giant oak trees stood and she'd had the gardener plant a botanical garden full of colorful flowers. There were a bunch of off-white outdoor loveseats arranged around a big wicker table, and fancy pitchers of lemonade and sweet tea with lots and lots of sliced lemons set the mood off just right.

Forget all that yang I had popped to Bunni about being on TV. I was hyped as hell to meet Okrah and I put on my precious little white girl voice and performed like a mutha!

"It's nice to meet you, Mizz Sinfree," I gushed all over myself after we were introduced. I went to give her a big hug like Selah had done, but Okrah checked me real quick before I could get too close.

"Yes, it's nice to meet you too," she said and gave me a fake little smile with her thin little lips.

I didn't know how to be with that. I wouldn'ta ate none of that mess she cooked, but I had watched her talk show plenty of times and everybody knew Mama O didn't have no shame in her game. As soon as the cameras got to rolling she was gonna be all up in my grill like we was best friends, asking me what color drawers I had on and when was the last time I changed them. The least she could do was show a sistah some love!

Her production crew got to work right away and they were real bossy with their shit. The show was airing live so they wanted everything to look perfect. They slapped a bunch of makeup on me and tried to mess with my hair and put it up in some old granny style, but I put the brakes on all that with a quickness. I didn't need nobody to tell me how to make my shit pop. I had danced on stage for thousands of ballers, and I knew what looked good on me and what didn't.

"Where's Viceroy?" I side-mouthed to Barron as they were telling us which chairs they wanted us to sit in.

"In the house," he said with his mouth all stiff. "Sleeping his drunk off."

Okrah took her seat on the couch next to Selah, and the next thing I knew it was lights, camera, and action time!

"Hello America, although The Okrah Sinfree Show usually broadcasts before a studio audience in Houston, I promised that from time to time I would bring you special live, on-location reports on topics that deeply affect me and the world at large. Today, I'm broadcasting live outside of Dallas, Texas, with a family who has experienced and endured what to many is their worst nightmare. At first glance the Dominion family appears to be living the American dream. They're one of the wealthiest and most successful families in the country, and they're pioneers in the crude oil industry. They live on this beautiful estate you see behind us, and they have all the trappings that their success has afforded them. However, like most Americans, the Dominions have also had their share of family secrets, heartache, and pain. As parents, they know what it's like to suffer, because eighteen years ago their three-year-old daughter, Sable, was abducted by a stranger, in part due to what some might say was the Dominions' own carelessness.

"Today, I'm happy to tell you that the Dominions have walked through that fire and come out on the other side scarred, but stronger. Due to something as simple as a milk carton and the efforts of those who labor tirelessly on behalf of America's missing and exploited children, the Dominions were able to find their missing daughter Sable, who is now known as Mink, and have been reunited with the child they never lost hope that they would see again.

"I'm pleased to bring you Selah Dominion, and her children Bar-

ron and Mink. Let's start with Barron, the eldest son of oil tycoons Viceroy and Selah Dominion."

Barron sat there trying to look polished and confident in his three-piece suit as the cameraman zoomed in on him. He was a little nervous because of course this was Okrah he was talking to, but some of it was because he was unsure about the type of questions she would ask as well. Barron knew Okrah was a master at interviews and getting the most out of her guests. Some called her a blond-haired box of tissues because she was known to jerk tears out of the strongest men, but she damn sure wouldn't be getting any out of him today.

"Barron thank you for being here on the live set with us on this beautiful afternoon," Okrah said warmly. "I understand your father is under the weather and can't join us, but I can only imagine that since coming out of his coma his health has been day-by-day to say the least. However, I'm so happy to have you as my guest, and on behalf of my entire crew I'm sending your father my prayers and well wishes."

"Thank you, Okrah," Barron responded, stunned by her warmth and sincerity. "My family appreciates your well wishes and we'll pass them on to my father. With love and care we're confident that he'll be back in great shape in no time."

Of course Barron was lying his ass off, but all of America didn't need to know that the great Viceroy Dominion had locked himself in his suite and was sleeping off a liquored-up rage.

"So, Barron, you had a pair of pretty big shoes to fill after your father's tragic accident," Okrah said. "How did you handle the pressure of suddenly being the CEO of a major company, and how well do you rank your performance?"

"Well, Okrah," Barron responded truthfully, "I feel as though my father has been grooming me for that position since I was a small child. He taught me the ins and outs of the oil business and when he was injured I gladly accepted the challenge. Of course, I'd already studied his tactics and his moves. As an attorney I learned to be assertive and to think quickly in high-pressure situations. To be honest with you, I'm still a work in progress and my performance could have been better, but I did my best. I didn't sink the ship and I think I actually helped the company see a lot of progress in many areas."

If they were in a studio the audience would have been clapping like crazy. Barron figured he had answered the question the way his father would have expected, and Okrah looked happy, like she appreciated his honesty.

"I'm sure your father was quite proud of you. Now tell me, Barron," Okrah moved on. "I know it was a long time ago but take me back to that day when you were watching your little sister, Sable. It was the last time you would see her for many, many years."

Barron thought he was prepared to the answer the question. He told himself that he would just say it was an accident and that he was young and Okrah would move on. But that's not how it turned out. Barron felt an emotional tug on his heart as he fought to keep his professional composure in front of Okrah and her cameras.

"Well, it was so long ago . . . I remember . . . I remember I was playing with my little brother Dane while my mom went into the store," Barron said, his voice dropping lower as the memories flooded his mind. "It was hot. There were a lot of people on the streets. We had walked around for a very long time."

The more he talked the more Barron's mind slipped further and further back to that day. His palms started to sweat and his legs began to shake as he zoned in on his past.

"I just kept playing with Dane, doing what big brothers do . . . annoying him. Then all of a sudden he got mad," Barron said as his eyes got very wide. "He started crying and I was laughing. But then I . . . I tried to calm him down."

It was like he was seven years old again. At that very moment Barron was right there in front of the damn drug store that haunted him for so many years. Everything seemed crystal clear to him.

"I picked Dane up and swung him around a few times," Barron responded slowly. "Just to stop him from crying. I only took my eyes off of the stroller for a second . . . just . . . a . . . second."

Before Barron knew it the flood-gates in his soul opened and tears started streaming down his face. His hands were clenched tightly together in sweaty fists as he remembered the pain on his mother's face when she came back out the store and realized Sable was gone.

"Do you think you should have been more careful, Barron?" Okrah asked. "Do you believe that had you been more attentive that you could have prevented what happened to your sister?"

"Yes . . . I should have been more aware," Barron said as anger rose in him and joined his sorrow. He was fighting back hoarse sobs as his plan to stay even-keeled went out the window. "I . . . turned around and . . . I saw the stroller rocking. For a second I thought Sable had jumped out. It was like a dark shadow had swooped down . . . and . . . snatched my sister away from us . . . and it was all my fault."

And then he broke down completely. The pain he had buried for so long and the barriers he had built around those emotions had finally collapsed. Barron was truly a mama's boy and he felt responsible for his mother's pain as well. She had never given up on the search for Sable and he felt real guilty for trying to convince her for years that her little girl was dead.

"I-I-I," he started.

Selah threw up her hand. "No, baby! That's enough!" She got up and sat beside him, pulling her oldest child into her arms. "It was not your fault, Barron! You were too young to be watching anybody. Everything that happened that day was my fault. I was the adult. I was the mother. I neglected all of you that day. I'm the only one responsible, so I need you to let that pain go. Right now. Let it all go, Barron, you hear me? You don't have to live with that burden anymore! It's not yours to carry."

Mink couldn't help the feeling that ripped through her gut. She didn't really fuck with Barron like that. He had been real shitty to her when she first came to Texas. But seeing his pain up close finally made her understand what Sable had meant to him and how much of the blame he placed upon his own young shoulders for her abduction. Tears welled up in Mink's eyes and she threw her arm around Barron as well.

"It's okay, Bump," she said as she hugged her brother. "You don't have to blame yourself anymore. I'm back now and I'm not going anywhere. What happened back then is over. The important thing is that we're all together now. That's all that matters. It's all good now big brother."

Okrah beamed. She knew her audiences at home were giving her guests a standing ovation as they saw a well-to-do family finally putting their demons to rest. What had just happened live on her show proved that no matter how much money you had, life could get real. The pure emotions had cast the Dominions in a good light instead of making them appear to be uppity tight-ass black folks. As a hostess she was well pleased. It was a powerful moment for the family and excellent ratings for television.

"We have to take a short commercial break, but we'll be back so please stay tuned for more. This is Okrah Sinfree Live."

Okrah was the shit! Selah was on deck last, so now it was my turn at bat! I felt bad for ragging on Bunni like I did because TV was all that and I was looking good as a mofo and I was so ready to work them cameras. I didn't know what O-Mama was gonna ask me or how I was gonna work her angle to my advantage. I had managed to squeeze a few fake tears outta my eyes, but I wasn't gonna get caught up in her trap or sit there slinging snot everywhere like Barron did, that's for damn sure.

"Today on Okrah Sinfree Live *we're bringing you a story about missing children. It's a heartbreaking topic because it's every parent's nightmare. Today's guests are the Dominions of Dallas, Texas. Viceroy Dominion, the multi-million-dollar oil tycoon and his wife experienced this tragedy firsthand. Their daughter Mink LaRue was kidnapped many years ago and her absence left a void in their lives that no amount of money could ever fill. But the strong-willed family never lost hope, and today after all these years they finally have their baby back.*

"Tell me, Mink. After growing up in the slum ghetto of Harlem, what is it like to wake up one day and suddenly find yourself an heiress to an oil fortune?"

Slum ghetto? Did this butter-fried trick really just tell America that *my* fuckin' town was a slum ghetto? I tried to stop my foot from tapping but Mizz O had some shit about herself and she needed correcting!

"Um," I said, poking out my titties and flashing my pearlies at the cameraman even though the producers had already told me twice not to look over there, "I don't know about all that slum ghetto mess you talkin', but I'm just happy to be back with my family and working on putting my life back together. I've been through so much and there's a big cobweb of lies in my mind that I'm still trying to clear out. Luckily, I have a lot of support from two wonderful and loving parents to help me through this process. I know it's been hard on them as well, and we're all taking it one day at a time trying to mend what was lost to us so long ago. I mean, all the money and the T.V. cameras are cool like that and everything, but all I'm really looking forward to is the future I'm going to have with the people who really love me and care about me."

I turned and smiled into the camera again, thinking I did pretty damn good with the lines I had practiced, but Okrah must didn't like it because right away she cued up for another commercial break. As soon as the camera cut away she turned toward me and blasted me with her cold blue eyes.

"Is there something wrong with you?" she asked me, and she said it real stank-like too.

I shook my head with a quickness. "Ain't nothing wrong with me! Why you asking?"

"Stop patting your foot and try to stick with the program," she said, dissing me like I was some little-ass kid. "Give me a little more sugar and a little less vinegar, okay? Try to concentrate and think before you answer."

"*Welcome back, America, today we are here on Okrah Sinfree Live with our guests, the Dominion family of Texas. We're discussing missing and abducted children who have been miraculously found and reunited with their families. The Dominions know the pain and the joy of losing and recovering a child firsthand and the immense grief and heartache it causes an entire family. You've already heard from Barron Dominion as he shared his personal experiences from a sibling's perspective on what it was like to lose his sister when he was merely a child himself, and now you'll have a chance to hear this story from a mother whose heart ached from the loss of her child for many years, only to discover that the daughter who was stolen from her was alive and well and living right there in New York City.*"

Okrah smiled and looked all misty-eyed as she reached out and took Selah's hand. "Thank you for being here on *Okrah Live*, Selah. We've heard from your son, Barron, now tell us what you remember about that day."

Selah took a deep breath. "It was just a normal day," she said softly, reciting all the stuff she had already said on all them other shows. "It started out wonderfully. My husband and I had taken our three children on what was supposed to be a vacation in New York City. But my husband . . . he was called away on business unexpectedly and the kids and I were stuck in the hotel room and they were getting very restless."

"So you left the hotel and just started wandering around Manhattan?" Okrah asked, her voice soothing and gentle.

Selah nodded. "Y-y-yes. The children needed some fresh air and so did I. We decided to go for a walk. The boys really liked being outside and seeing the sights. I happened to spot a drug store and I left my oldest son outside to watch my younger kids. I ran in the store just for a bit. I couldn't have been gone for more than three, maybe four minutes tops. But when I came outside my three-year-old daughter was gone. Someone had walked up and lifted her out of her stroller without saying a word. I screamed and searched all over, but . . ." Selah dabbed at her eyes with her lace hanky, "she was gone."

That shit felt so raw to me. Just because I had loved my mama Jude and I didn't remember a thing about getting took, it didn't mean I couldn't feel mad sympathy for Selah every time she told that story. All that pain I was hearing in her voice was there because she had lost a kid she really loved. Because she had lost *me*. And that's why I copped a real stank 'tude when Okrah opened her mouth and bit her like that.

"But it really wasn't that simple, was it, Selah? Tell the truth. It wasn't that you just ran in the store for a moment and then a tragedy occurred, as you've led everyone to believe. The truth is, you were *drunk,* weren't you?" she accused, turning on Selah like a pudgy pit bull. "According to the police report and statements our producers uncovered, you had been walking around consuming large amounts of alcohol in the middle of the day. So, you're telling the world that knowing full well that you alone were responsible for the safety and well-being of three young children, you were out there *drinking?*"

You bubble-eyed bitch! I wanted to come up outta my seat on Okrah! She didn't *even* have to go her ass there! We had been on plenty of other talk shows and nobody else had put Mama Selah's shit on blast like that! I was about ready to leap up and get real ratchet on Mizz O because I wasn't scared of her ass!

"Y-yes, you're right," Mama Selah admitted quietly. "I was drinking and it was my fault that Sable was taken."

"Because you were *drunk,*" Okrah repeated. "Say it and own it! You were falling down *drunk!*"

Selah lowered her head in shame. "I admit I was drinking and I take full responsibility for that. But the worst part is"— her lips started quivering face crumpled in a million pieces. "And as you just saw, for almost twenty years my son Barron blamed himself, but he was only seven years old and there was no way he could have stopped that crazy woman from doing what she did."

By now I was swole like a muthafucka and there was no way nobody coulda stopped me from doing what I was about to do neither!

I jumped up outta my seat and blasted that heffa with both my guns. "You's a hater!" I screamed on Okrah as I grabbed Mama Selah by her wrist and yanked her to her feet. Barron jumped up too and he got on the other side of Selah and wrapped his arm around her protectively.

"Faker!" I yelled at Okrah. "Coming up in here pretending like you cared about her! Well we ain't gonna sit here and let you disrespect our mother like that! As much loot as you got you still ain't nothing but a ratings rat! That's why all that food on your show looks like hot buttered dog shit! 'Cause you fake, Okrah! You *fake!*"

You shoulda seen the way her security people tried to swarm all over us.

Barron jumped in front of me and Selah and looked crazy as hell posting up in his three-piece suit as he threw up his dukes.

"Put ya fuckin' hands on me and your narrow ass is gonna be taking a nap out here in this grass," I peeped out from behind Barron and warned a tall white dude who looked like he wanted to step to me. I snatched those clip-on mics and little black boxes off of me and Selah and tossed them shits into the flower bed.

I pointed my finger at Okrah as her team started packing up their shit and her security squad tried to rush her away. "That's why I stole a whole box of your stupid magazines off a truck one time and ripped out the pages to soak up pee-pee water when my toilet overflowed! Lemme give you a hint, witcha high and mighty stuck-up ass," I hollered as I ran her nosy tail up outta there on live TV. "Put *somebody else on the goddamn cover of that thick-ass telephone book!* 'Cause America is sick and tired of looking at your old ass!"

CHAPTER 8

"*Today on* Okrah Sinfree Live *we're bringing you a story about missing children. It's a heartbreaking topic because it's every parent's nightmare. Today's guests are the Dominions of Dallas, Texas. Viceroy Dominion, the multi-million-dollar oil tycoon and his wife experienced this tragedy firsthand. Their daughter Mink LaRue was kidnapped many years ago and her absence left a void in their lives that no amount of money could ever fill. But the strong-willed family never lost hope, and today after all these years they finally have their baby back.*"

The television was blaring in the living room while Gutta was at the kitchen table breaking down bricks of weed for sale. Fresh home from a state bid, he was trying to get back on his feet and get back in the freedom swing. Places like Attica, Sing Sing, and Greenhaven were a rite of passage for criminals like him who scavenged the streets of New York. Most were lucky to make it out from behind those walls.

"Ayo," Gutta yelled to his partner Shy who was in the living room bagging up. "Turn that fucking TV down, nigga! Ain't nobody tryna hear what the fuck Okrah talking about!"

The streets hadn't changed much while he was gone, only the players. A few niggas got deaded, a few more got locked up, and some who was at the bottom when Gutta first went in had come up and were now trying to run the show.

But none of that mattered to him now because he was ready to put in some work. As a street nigga just coming home, most of the time you had to re-establish your power and get your weight up. Gutta didn't have a problem knocking a few heads off shoulders and kidnapping a few kingpins. The time he'd spent in jail had enhanced his grimy tendencies, and it had also made him more ruthless and more determined to put the block back in the bear hug that he once had it in.

"I'm pleased to bring to you Selah Dominion, and her children Barron Dominion and Mink LaRue! Let's start with Barron, the eldest son of oil tycoons Viceroy and Selah Dominion of Dallas, Texas . . ."

"Yo, Gutta! Come in here, nigga!" Shy yelled from in the living room. "I think ya honey Mink is on *Okrah*, yo!"

The sound of her name made Gutta growl in anger. He had been trying to find that bitch ever since she escaped from that back room he had tossed her in down near the garment district. His slime Petro had let her get the slip on him, and it had earned him two claps straight to the dome. Nobody in the hood had seen or heard from Mink ever since, and he couldn't catch up with that bitchy nigga Peaches she used to stay with neither. He had vowed to make Mink pay for fucking with his money and losing his apartment when he went to prison. He had fallen for that sweet sex game she used to put on him but he should have known that sexy little liar couldn't be trusted.

Hold up, did this nigga just say Mink was on Okrah?

Gutta got up and headed into the living room and sat down on the couch across from Shy. He had to rub his eyes because he couldn't believe what he was seeing. Sexy Mink LaRue was looking like a million bucks sitting there across from Okrah. Gutta grinned. That sherm nigga Barron who had paid him to kill Mink over a DNA test had been dead wrong. That slippery little Harlem chick really *was* the daughter of some rich-ass oil family. Deep inside Gutta couldn't help but smile with pride at his slick get-money honey, although he still wanted to see her dead body floating in the East fuckin' River!

"I'm just happy to be back with my family and working on putting the pieces back together. I've been through so much and there's a big cobweb of lies in my mind that I'm still trying to clear out. Luckily, I have a lot of support from two wonderful and loving parents to help me through this process. I know it's been hard on them as well and we're all taking it one day at a time trying to mend what was lost to us so long ago . . .

"Damn son," Shy said in amazement. "I didn't know your girl was sweet like that. That bitch is down in Dallas now, hella paid son!"

"Yeah," Gutta said as he gritted his teeth and started plotting like a mutha. *Texas.* So that's where the fuck she ran off to after he stomped that mud hole in her ass. "It's a big surprise to me too, Shy. I don't know how the fuck it's even possible, but if she's sitting her ass up there with Okrah then it's looking legit."

Gutta didn't give a fuck about none of her family ties. All he saw was an opportunity to tap into some big-time cash. Sitting up there looking delicious, Mink mighta had them rich mothafuckas wrapped around her pinky finger, but he wanted his whole hand wrapped around her scrawny neck.

"So what you thinking, bruh?" Shy asked. "How we gonna get at her now?"

Gutta shrugged. "Easy. We gonna take us a trip to the dirty D," he said, smiling as his mind worked up some very crooked angles. "If that bitch Mink got some money—then that means *I* got some money. She gonna pay me what she owes me plus pain and suffering. This could be our ticket to the big time, Shy. If I line this shit up right we could come out on top. We need to get us some of that muthafuckin' oil money cuz ain't none of that black gold bubbling up in Harlem."

His face split in a vicious grin. "You think my girl is gonna be happy to see me?"

Shy hollered. "Hell no, nigga!"

Gutta agreed. "Me neither, my nigga. Me neither!"

CHAPTER 9

"I've got some important news to share with you two," Viceroy called Barron and Dane to his office later that night. He had just woken up and got his head right, and his eyes were still bloodshot and his breath still smelled like gin. He had missed the entire *Okrah* filming but he didn't care. That fire-water had had his ass calling cows in his sleep, but it wasn't enough of a drunk-fest to ease the pain of what Selah had done, or of knowing that Ruddman had dipped his spoon deep into his private pot of honey.

Dane took a seat in one of the chairs across from his father's desk, but Barron stood with his back stiff against the wall, refusing to sit down. He could still hear the anguish in his mother's voice when she'd called to tell him that Viceroy had put her outside in the pool house, and he was straight up pissed that his father had confirmed that shit and said Selah wasn't going to be welcome under his roof no time soon.

"I had a meeting with my advisors today and I've decided to run for political office," Viceroy said without fanfare. "It's a state-level position with the Railroad Commission with top seats on several commissions and strong ties to the regulatory board. I've got some key backers standing in my corner and they really think I can get the win."

Dane nodded like it was a cool idea, but Barron frowned and raised an eyebrow like dude was buggin'.

"So what does that mean for us?" Dane asked. "Is there anything we can do to help you win?"

"Definitely." Viceroy nodded. "Y'all can make sure folks around here start getting their shit together like right now! Everything's been going to hell in a handbasket up in this place and all the craziness and drama has gotta come to a complete halt. The election is in three weeks and it's gonna be real close. My political foes are experienced and they're gonna be all over us like stink on a fart. They'll be digging for dirt all up under our fingernails, and the media will put our entire lives under the microscope. I'm gonna need everybody to be on their absolute best behavior, and that means you too, Dane. All that drug smoking and chick banging is gonna have to be over with because if one of you comes up with so much as a shit stain in your drawers it's gonna cost me the election."

Barron had stood by silently mean-mugging his father all this time, but he was way too amped to stop himself from blasting on the man.

"So what the hell brought all this on, Pop?" he asked, throwing up his hands. "I mean, there's a whole lot of chaos going on in the family right now. *Okrah* was broadcasting live in our backyard today and she talked shit to Mama on national TV and said she used to be a drunk! Between us filing charges against Dy-Nasty and sending her to jail, and that thing named Peaches that you let Bunni bring up in here. Not to mention the fact that you have my *mother* sleeping out in the pool house like some common piece of ass off the streets." Barron shook his head. "We ain't got nothing to be proud of so I don't understand why you would wanna shine any kind of spotlight on the Dominion name right now."

Viceroy scoffed dismissively. "For one thing, Peaches is getting his or her ass up outta here pronto, and for another thing, your mother is sleeping exactly where she deserves to be sleeping! Nobody outside of the family has to know anything about where she lays her head at night and I plan to keep it like that."

"But Bunni is trying get a reality show going," Dane reminded them. "Once that goes down this entire joint is gonna be crawling with strangers and cameras, the whole nine. You think you can run a campaign with all of that going on?"

"Won't none of that bullshit be going on!" Viceroy snapped. "Bunni can kill that reality show nonsense. It ain't happening. Bob Easton said everything around here has got to be squeaky clean. I plan on winning this election, goddammit, and I can't have any distractions or disruptions knocking me off course."

Barron shrugged but he still looked doubtful in the face. "Whatever you say, Pops. I think it's a risky move and you're trying to do too much, but hell, it's your move to make."

"You got that shit right," Viceroy said, grilling the hell out of his oldest son, who, to his great displeasure, had always been too much of a mama's boy. "It's my move and I'm calling all the shots. All of them! Now, my paperwork has been filed and my public declaration is being announced first thing tomorrow morning, and that's when the shit's gonna get real hot and funky. Don't worry about me and your mama, boy." He clapped Barron on the back as he dismissed him from his office. "I got this shit. Remember, I'm the captain and your ass is just one of the crew. All I need you to do is hold the lil yellow chicken down and let me choke him, son. You just hold his ass down and I'll choke his goddamn lights out."

Now that I was officially a Dominion it was gonna take a whole lotta lying and sneaking around in order for me and Suge to keep getting our mash on. Hooking up and fucking like rabbits had been all well and good when Viceroy was laid up in his coma and I was busy running my lil get-money scheme on the Dominion goldmine, but now that I was a certified member of the crew it looked like our delicious little grind game was gonna have to come to a screeching halt. Unless we took it underground on the sneak tip, that is.

"Don't tell me you cussed Okrah Sinfree out." Suge laughed as we ate donuts in his office early the next morning. We were planning on going down to the racetrack when it opened up in a couple of hours, but first he had some work he needed to take care of at Dominion Oil headquarters.

"Oh yes I did," I said proudly as I bit into a vanilla custard bowtie. I was wearing some hip-hugging booty shorts and sitting my rump on the edge of his desk while he shuffled through a stack of paperwork. I had started out porno-posing on his butter-soft couch, but he had been igging me, busy tryna work, so I had jetted over to him and plopped my hot lil honeybuns right down on his desk.

"You shoulda been there. I straight wigged out on her ass! I don't care how rich and famous she is, I didn't appreciate the way she tried to put Mama Selah and all our family bizz on front street. The sun was shining real bright outside but that hater chick was just bringing too damn much shade!"

Suge grinned as I raised my knee and stuck my bare foot in his lap, wiggling my toes all on his dick and fuckin' with him. I didn't give a damn what kinda work he was doing with all those boring papers. I wanted his cock-strong ass to work on *me!*

"You're a real loyal chick, Mink," Suge told me as he pushed his papers aside and put his big ol' paw down on my thigh. "C'mere." He scooted his plush armchair back from his desk and swiveled me into position until my coochie was staring him in the face. He pulled me toward him and slid his thick fingers up the inside leg of my shorts. I scooted my butt closer to the edge of the desk and his fingers found my naked pussy and slid straight through my slick, curly hairs.

"Oooh, *shit!*" I bit my lip, happy that I didn't have on no drawers as I gapped my legs open wider and leaned back as he played with my pearl. Suge gripped my hip with his other hand as he slipped his middle finger deeply inside me and slowly fucked the shit outta me.

"This what you wanted?" he asked me quietly.

I nodded like crazy.

"Here!" I whispered and pulled up my shirt and bra and let my titties fly free. Them bangin' twins jiggled and bounced like a mutha as I humped and grinded on Suge's finger, and when his lips clamped down on my nipple and he damn near sucked my whole titty into his mouth, I arched my back and bucked my hips real hard a few times and came hard as hell!

It was a real quick nut, just enough to hold me off until I could get that big black dick up in me, and as Suge sat there licking my juices off his fingers I pushed against his shoulders until his chair was back far enough for me to stand up. I peeped that boulder bulging in the crotch of his dress pants and my greedy fingers moved quick as shit as I unbuckled his belt and slid his zipper down.

I lifted that thing outta his drawers like it was made of pure gold, and then I slipped one leg outta my shorts and let them fall down around my ankles. I spread the lips of my triangle and let Suge look at my pretty pussy as I rubbed my throbbing clit, then I turned around slowly and leaned forward with my elbows on my desk so he could get a good look at my yellow banana ass.

"Beautiful," I heard him whisper behind me, and then I felt the tickle of his moustache and his warm lips on my skin as he gently kissed my ass in about a thousand places. By the time he lifted my booty cheeks up in his hands and spread those lumps east and west, my stuff was purring and dripping in anticipation.

I put my head down on his desk and whimpered like a kitten as he lapped at my cheeks, my hole, and then my pulsating split. Suge got down on his knees and lifted my ass cheeks even higher as he ate me out from behind. His wet tongue was everywhere, whipping back and forth deliciously over all my most sensitive spots.

This time when I came there wasn't no small time gasping and moaning. "Yeah! Eat this pussy! Munch me out!" I cried, poking my ass out and humping my hips up and down on his face as I squeezed my titties and pinched my nipples until I creamed over and over. Suge lapped my cum up with his tongue, then gripped my hips and gently urged me backwards, into his lap.

That dick was standing up like a street pole as I lowered myself down on the firm, thick crown. I heard him grunt as I arched my back and let him get up in my na-na until my ass was on his thighs. We moved together in a sweet, funky rhythm as I held on to the arms of his chair and he reached around and massaged my breasts. We had that big ol' office hot and steamy as my pussy made wet, sloshing sounds every time I down-stroked on that chocolate dick.

"I got one for you," Suge muttered behind me as he played with my titties and licked and sucked on the back of my neck.

"Well give it to me then," I whispered, squeezing my pussy muscles tightly around his shaft as I shimmied and bounced on his pole. "Gimme that shit, big boy. Gimme all of it!"

Suddenly that beast gripped my hips and lifted me straight up offa him!

He pushed me forward and leaned me over the desk, then drove that iron dick back up inside me and pounded so hard my whole face bounced off the wood.

"Oochie! Oochie! Oochie!" I yelped with pleasure-pain and slobbered all over his papers as he rammed his dick up in me like he was aiming for it to bust outta my throat. Suge slid his finger down the crack of my ass and massaged my back door, then grunted and plunged deep up in my guts and shot a full load of buckshot in my tunnel as we collapsed on his desk together, just a-panting and grinning.

"Hey, how about you give me a job up in this joint," I joked a few minutes later as we took a shower in his private bathroom and Suge gently rubbed my soapy pussy with his thick fingers. "If you let me be your assistant then I could come to work with you every day, dude."

He kissed me on my forehead and shook his head as he aimed the spray of warm water down at my crotch. "Hell no. You ain't bringing your fine ass up in here every day." He slapped me on my wet booty. "The only work a nigga would ever get done would be working on you."

CHAPTER 10

It was ten a.m. on Wednesday morning when the urgent email popped up on his screen. The man sitting in front of the computer read the message three times before he got up from his chair and walked into his boss's office.

"You're not gonna believe this shit but we just got ourselves a legitimate challenger for Cooper's vacant chairman's seat," Larry Dawkins announced as he walked into Railroad Commissioner Stewart Baker's office. "His name is Viceroy Dominion and he's out of the Houston district. He filed his ballot paperwork late last night and he made his public declaration this morning."

"So?" Stewie hunched his shoulders and looked up at his campaign manager unconcerned. "It's my turn to get the chairman's seat. Perry's only appointed this guy for the next three weeks. Even if he's stupid enough to run, there's no way he can win in my district."

Larry shook his head. "Apparently he thinks he can. This Dominion guy is the real deal, and I'm telling you if we don't do something drastic he might just win, Stewie. He's got nearly every card in the deck stacked in his favor. He could beat the socks off you at the polls and win this thing hands down. That is, unless we can come up with a plan to stop him."

Viceroy Dominion. Stewart Baker turned the name over in his mind as his stomach twisted and turned in big knots. Reaching into his top drawer, he took out a container and popped two extra-strength Tums in his mouth and crunched them between his back teeth.

He'd been the front-runner during every election cycle for the past eight years, which was no small feat for a liberal Democrat in a southern red state. As the chairman of the Texas oil board he'd twisted a lot of arms and exerted a lot of influence over the state's refinery regulatory body, and he had cronies in his pocket from one end of the Lone Star state to the next.

He sighed as he looked down at the press announcement his white-haired campaign manager had printed out and slid in front of him. A color photo of a smiling Viceroy Dominion stared back at him. Stewie was accustomed to some redneck from the local saloon putting up a halfhearted fight and running for office every other year, and he enjoyed smashing their asses like ants on election day too.

But the world was changing and this was something different. Not only was it the first time that a darkie had ever dared to cast his hat in the ring and put his name on the ballot, it was the first time anyone with loaded pockets and a great public persona had ever challenged his position too.

"What makes you so sure he can beat me?" Stewie huffed, trying to sound tough. "He's got some decent credentials, but I've got quite a bit of political capital around here too, Larry. Just 'cause he's running doesn't mean he can win."

"Dabnabbit, have you seen the stats on this guy?" Larry blurted. "He's the richest darkie in the whole damn state, Stewart! He's a black oil man, and he's got the perfect public story. This is the guy who got blown all to hell when that rig went up in the Gulf of Mexico last year. The media bom-

barded us with so many pictures of him wrapped up like a
mummy with his beautiful wife weeping at his bedside that
the whole damn world cried with her. And his kids are perfect,
man. Not so much as a crooked tooth on any of them! In fact,
one of the girls went missing about eighteen years ago and they
put her picture on the back of a milk carton to try and get her
back. And it worked too! They found her recently and brought
her back home. Trust me. I've been doing this job for a long
time and I can promise you that Viceroy Dominion is going to
poll higher than you can shoot a space shuttle. Short of rushing into a burning building and rescuing some kids, some kit-
tens, and a couple of old soupy-mouthed grannies, there's no
way you can beat him by playing politics as usual, Stewie. No
fucking way."

Stewart flung his drawer open again and snatched out his
bottle of Tums. "Well, if there's no way I can beat him then
what the hell are we doing here? If I've already lost the election
then I might as well pack it up and take it on home right now!"

"Now hold on," Larry said, grinning slyly. "I didn't say
you've already lost. I said there's no way you can beat this bastard by doing things the usual way. You've got to sharpen up
your knife and tighten up your strategy, Stew. You've gotta be
willing to dig in the mud and get your lil soft white hands dirty.
Politics is a grimy business, as you very well know. If you're
gonna beat Viceroy Dominion you're going to have to run a
different kind of race."

"And what kind of race is that, Larry?"

"Well," Larry said with a devious twinkle in his eye, "the
kind that always wins, of course. The kind that always wins."

Selah couldn't believe this shit. While Viceroy had every
right to be pissed behind the crazy stunt Ruddman had pulled,
homeboy was taking this drama a little bit too damn far. Not
only had he banished her to the pool house, he had forbidden
her to so much as step foot inside their lavish bedroom suite.

"Just tell me what you need and I'll hand it to you," he barked, blocking the doorway with his body two nights after putting her out. She'd come upstairs to see if she could throw some sweet talk and a slice of ass down on him and saw that he'd changed the locks on their suite and even installed a motion-sensor-operated security camera outside their door.

"Are you serious?" Selah said like, *nigga you must be kidding!* "I need some of my bathroom items, Viceroy! My toiletries and a few other personal things. Open the door, baby. It will only take me a quick second to get them."

"Open, hell," Viceroy bitched, standing his ground as he glared at her like he wanted to deck her in her other eye. "You ain't getting your ass up in here, Selah. I don't trust you and I don't want you nowhere around me. I wanna say I don't know where the hell you been, but I *do* know. I know like a mutha-fucka!"

"Viceroy, *please*," Selah pleaded. She had never in life begged a man for a damn thing—except Ruddman of course, she had gotten all on her knees and begged him for that dick—but she was worn down and ready to beg Viceroy now. Somehow the sweet taste of revenge she'd always thought would tantalize her tongue instead burned her throat like hot peppers and she was desperate to get back in her husband's good graces. "This is ridiculous. You know I'd never betray you. Never!"

"I don't know shit about you, Selah," Viceroy barked, slamming the door in her face. "For all I know you could be a scallywag, a chicken, a trollop or a tramp! Until you produce your engagement ring and show and prove that the one Ruddman has ain't yours, then I don't know *what* the hell you would do. I don't know how you living, I don't know how you roll, I don't know a goddamn thing about you!"

Back in his office Larry Dawkins leaned back in his chair and propped his three-thousand-dollar cowboy boots up on his desk. As a long-time campaign manager he had been a student of Texas politics for nearly forty years and he was damn proud of the fact that he had never run a race that he couldn't win. And if he had anything to say about it, this battle between his guy Stewart Baker and that black-ass Viceroy Dominion wasn't going to be any different.

He lit a cigar and glanced through the dossier of information that he had compiled on the private affairs of his current political foe. Larry was as shrewd and resourceful as any snake that had ever slithered the face of the earth, and he took great pride in rooting out the nitty-gritty nuggets of information that most people would give their last dime to keep hidden.

A frown creased his brow as he flipped through the folder and absorbed what he found. Everything he had told Stewart about his contender was true. Viceroy Dominion was super black and super rich. He had been born and raised in the slums of Houston, and through a shit-load of hard work and dedication, he had pulled himself up by the bootstraps and made a way out of no way. He'd gone from being a penniless gutter thug who barely scraped out enough to eat, to the CEO of a multi-billion-dollar oil company. All while maintaining a marriage to his college sweetheart and raising a stable of five decent and well-behaved children. At least that's what the report said.

But Larry had never been one to take things at face value. Over the years he'd discovered that things were hardly ever what they looked like, especially from the outside peeking in, and that people were willing to go to great lengths to maintain a certain public image that didn't have a damn thing to do with how they truly lived their lives in private.

Larry shut the folder and scrolled through the contacts in his cell phone. He wasn't interested in Viceroy Dominion's public fucking image. He didn't give a damn how much the man dropped into the collection plate at church or how often he flossed his fuckin' teeth. It wasn't what Dominion did while the world was watching that was going to cost him this election. No, it was the dirt under his fingernails that Larry was after. The shit he dragged home on the bottom of his shoes.

Politics was a filthy game, full of dirty, disgusting players. It didn't matter who you were or how you rolled, there was always something dark and grimy hiding in the back of your closet, and if you were running against *his* guy, then it was Larry's job to find out exactly what that something was.

He chuckled under his breath as he paused at a name displayed in his phone's index. Larry knew exactly the type of bloodhound he could send in to stick a wet nose up the crack of Viceroy's ass. Thanks to Stewie's insatiable taste for redheads they had an ace in the pocket that made an ordinary gumshoe dick look like the Avon lady. He clicked on the phone number and grinned when it was answered on the other line.

"Yeah, let me speak to GiGi," he drawled happily. "GiGi Molinex."

CHAPTER 11

Rodney Ruddman was putting in some mean work on a tall stack of banana pancakes. The chewed-up rinds from several slices of salt pork lay discarded on the side of his plate, and the bright yellow guts of his over-easy eggs sat congealing in the morning air.

He was gulping down a glass of chilled apple juice when the door to his private dining area burst open and Kris Sanfrass, his longtime business partner, rushed in.

"Have you heard yet?" Kris asked excitedly. "Can you believe it?"

Ruddman jabbed his fork into the last mound of pancakes and shoveled it into his mouth.

"Heard what?" he said as he chewed.

"About your old friend. He's been running around the media circuit from *Good Morning America* to *Okrah* and *The View*, and now he's sticking his fingers in the latest local political pie."

Sanfrass pushed his smart phone into Ruddman's hand. "Here it is. He just entered the race against Chairman Stewart Baker. Check out my Twitter. It's all over the news feeds."

Ruddman peered down at the phone and scrolled through

the multitude of tweets. The more he read the hotter he got, and by the time he had scrolled halfway through the list he was good and fuckin' mad.

"Uh-uh." He shook his head as a dark look crossed his face. "Hell no! This can't happen. With that bastard chairing the board he'll regulate Ruddman Energy right out of business."

"We're not gonna let him get away with this, are we?"

"Hell fucking no," Ruddman growled, picking up his embroidered cloth napkin and wiping his hands and mouth. "Dominion is trying to be slick. As if I can't see right through his shady ass. He must have forgotten that I know where he chopped up all his bodies and where he buried them too! He'll never get that goddamn seat! *Never!* I'll run for it myself before I allow him to have it. In fact, I'll beat his ultra-conservative ass at his own dirty game. When's the deadline to put my name on the ballot?"

Sanfrass glanced down at his watch. "In about thirty minutes."

"Well get on it, goddamn it," Ruddman snapped. "First file the paperwork at the courthouse and get me in! And once that's done then I want you to contact that other guy who's running for the seat. What's his name again? Stewart Baker! Yeah, get Baker on the horn and arrange a meeting with him."

"A meeting?" Sanfrass looked confused. "With the guy you're about to run against?"

"Wake the hell up, dammit!" Ruddman snapped. "I'm running this race against *Viceroy Dominion*. With his kind of political story he'll beat the brakes off me and Stewart Baker both. No, forget about Stewart. He can't do me any harm. Baker is now the enemy of my enemy, and that makes him my friend. And by the way," he added as a crafty look crept into his eyes, "who's Viceroy Dominion's campaign manager?"

"Er—that contractor fellow who works for him, I believe. Bob Easton."

A sly smile crossed Ruddman's face. "Is that right? My old

friend Bob Easton, huh?" he said, remembering the last time
he had twisted the old man's balls. "Well, get on the horn and
get me a meeting with him too."

Dane Dominion pulled up outside of Dominion Oil headquarters and climbed out of his 2014 hot red Camaro ready to
report for work. Unlike the elder men in the family he didn't
have a designated parking spot, but he was cool with it because
he was only planning on slaving on the family plantation for a
quick minute.

Snuffing out the blunt of sticky he'd been puffing, Dane
retrieved a small bottle of Visine from his console then flipped
his overhead mirror open and squeezed a few drops in each
eye. Unwrapping two sticks of Big Red cinnamon gum, he
stuck both pieces in his mouth and chewed until the smell of
booda disappeared from his breath, then he hit his suit jacket
with a blast of Clive Christian No. 1 that he kept under his
seat.

He climbed out of the car feeling lifted with his head
buzzing nicely. Working a full-time job was going to be a real
challenge for him and he was gonna need to jet back to his
ride to hit the rest of that dro before lunchtime. His pops had
fucked his head up when he ran him that "start at the bottom
and work your way up" shit, but with debts racking up with
every major drug dealer in town and nothing but chicken
change trickling into his bank account, he had no other choice
but to follow orders and take the damn job that Viceroy had
offered him.

He strode toward the entrance of the stately building looking handsome and well-dressed in his sharp business attire. A
stylish Fioravanti jacket, a matching pair of slacks, and a five-
thousand-dollar pair of custom made Lucchese Classics black
belly American alligator boots.

Stepping up to the door, he was greeted by the longtime

doorman who had been working for Viceroy way before Dane was born.

"Hey there, young blood!" Dude dapped Dane out then reached out and gave him a big hug. "Long time no see, stranger! How's the college life been treating you man?"

"Aw, you know how it is," Dane said, playing it off. All those sweet milk and honey days of chillin' in college were over. He had slid his joint up in the wrong damn chick and all the good times had rolled.

"I'ma outta school now, man. Pops got a lil gig he needs me to handle for him here at the company so I'ma put my skills to work for the family for a quick minute."

"That's what I'm talking about," the old man said with approval. "Use that good education for the benefit of your family. Your father is a good man and a smart one too. Look at you! Bringing all that knowledge to the family fold!"

The receptionist in the lobby greeted Dane like he was royalty, and he got nothing but love from the Dominion employees as he walked around smiling and shaking hands with the staff. He had no idea which department Viceroy was going to put him in charge of, or which of these people would end up working for him, but it didn't really matter. He was a Dominion, and that meant he was automatically a big willie up in these parts. But that didn't mean he wanted a piece of the corporate head-game. His team could just keep on doing whatever the fuck they'd been doing all along because Dane wasn't trying to come in and take over a damn thing. *Sheeit*, his plan was to lock himself in his office where he was gonna be busy writing lyrics and having phone sex with a few honeys all day, so whoever ended up being his right-hand man was gonna have to juggle all the company balls on his own.

Dane rode upstairs to the eleventh floor where the senior executive offices were housed. His father, his uncle Suge, and his brother Barron all had plush-ass corner offices up here and Dane didn't expect anything less for himself.

"Good morning, Mr. Dominion," the secretary greeted him the moment he stepped off the elevator. "Your father is in his office. He's expecting you."

Dane passed through a gauntlet of high-powered oil executives who worked for his father. Some of the smartest mofos in the country were up in here damn near bowing down at his feet, and even without his college degree Dane felt grand as hell.

Viceroy was on the telephone engaged in a heated conversation when Dane walked in. Viceroy acknowledged him with his eyes and held up one finger, and Dane sat down on a buttery leather sofa and chilled while he waited. He sat back and closed his eyes and let a few lyrics run through his mind as his father conducted business over the phone. He didn't bother to listen in or to try to follow the conversation because he didn't give a damn about none of it. The only reason he was there was because his father thought it would look good on paper during his political campaign, but once Viceroy won the election and shit went back to normal at the mansion, Dane was gonna be ghost.

"You're late," Viceroy barked as he hung up the phone and turned to his second son. "Business, business, business. That's the name of this game."

Dane got up off the sofa and grinned as he went over and shook his father's hand. "Sorry about that, Pops. My alarm didn't go off this morning, but no worries. I'm here now and I'm gonna be here all day."

"Yeah," Viceroy nodded and agreed. "You sure will. Give me a minute and I'll take you downstairs and get you started on your new job."

"Cool," Dane said as Viceroy shuffled through some paper on his desk. "Where are you putting me? Acquisitions? Marketing? Product development? What department do you think I'll fit in the best?"

Viceroy glanced up from his desk like he was looking at a

damn fool. "Kill all that stupid talk," he growled. "You're going to the mail room, son. I'm putting your ass to work down in the mail room!"

Bob Easton had been summoned by a billionaire and he was skulking to his meeting under the cover of night. He had parked more than a mile away from the Omni Hotel, and by the time he slipped through the service entrance his seventy-two-year-old knees were killing him.

It had taken him by surprise when he'd gotten the call that Rodney Ruddman wanted to see him. The two men had more than forty years of history together, but they had never been friends. Ruddman was close to Bob's sons and when they were younger he had given both of them summer internships at his firm every year. Bob's wife had been pretty close to Ruddman's wife in the years before she died, and it was she who had helped plan the poor woman's funeral.

They were familiar, even if they weren't close. But still. There had always been something about Ruddman that rubbed Bob the wrong way, and his dislike of the man had only intensified during the years he'd been under contract with Dominion Oil. He figured Ruddman was making a ploy to lure him away from Viceroy just like he'd done with Dominion's brother-in-law, Digger Ducane, and his first reaction was to tell that uppity nigger to go to hell. But when he was told that Ruddman wanted to discuss a few family matters Bob had quickly agreed to meet him right away.

He made his way to the lobby of the Omni and over to the desk where he announced his presence. He was escorted to a bank of elevators that took him to the third floor where he was ushered past guest suite after guest suite, down several long and winding hallways until he was finally led into a freezing cold guest room that held two single beds but wasn't much bigger than a coat closet. A small round table was set up in the space in between the beds, and two plastic chairs were on either side of the table. Other than that, the room had been stripped bare. There was no television, no clock, and no sheets or blankets on the naked mattresses.

Bob was seventy-two years old, and his next birthday was in less than a month. He had been a fixture in the oil industry for more than fifty years, and had worked for various firms before investing in a company that mass-produced drill bits for offshore oil rigs. During his fifty-plus years in the business he had earned the respect and admiration of powerful men at all echelons of state and federal government. He even had a pipeline to the desk of the Attorney General of the United States. Which is why, after sitting in that cold, godforsaken room for over forty-five minutes, freezing his wrinkled nuts off on a hard plastic chair as he waited for some fat, arrogant black turd to bless him with his presence, he was ready to explode like a cannon from his aching feet on up.

"Good evening, Bob," Rodney Ruddman said with a smile as the door swung open and he rolled into the room on an air of self-centered confidence. "I'm glad you decided to accept my invitation," he said, sitting down on the other side of the small table. "It's chilly in here. Can I call downstairs and get you some coffee?"

Bob shook his head. It was nearly midnight and he didn't want Ruddman's goddamn coffee! What he wanted was the ugly bastard's head on a platter!

"What the hell is so important that you called me down here at this time of night?" Bob asked stiffly.

Ruddman's face creased in a slight grin and he raised one eyebrow and shrugged. "What's so important? Do you mean to you or to me?"

"To me, dammit!" Bob slapped his palm down on the table and the cracking sound echoed in the tiny room.

Ruddman was really smiling now. "Well," he began, "let's just say I'd like to have a conversation about someone who's very near and dear to both of our hearts." He paused for a moment, staring at Bob like a cat gazes at a trapped mouse as he waited for the gravity of his words to sink in.

"What the hell is this about?" Bob growled.

"It's about your son," Ruddman said simply. He looked up at the ceiling and started counting off on his fingers. "Your no-count, trifling, dope-sniffing, bribe-taking son." He looked back at Bob and laughed. "Damn. For a moment there it sounded like I was describing a black man, now didn't it?"

Bob's facial expression never changed, but inside his blood ran cold. "I'm not amused, Ruddman. In fact, I don't find any of this funny in the least."

"Well, you wouldn't," Ruddman shrugged. "I mean, you're the inadequate parent who raised that little bastard, and you know which son I'm referring to. If he was a kid of mine I wouldn't be laughing either."

Bob bristled. "You've known Brandon and Billy all their lives. If you called me down here just to insult me and my family, I've heard enough."

He leaned heavily on the table as pushed himself into a standing position and he was startled when Ruddman screamed, "Sit your ass back down! Did I give you permission to leave? Unless you want to see Brandon bent over a bunk in the penitentiary you'll sit right there and listen to what the fuck I have to say!"

Bob's hands were trembling as he gripped the table and lowered his wide ass back down onto the hard plastic chair.

"W-what do you want? What does my boy have to do with any of this?"

Ruddman smiled, his anger suddenly dissipated. "It's not just your son, Bobby Boy," he said. "It's that bribe money that he took on your behalf from Lynch Corporation last year. You got your son to do the dirty work for you, perhaps because he could be trusted above anyone else. But that idiot picked the wrong hotel to do his dirt in."

Bob's nose flared and he balked. "How dare you, you rotten bastard! I would never do such a thing, and nor has Brandon been involved in anything illegal! I've run a legit business my entire career, and you know it! You have some nerve calling me here and accusing me of using my own child in some cockamamie underhanded scheme! I've built my reputation on hard work and dedication, not bribery and back-door shady deals. So don't you dare insult me!"

Ruddman had let the old man run on and on at the mouth, and now he gave him the *muthafucka are you serious look* and sucked his teeth.

"You can save all that glamorous good-guy shit for the cops when they bust your ass, okay? I know all about your back-door business dealings, Bob. This isn't anything new."

Bob's voice trembled as he asked, "What's that supposed to mean?"

Ruddman pushed a few buttons on the iPad he carried and a grainy color video began to play. Bob watched as a series of security cameras recorded a man who was undeniably his son entering the elevator with a tall older man wearing a business suit and carrying a briefcase in his hand. When the elevator door closed, the man handed Brandon the briefcase and watched him open it. Stacks of money filled the briefcase and once Brandon was satisfied with an eye count, he reached in his jacket and handed the tall man a large envelope. The two men then shook hands and Brandon took the briefcase and got off on the ninth floor.

"Of course you know the man you see here with your son Brandon is none other than Lance Hollister from the Lynch Corporation," Ruddman smirked and then told a lie. "We have audio recordings of him confirming the transaction with his boss. Would you like to hear it?"

Bob's breathing grew heavy and he clenched his ass-cheeks together as his stomach went loose and his bowels began to rumble.

Ruddman was right. This shit could send Brandon straight to prison. And him too!

"No, goddammit," Bob managed to say hoarsely as his left eye began to tic. "I've heard enough."

Ruddman pinched harder. "We also have the license plate of the limo Mr. Hollister arrived in. Let me show you," Ruddman said as he advanced the film with a swipe of his finger.

The hotel's exterior cameras had caught Lance getting out of a limo, and Ruddman swiped his fingers and zoomed in on the license plate.

"That plate comes back registered to your company, Bob." Ruddman smirked. "Now did you really think a man of my intelligence wouldn't catch this juicy move?" He laughed. "Bob, Bob, Bob. You gots to be mo' careful, boy, as my granny used to say."

"What do you want from me?" Bob said weakly, his words hollow in the frigid room as beads of sweat dotted his nose and the crown of his balding head.

"Oh, I don't want anything from you," Ruddman said jovially. "Or from Brandon either. It's ya boy Viceroy," he told him. "What I want has to come out of Viceroy Dominion's pompous ass."

"And what's that?" Bob ventured.

"I want a *loss*," Ruddman said. "I want that bastard to lose the goddamn election, and I want him to lose it bad."

"You want him to throw it?" Bob asked incredulously.

Ruddman nodded. "Like a goddamn hand grenade."

Bob sighed. The thought of tricking Viceroy Dominion into throwing the election sent his heart into a tizzy. He rubbed his knees and mopped his thinning hair off his forehead and stood up to leave. "All right, but you know, we're really too old for this shit, Rodney,"

Ruddman looked at his old comrade and chuckled. "Naw, Bob. Your ass is old. I'm just getting started."

CHAPTER 12

I'm a buh-buh-beast, my nig! I'ma muthafucka beast, ya dig?
In the sheets, on the beats, and the muthafuckin streets, my nig!

The bass pumping through his ride was rattling the windows as Zeke Washington pulled up to the valet outside of the Omni Hotel in Dallas. He grinned as he hopped out of his beat-up 1999 Hyundai, which was covered with dents, dings, and large splotches of dried-up bird shit.

"Make sure you take good care of her," he said, tossing the uniformed valet the keys as he chuckled and headed toward the revolving front doors.

Two days earlier he had been boning this bad-ass Mexican bitch from the south side when he got a call from somebody claiming to be a representative of Rodney Ruddman, the CEO of Ruddman Energy.

"Is this Zeke Washington?" the female caller had asked in a professionally crisp voice that screamed, "Bill collector! Nigga-I-Found-Yo-Ass!"

"Nooo." He'd held the phone against his ear and kept right on stroking that hot pussy as he replied with a fake Spanish accent. "Zeke no lib here! Theese is Who-leeo's pone number now!"

"I have an important message for Zeke Washington concerning the financial assets of his late father. It's believed that

Earl Washington was the rightful owner of a substantial share of crude oil stock before he died, and as his heir, Zeke Washington could potentially be the rightful owner of those assets."

"What?" Zeke had blurted, pulling his wet dick out of the chick and tossing her jiggly ass to the side. "Yeah, this is Zeke. Who the fuck is this? What's the message, yo?"

"The message is that Mr. Ruddman would like to meet with you. As I mentioned, he believes your father's estate may have a right to a major portion of lucrative stock. Would you be willing to sit down and talk to Mr. Ruddman?"

"Sheeiit!" Zeke had laughed. Growing up, his mother had hammered him with stories about how his father had been dumb enough to trust the word of his shiesty friends and ended up getting fucked out of a fortune. "I'd sit down with Jeffrey Dahmer if he could help me get my daddy's dough back!"

"You wouldn't happen to have any of your father's old business documents still sitting around, now would you?" the female on the other end asked.

Zeke thought about the two boxes filled with his father's papers that sat catching cobwebs in the storage shed he lived out of.

"Yeah, I still got some of his stuff," he said, grabbing the Spanish chick by her hair and guiding her wet pink mouth toward his rock-hard dick. "Matter fact, I got all that shit."

"Good," the woman had said with a note of authority in her voice. "Bring it with you."

Bunni was gritting hard on some fried pork skins in the kitchen of the Dominion mansion when the house phone rang in the middle of the afternoon. Sliding off her stool, she shimmied over to the counter and saw the word "Private" pop up on the caller ID screen. Her eyes bucked open wide and she crossed her fingers and hoped like hell that this was the call she had been waiting for.

Now that she was rich Bunni wanted to be famous too,

and she gave less than a damn about that yang Mink was spitting. She wanted that big-time F.A.M.E, the shit that Fake-Ass-Muthafuckas-Envied, and taking matters into her own hands she had come up with a unique angle and drafted a lil write-up about how grand it would be to launch a reality show about her crazy new family the Hood Rich Dominions.

Bunni had sent out promotional blasts everywhere from Facebook to Craigslist, and she also emailed all the producers who had already turned her down and gave them a second chance at landing such a prize deal. She definitely hit up all the major cable networks like VH1 and Fox, and she was hoping Showtime would jump on their tip too.

Mink said she was bugging out and doing way too much, but Bunni felt she had a personality that was made for television and she was dying to show the world how a down-ass chick from Harlem could represent on a TV screen.

"Hello?" Bunni answered the phone with a big wide grin.

"Good afternoon! My name is GiGi Molinex. Is this the Dominion residence?"

"Yes!" Bunni screeched, jumping up and down so hard she damn near broke her toe. "I knew somebody was gonna call me today! I *knew* that shit!"

"I'm sorry, the woman said, sounding so cheery-o and wholesome that Bunni could tell right away that she was white. "May I ask who I'm speaking to?"

"Bunita Baines, baybee!!!"

"I'm sorry, did you say your name was Bunita Baines?"

"Yes!" Bunni screeched again. "This me, this me, this *me*! Whooop! Whoo*ooop*! Thank ya, Jeezus! I knew you would answer my prayers. Yes, yes, *yes*, Miss Moldiness! You a producer, ain'tcha? You wanna get my fam on your reality show, don'tcha? Gurl, I been expecting your call for *days*. I knew it, I knew it, I *knew* I would get my shot on TV! Did your office get them emails I sent? Did you like that beast-ass bio I wrote?"

"Well, errr . . . yes, Bunita, that's exactly why I'm calling," GiGi said, switching gears as a sneaky smile curled her red-painted lips. She had been flying totally off the cuff hoping something would come out of this cold call . . . and it did!

"Again, my name is GiGi Mo-lin-ex and I wanted to touch base with you because that bio you mentioned sounded very intriguing to me and my fellow producers. I'm glad you're interested in having us showcase your family on a reality show, and I'm calling to get a deeper insight into your story. Can you tell me a little bit more?"

"Oh *Lawwwd!*" Bunni shrieked all in the lady's ear. Mink had the moolah and now *she* was 'bout to have the spotlight!

"Well like it says in my bio," Bunni said, out of breath and barely able to contain herself, "me and Mink came down here from Harlem, but now we're part of the filthy rich oil family known as the Hood Rich Dominions! Us hoochies are live, full of jive, and we have *arrived,* baybee!"

"Great!" GiGi chirped. "But what makes you think your family has what it takes to float a reality show? What's special about the Dominion family that people don't already know?"

"Oh, we got what it takes," Bunni puffed her chest out and assured her. "Plus, it's so much shady shit that be going on with these mofos around here that people won't hardly wanna turn off the TV! We wanna bring those cameras into our mansion so America can see how black folks with a lotta money, a lotta soul, and a whole lotta attitude get down with each other, ya feel me, GiGi?"

"Oh, I certainly do," she replied. Bunni was ecstatic and GiGi was laying the game on her thick. "You and your family seem to be exactly what my team is looking for. Is it possible that I could get another copy of that bio you sent out? I need to reference it with my boss and my email server seems to be down right now."

"That ain't no problem," Bunni said. "You on Facebook,

right? Just go to my page and check it out. I put the bio up there and I posted a bunch of pictures too."

"Great!" GiGi chirped again, playing her role. Bunni had just threw the alley-oop, and now all GiGi had to do was slam-dunk that shit. "I believe we have room on our production schedule for one more slot, and from what you've told us we'd be very interested in getting you some air time."

"Yes! Air time! That's *exactly* what we want!"

"I can tell you're very excited, Bunita, but as I'm sure you already know, TV networks get a lot of bogus stories and people claiming to be someone they're not. It's my job to filter through these stories and see which of them are legitimate and exciting enough to grasp the minds of America and keep the ratings rolling in. If you don't mind I'd like to set up a meeting with you and your family at your earliest convenience."

"*Sheeeit.*" Bunni sucked her teeth. "You can brang yo ass over here right dammit now, while ya bullshittin'!"

"Excuse me?"

"Oh sorry," Bunni said with a chuckle. "I meant umm . . . I'm down to hook-up whenever you are, GiGi. You calling from Hollywood, right? Prolly somewhere over there on Ro-day-yo Drive, right?"

"Er, no. I'm a Texas affiliate with the network so I'm actually located right in the Dallas area."

"Cool! So tell me what I gots to do to get my peeps ready for this meeting?"

"Oh, please don't worry about any preparations. The meeting will be interview-style but," the white chick warned, "you need to be aware that there are several other families who are competing for that time slot as well. We're going to be using some very invasive pre-screening evaluations to help us decide who gets on the air. Do you have a problem with that?"

"Pre-screening evaluations?" Bunni repeated dumbly. "What the hell is that and why would I have a problem with it?"

"Well, for one thing, we have to come on site and interview the entire family. We have to ask some pretty probing questions in order to determine whether or not your particular story resonates with our target audience. People thrive on drama you know, and our viewers want plenty of it. If your family isn't exciting and a bit dysfunctional with lots of juicy, scandalous secrets that you've been hiding, well . . . sorry to say it but we can't use you. And the other thing is, we don't compensate you for these pre-screenings. You won't get any money out of it."

Bunni narrowed her eyes.

"Um, lemme hit you with a lil something, Mizz GiGi. Must I remind you about who you talking to?" she demanded.

"Pardon me?"

"I mean, do you really, really, really know who the hail you talking to?"

"I'm sorry, you said your name is Bunita Baines, did I get that correct?"

"My name might be Bunni Baines, but my best friend's name is Mink Domino! Domino, ya feel me! Like in Viceroy Big Daddy Drilling For Dat Oil Domino and Mama Selah Laced Out the Ass And Got it Going on Domino?"

"I-I'm afraid I don't understand what you—"

Bunni laughed. "I'm just messing with you. Don't nobody around here care about making no money, honey! We ain't concerned about getting paid because we already rich, ya dig? And we ain't stuttin' ya little 'evaluations' neither because we already know we the shit! So come on wit'cha cameras and all ya nosey-ass questions too! We rollin scandalous like a mug 'round here, baybee! We ready!"

I'm ready too, GiGi thought as she giggled inside. *Thank you, Bunni Baines for giving me such an easy way to screw your family from the inside out! This job is gonna be way easier than I thought!*

"Awesome!" GiGi said in a wholesome tone. "I'm glad you understand and I apologize if I offended you. Not every family who contacts us qualifies for a reality show, so I like to make sure everything is clear and concise up front. This is an opportunity for your family to let the world know who you really are and how you live, and for my company to bring something new and exciting to reality television. So trust me, I hope you have a *very* scandalous story and everyone in your family is just as fascinating as you say they are. I have a very important meeting to attend right now, but I can swing by your place for an initial assessment early this afternoon. How about two o'clock? Does that work for you?"

"Hell to the yeaaa!" Bunni said jovially. "I appreciate you for reaching out to a sistah, Mizz GiGi, and we will damn sure be ready to get this TV interview thang rollin. I promise you girl, you won't be disappointed 'cause we got just what your TV station needs."

"I'm sure you do, Bunni." GiGi smirked as she stared at the ratchet Facebook profile she had just pulled up on her computer screen and prepared to zero in on her next victim. "I'm sure you do!"

CHAPTER 13

I was crawling six feet deep at the bottom of a nightmare when Bunni woke me up and scared the shit outta me.

"Guess what?" she shrieked all loud with her lips right on my ear. "I just got a call from a TV producer, baybee!"

"Bunni, please!" I wailed as I rolled over in bed with my whole body sweating. I had been tossing and turning and dreaming that Gutta had his big hands wrapped around my throat tryna choke me out, and I was scared and mad at the same damn time. "What did I tell you about waking me up like that? Go somewhere and lee'me 'lone, girl!"

"C'mon, Mink!" She snatched my pillow. "I finally got one of them stuffy Hollywood mofos to agree to come out here and check us out so we can get our own reality TV show! Get in that bathroom and brush your teefus so we can get stupid on our grind today. The producer is coming over this afternoon to interview us and see if we're the type of peeps who can hold down a reality TV show for more than a couple of episodes."

I lifted my head and peered at her from one eye. "We? We *who*?"

"Me, you, and Peaches, that's who! Keep up, dammit!"

Snatching my pillow back, I rolled back over and mumbled. "Bunni, please. After that bullshit with Okrah you know I ain't feeling no more TV shit and Viceroy done already said Peaches can't stay here playin' all them tight skirts and high heels he be rocking. He swore to God he could see P's dick print through his dress and it freaked him straight out."

"So what?"

I flicked my hand at her. "So you scammed him, Bunni. You told him your manly brother 'Paul' was coming for a little visit! Viceroy practically shit on the couch when Peaches pranced up in here in that fly-ass pink Chanel suit."

"So what?" she said again.

"So you can just kill all that reality show noise, okay? It ain't gonna happen."

"But P's gotta be living right here in the mansion in order for us to get the show, Mink! That's what's gonna get us on, girl! People are gonna wanna see how all of us different types of rich black people live together under one big old gigantic roof."

"That ain't happening." I shrugged. "Viceroy wants Peaches out the door like yesterday, and besides, none of them other producers who was blowing up your phone at first ever called you back again, now did they? I'm telling you I am *not* with this reality bullshit, Bunni. All they want us to do is talk shit about each other and stab each other in the back. Who they think we are? The Braxtons? Nah, I ain't tryna put on no front and walk around with no camera stuck up in my face twenty-four/seven."

"Trick is you serious?" Bunni shrieked as she plopped down at the foot of my bed. "Uh-uh, Mink! You cursed Okrah out on live TV so I know damn well you ain't tryna act camera shy! Me and you *belong* on TV! Remember how we used to wanna be the hosts on *Wildin' Out* so we could show off all the fly clothes we stole?"

I smirked. "Getting seen and being noticed ain't every-thing no more, Bunni."

"It is to me, goddammit!" My Harlem rowdy crossed her arms and poked out her lip. "I don't know about you, but it is to *me!*"

Gutta and Shy stood outside the dirty Greyhound station smoking Newports and chillin' as they waited for the bus to arrive. They were planning to take a long-ass ride down to the Lone Star State since going up in an airplane scared the shit outta Gutta. The bus station was filled with all kinds of people coming and going from one destination to the next. There was always an under-current of griminess and shady characters that rolled low-key among the ordinary travelers, and Gutta and Shy fit in perfectly with that set.

"Yo, son," Shy said as he flicked the butt of his Newport on the ground and crushed it under his foot. "What's the plan once we get down there, bruh? How we gonna get up close to these silver spoon-ass muffuckas?"

Gutta was already two steps ahead of his comrade. In his mind he was already in Texas puttin' in work. He knew they were gonna have to do some scoping in order to find out where Mink's family lived and how they moved. Gutta was gonna use every tool that predators in prison used to manipulate people and situations and to exploit any weaknesses they might have. He had spent enough time in the joint to know how to get up close on a target with a smile and a handshake, just to shank 'em in the back as soon as they lowered their defenses.

"Don't worry 'bout it. I got this. We gonna make some-thing happen, son," Gutta said confidently to his young soldier. "We gonna go down there and show these niggas how Harlem get it in. Once I put the murder or the kidnap game down on Mink and her coward-ass fam, they gonna be begging me to take their money and get the fuck up outta Texas."

Shy was about to ask another question when some mangy-looking white woman approached them pulling a shopping cart loaded with junk. She bore all the classic signs of a drug fiend. Her dirty hair was matted to her scalp and her clothes were ripped and raggedy.

"Hey fellas, how ya'll doing," she walked right up on them and greeted them. "Umm, I don't mean to bother you guys but I was wondering if you . . . umm . . . if you know where I can cop a little bit of scag."

Shy started to answer her but Gutta cut him off.

"What the hell is *scag*?" Gutta snapped, knowing damn well the bum-fiend wanted some heroin. "Yo, do I look like a fucking drug dealer to you?" he demanded, pretending to be mad. "I'm fucking offended, lady! It's junkies like you that lower the value of our great city."

Gutta took an aggressive step toward the woman and raised the intensity in his voice.

"Yo, why don't you go ask your fuckin' cop-buddies over there chewing on them dirty franks where you can get you some scag! Niggas over there tryna act like they ain't been scoping me out for the last damn hour," Gutta said as he pointed at the two undercover agents who were standing near the hot dog vendor eyeing him. "Miss Officer," he said to the dirty white woman, "your shit is very sloppy. Next time tell those muf-fuckas to stop stuffing that mystery meat down their throats while they're on the job, you fucking rookies!"

The white woman's face turned Kool-Aid red with anger as she got busted out in front of the entire bus station. She was definitely a cop trying to make a buy and bust, but Gutta had just shot her cover straight outta the water so she turned around and grabbed her raggedy cart and jetted out of the terminal. People started laughing and clapping and finger-pointing like crazy. The undercovers at the hot dog stand had no choice but to pack it up and get the hell out too.

"Yo, you peeped the fuck outta that shit, son!" Shy grinned

at his manz in amazement. "How the fuck did you know ol' girl was a fucking cop? I was just about to serve that bitch!"

"You gotta be observant, my nigga," Gutta told his young partna. "Remember that shit when we get to Texas. Keep ya eyes open when we get down there and learn to scope everything around you. Not just the obvious shit in front of you. Ya dig?"

A half hour later Gutta and Shy were on their way. The bus wasn't too crowded yet so Shy got up and went to the bathroom. Gutta sat in the aisle seat with his headphones on rapping loudly to the music on his iPod. Soon, the unmistakable scent of Sweet Grand Daddy Purp was floating all throughout the bus. An old black lady and two middle-aged Hispanic women complained to the bus driver that someone was smoking in the bathroom so the driver pulled over.

"Ayo," Gutta said, snatching his headphones from his ears as the bus came to a halt on the edge of the road and the driver stood up. "What you stopping for old man? I need to be somewhere on time and you holding us up."

"Somebody is smoking weed back there and I ain't having that type of shit on my bus," the heavyset black man responded as he headed down the aisle. "Whoever is in that bathroom better come the hell on out right now!"

A few moments later the door squeaked open. Shy came out with a thick cloud of smoke trailing behind him with his red eyes looking like he was part Chinese. Gutta looked at his boy and shook his head. That nigga was higher than a light bill after Christmas.

"I'm going to need you to exit my bus, young man," the driver said as he huffed and puffed his old chest out. He pointed toward a red and white billboard overhead. "Smoking is strictly prohibited on this bus, can't you fucking read the signs?"

"Man, go sit ya old ass back down and drive this bus." Shy waved him off lazily as he got back in his seat. "I ain't getting offa shit!"

The driver frowned and nodded. "Okay then, smart-ass.

Have it your way, but this bus won't move until you get to stepping," he said defiantly. "Now you can take that shit up with all these other passengers and see what they say. I'ma get paid either way, mothafucka."

The passengers started getting real rowdy and cursing at Shy to get off the bus. One tall, light-skinned dude sitting across from Gutta got out of his seat and confronted Shy directly.

"Yo, you gotta get the fuck off the bus, homey," the dude said in a real brolic voice. "I gotta go see my goddamn son and you holding us the hell up."

Shy was high as shit and found the whole scene funny as he grinned from ear to ear.

"Man, fuck you light-bright!" Shy laughed. "You gotta problem come handle it."

Before the tall nigga could react a swift hand of lightning came down and struck him across his face.

Whackkkk!!

The monumental force of the slap dropped him perfectly back into his chair and he slumped over with his forehead leaning on the seat in front of him. That nigga was asleep just that fast. All he needed was a pillow.

It got so damn quiet that you could hear a pin drop on the bus. Folks were wide-eyed and silent as Gutta stood over the sleeping guy and grilled the rest of the passengers.

"All ya'll shut the fuck up and stop that bitching and moaning," he barked, putting the entire bus in check. "The next mothafucka who got something to say is going straight to sleep just like this clown right here!"

Gutta turned his murderous attention to the driver.

"Nigga if you don't get this bus moving right now I will body yo old ass, stuff you in the back of that dirty-ass bathroom, and then drive this bitch myself to where I gots to go. You feel me?"

The driver looked horrified at the huge brolic nigga with

fire in his eyes, knowing he meant every word he had uttered. He needed that paycheck he got every two weeks, but Greyhound didn't pay him nearly enough to handle these types of problems.

"Y-y-yes sir," the driver stuttered as he headed his ass back down the aisle to his seat. "We're out of here right now, sir. No problem at all."

"Now." Gutta turned to the frightened passengers again. "If anybody else got some smart shit to say I can make ya'll asses go night-night too. My right hand is better than Nyquil, dammit! I will put you smooth the fuck out, free of charge."

Nobody even looked in Gutta's direction as the bus cranked back up and everything got back in motion.

"Fuck you, nigga!" a tiny voice came from the back of the bus. "Ain't nobody scared of yo' big head Incredible Hulk–lookin' ass!"

Gutta whirled around ready to kill a mothafucka and then he saw Shy cheesin' his ass off. Gutta's scowl melted into a smile as he laughed at his homeboy and shook his head.

"Don't be playin with me like that, man," Gutta said, cracking up. "All this was yo dumb-ass fault anyway! You got me on the Greyhound wildin' out and shit, nigga!"

"We Harlem, baby," Shy said, still cheesing from the weed. "We do what the fuck we wanna do. It's a Harlem world."

"We've got a small problem," Bob Easton said the moment Viceroy stepped into the executive boardroom at Dominion Oil. He was sitting in Viceroy's chair with his feet up on the desk. The rest of the crew sat randomly around the conference table. They were an informal bunch today, this Gang of Five. They sat around in their shirtsleeves with their collars unbuttoned, smoking Havana cigars and pondering the political futures of the candidates like a think tank full of vicious sharks.

"What's up?" Viceroy asked as he walked past the white man lounging in his chair and took a seat in the middle of the pack. When he stood at the head of the table and conducted board meetings and dictated company policy he was the HNIC. The oil business was his specialty, but the arena of big-time politics belonged to the elder white men in the room, and today Viceroy knew to stay in his place.

"It's Ruddman. He's running against you, Viceroy. He filed his paperwork ten minutes before the deadline, and now he's in the race."

"That greasy bastard!" Viceroy sneered. "That fat-head fuck!"

"Now, now." Bob held up his hand calmly. "There's no need for all of that. This isn't a game of emotions, Viceroy. It's a game of cunning and skill, and obviously Ruddman is using a bit of both."

"But if he's running against me then that could split some of the votes. Folks who are against Larry Dawkins and want him out will now have to choose between a rich black man and another rich black man!"

"That's the whole idea," Bob said, nodding. "Ruddman's being smart and strategic. He's got some top-notch advisors who are setting him up for big-time success."

Viceroy balked. "So if his cats are setting him up for success, what the hell are you guys setting me up for?"

"A killing," Bob said quietly. "We're not just setting you up to win, we're setting you up to conquer and annihilate! When we get done throwing rocks in Ruddman's campaign he'll go crawling back into his cave at the Omni and never come out again."

"So how are we gonna do that? What's our plan?"

Bob smirked and waved his hand. "Plans are for the weak and vulnerable. What we've come up with is a *scheme*. Watch this."

Bob picked up a small remote and clicked it, and a film began to roll on the conference room's back wall. Viceroy watched as a political advertisement for the support of undocumented workers filled the screen, showcasing none other than the CEO of Ruddman Energy himself.

"Undocumented workers are not your enemy," Ruddman spoke into the camera. "They are the lifeblood of this great country, the backbone of our industry. They do the jobs that ordinary Americans do not want to do, and they provide reliable services and resources at every level of American life." Big color photos of Mexican fruit pickers, bus-boys, child care providers, and elderly companions flashed by on the screen.

Ruddman smiled, then drove his message home strongly by saying in Spanish, "Here at Ruddman Energy we respect and support our undocumented workers. We will ensure their jobs remain safe."

When the sixty-second spot went off, Viceroy turned his glare on Bob expectantly. "That bastard doesn't speak a word of *español*, but he's probably just pulled in a major hunk of the Latino vote with that one. How the hell am I supposed to fight that?"

Bob was ready. "By hiring a few undocumented workers on your staff and making your own video," he said. "And," he added quietly, "by showcasing your new houseguest. The cross-dresser. As distasteful as I find his lifestyle he can get you a shitload of votes that Ruddman could never touch."

"Who you talking about? Peaches?" Viceroy balked with his lip curled down in disgust. "But I thought you told me to get rid of him and now you're telling me to shoot a commercial and go on the air with that skirt-wearing, perfume-stanking, makeup-sporting, sissified-drag-nasty-go-rilla muthafuckin' fa—"

"Transvestite!" Bob cut in. "Yes, we want you to go on the air in support of Peaches and show the world that just because you're a Republican who believes in small government and fiscal responsibility, it doesn't mean you're a heartless cad who would turn his own family member away just because he happens to have a different lifestyle."

"Peaches ain't none of my goddamn family!" Viceroy exploded. "He's a gorilla freak from New York City! There ain't none of that funny stuff going on in my family tree!"

"It doesn't matter," Bob said firmly. "Ruddman has bitten into the Hispanic vote and now we've got to take a major bite of the gay and lesbian vote and force ourselves to chew it. I've arranged some studio time for you to shoot the ad spot tomorrow morning. Your speech is being written up as we speak, and I'm sure it'll say something about how you respect and support all members of your Republican constituency, even if they are gay cross-dressers like your favorite nephew."

"Nephew? I already told you, that fruitcake ain't no kin to me!"

"Well, if you want to win this election you'd better start acting like he's one of your kin. Your initial polling numbers are way down, Viceroy. Perhaps you should start treating him like he's your son."

"*Shit*!" Viceroy whined with his face screwed up. "The next damn thing you'll be telling me is to let some fools come up in my house to shoot that damn reality show!"

"You're exactly right." Bob nodded firmly. "That's precisely what I was planning to tell you. One reason your poll numbers are so low is because people don't know enough about you. A reality show might be just what the doctor ordered, especially if they can air it right away. It's time to stop hiding behind your walls. Go ahead and give America an up-close-and-personal look at what your life is *really* like, Viceroy. Let them see your frailties and your faults. Everybody loves to watch a good train wreck. Let's see how close you can get to the edge of the tracks without jumping off."

CHAPTER 14

Rodney Ruddman wasn't above a good-old-fashioned ass-fucking. Especially if he was the one supplying the stiff meat.

"Mr. Washington has arrived, sir," his longtime secretary at Ruddman Energy poked her head in the door and informed him in a hushed tone.

Rodney glanced at his watch and nodded. The young man was exactly five minutes early and that was a good sign.

"Make him wait a half hour and then send him in," he instructed his secretary, and then opened a folder on his desk that was labeled *Confidential* in big black letters.

A slick smile of satisfaction played along Rodney's lips as he thumbed through the photocopied documents inside. It had taken some arm-twisting and a nice chunk of change to get his hands on this folder, and now that he had it he was gonna use it to his full advantage.

Rodney shook his head as he read through the documents. That Viceroy was a bad mothafucka and as shrewd and crafty as they came. As much as he despised his ass, Ruddman had to admit if you were gonna dog-fuck your friend, then this was definitely the way to do it. His arch-enemy had earned his full respect for this particular ploy because only a cold-blooded bastard would lie, cheat, and swindle a homey the way Viceroy Dominion had done.

"It's been thirty minutes," his secretary said softly as she opened his office door once again. "Shall I send him in?"

Rodney glanced down at the eight-by-eleven photo of Earl Washington, Viceroy's former business partner. He wondered if the son's balls were any tinier than the father's had been, or if the young man had been cut from a thornier tree. Either way, he was about to find out. "Send him in," Ruddman said with a cold, calculating grin. "Yes, send young Mr. Washington right on in."

Zeke Washington sat back in the soft leather chair with his mind in moolah heaven. A pretty white escort from Ruddman Energy had led him over to a private elevator and used a card key to access the skylight suite on the top floor. He'd given the secretary the box of his father's papers and told her that he had an appointment with Rodney Ruddman, and in return she'd given him an iPad that had been loaded with all the latest movies and had all the best games available on it as well.

She left him in the lounge area for a good minute, but waiting around didn't mean a damn thing to him. He was unemployed and the clocked ticked the same way for him every single day. He was busy playing *Call of Duty* and making loud action noises with his mouth as he slayed muthafuckas left and right when he glanced up and realized the secretary was standing over him, calling his name.

"Mr. Washington?" she said with a small smile. "Sorry to interrupt you but Mr. Ruddman is available to see you now."

Zeke flashed her a big smile and tossed the iPad carelessly down on a chair. "Oh, yeah?" he joked. "That's cool, because I'm ready to see him now too."

Following the secretary down a long hall, Zeke smoothed down his cornrows and hiked his baggy jeans up by the belt loops. His bop was full of confidence as his Timbs sank into the plush carpet that felt like soft cotton under his feet. The smell of big-time money was in the air as he added a little dip to his gait and a masculine swing to his arms.

At the end of the hall they entered an office that was nearly five times the size of the U–Store–It shed that Zeke rented for a hundred and twenty-five dollars a month and crashed on a cot in every night. The office hollered "pure money" loud and clear, and the desk was so damn big he had to look twice to find the little round dude who was sitting behind it.

"Zeke Washington," Rodney Ruddman boomed, his voice filled with power and authority. His snake eyes swept over the young man as he studied him intently. He was from the streets. A handsome and fit young man with an athletic build. He was a two-bit criminal too, Ruddman knew. He had already pulled up the boy's rap sheet and it was longer than his dick.

Dressed in the trappings of cultural poverty, Zeke sported what Ruddman referred to as "corner clothes" and while his gear screamed BROKE AS SHIT, the look in his eyes said, HUNGRY AND AMBITIOUS.

"It's good to see you. You look just like your father."

"Is that right?" the young man replied smoothly. "What? You used to run with my pops back in the day or something?"

"Yes, I knew your father well," Ruddman lied. "Or at least well enough to be pissed off when he caught that raw deal. I called him up and offered to have my attorney help him out, you know. But unfortunately he died before we could put something together. Have a seat," he said, nodding at a leather chair on the other side of his desk. "I've ordered up some lunch for us. Make yourself comfortable until it arrives."

Bopping over to the chair, Zeke plopped down on the edge and then leaned back like he was low-riding in a sporty whip. His legs were cocked open wide in his baggy faded jeans, and he sat there trying to look hard as hell as he lounged across from one of the richest men in America.

"So, you're probably wondering why I asked you to come here," Ruddman said.

"Um, yeah." Zeke grinned. "I mean, I ain't exactly the type of cat who slums with the oil willies ere' day, so yeah. The thought crossed my mind."

Ruddman sat back and nodded, pleased by what he saw. Earl Washington had been a quiet brainiac, but his kid was all ruthless street charm. He looked just like all the other young un-educated black men who were caught up in a cycle of poverty and hopelessness, and whatever potential greatness he might have tapped into had his father lived and Viceroy Dominion not fucked him out of a fortune, was way in the past.

Two waiters entered the office quietly. They pushed cov-ered platters ahead of them on carts and busied themselves set-ting up lunch for the big boss and his guest.

"So, what are you doing with your life?" Ruddman probed as Zeke pounced on the food the moment the waiters were done. He took the top bun off both his cheeseburgers and stacked a fistful of French fries on top of the thick and juicy chopped steak patty. Ruddman watched in amusement as the young man slathered ketchup all over the mound, then smashed the buns back on top and choked the cheeseburgers down two at a time.

Yeah, he's hungry all right, Ruddman smiled inside as he watched the young cat grub. *Now let's see if he's ambitious.*

Barron stared down at the folder in his hand then flung that shit on his desk like it was a hissing snake. Somebody was trying to fuck the shit outta his father and it damn sure wasn't his mother. Barron's mouth wanted to fall open as he thought about what he'd just read but he knew better than to let a mofo see him sweat.

They were in the middle of a heated political campaign and not only had that bastard Ruddman dug up some skeleton bones on Viceroy that could put him in a legal bind due to his shady business dealings with his late partner, he had also called in Earl Washington's son to help him bury Dominion Oil in the dirt.

"It's hot off the press," Digger Ducane said with a shiesty grin. "In fact, my sources tell me Earl's son is eating lunch in Ruddman's office right now."

Barron shrugged and angled his chin at the folder on his desk as he played it cool. "So what, Unc? Is this shit supposed to scare us?"

Digger had torn his drawers raggedy with the Dominion family. He had once been a trusted member of the fold, but when Viceroy was in a coma he called himself pulling a slick move by jumping ship and going to work for Rodney Ruddman. Right now the look in Digger's eyes told Barron that his reaction wasn't the one his uncle had expected, but Digger played his hand just as cool.

"It ain't supposed to scare you, Barron, but it is supposed to make you think and plan. Ruddman got these papers from Zeke Washington. He's planning to turn them over to the commission as proof that the documents Viceroy filed with the state thirty years ago were forgeries."

Barron was an attorney and he shrugged like he had icewater in his veins. "These papers don't mean shit. They're not notarized or executed. I could sit down at my computer right now and type up something just like this myself."

"But these papers are *signed*. Any handwriting expert could prove that's your father's signature."

Barron nodded. "So what? They may be signed but they're not executed. The only version of this contract that counts is the one that's on file at the county office. People sign shit every day and then revise different drafts of the same document. That's how it's always been in this business, and I doubt if this is any different."

"Oh, it's different," Digger assured him with a smug grin on his shit-eating mug. "Have you ever heard of a gentleman by the name of Wally Su?"

Barron shook his head. "Nah. His name doesn't ring a bell."

"Well, it should," Digger said. "I'm sure your father could tell you a whole lot about old Wally Boy."

"Oh yeah? And why is that?"

"Because Wally Su is his dear old friend. He's also the former county clerk who signed as a witness to the documents drawn up between Earl Washington and your father all those years ago. Wally's on his deathbed now, and he's been convinced that confession is good for the soul. He's prepared to testify that the documents he filed thirty years ago when he was a clerk were forged, and to air every piece of dirty laundry he has on the swindle that sent Washington to a poor man's grave and made your father filthy fuckin' rich."

Barron stood there looking like a statue. From the outside he appeared to be etched from granite, but inside he was enraged and his blood swirled around in his veins like hot lava.

These muthafuckas were gonna *do* his daddy. Not only were they gonna hit him with a prosecution and a public shaming, they were gonna rip off his pants and yank his drawers down, and then bite off a great big chunk of his big black dick. If this Wally cat testified in front of the commission then the carefully built walls around the empire that Viceroy had built were gonna come tumbling the fuck down right on top of their heads.

Unless Barron was able to stop them, that is.

As furious as he had been with Viceroy's bullshit lately, he was still his father's son.

This was some serious shit, and there was only one man in the state of Texas who Barron knew could save Dominion Oil and get his father's ass out of this sling. One man in the country, in fact. Hell, in the whole fuckin' world.

"All right. I'll make sure my father sees this."

"You're gonna let him know I was looking out for him right?"

"Yeah. I will."

"You be sure to tell him I'm still his boy and I still have his back."

"A'ight."

Leaving his uncle in his office, Barron strode down the hall to the private conference room. He slammed the door shut, then locked it with both bolts. Pulling the curtains closed, he took out his cell phone and hit the speed-dialed number of the best damn closer on this side of the Atlantic.

He dialed his *other* uncle. The brolic nigga who moved the mighty mountains and held back the raging seas.

He called Suge.

CHAPTER 15

Miyoko Su sat motionless by the bedside of her dying father and gazed down at him with loving eyes. At the age of fifty-four, Wally Su's body was wasting away from the ravages of stage four cancer, while his mind remained alert and strong.

The hospital room was large and serene, and as a multi-billionaire Mr. Su was benefiting from cutting-edge medical expertise and every man-made comfort that money could buy. Each morning his attendants read to him from the business sections of all the major newspapers in order to keep him engaged with the outside world, but Wally Su was dying, and the end was very near. He knew it, his doctors knew it, and his beloved daughter Miyoko knew it too.

"You must drink a little water," Miyoko urged him gently as she held a paper cup to his lips and patted his burning face with a damp cloth. It pained her to see her once strong and powerful father reduced to such a diminished condition. His sallow skin stretched tightly across his hairless skeleton, and his muscles had long since turned to mush.

But his eyes. His eyes still burned with intelligence and awareness, and the force of his will was ever strong. Wally Su had once been considered one of the most powerful men in the state. He had graduated from the University of Texas Law School and gone to work at a premiere law firm where he learned the ins and outs of contract law from the very best minds in the nation. But it was during his tenure as a law clerk that Su formed the most lucrative alliances of his career. He had built his financial empire by trading favors under the table with those who were even greedier and grimier than he was, and now, with the last of his life hanging by a thread, all Wally Su wanted to do was to confess to his crimes and let the chips fall where they may.

"It's almost time," he whispered to his beloved daughter. He had spent the last thirty years of his life protecting her, and he was well prepared to protect her in death as well. But everyone else who would be affected by his deathbed confessions? Too fucking bad for them. It was only right that when the tree died, its tainted fruit died right along with it.

"Are you certain you want to do this, Papa?" Miyoko asked softly. Ever since he'd met with the young black man sent by Rodney Ruddman, Wally had been restless and filled with anxiety. The young man had asked him to make his confession during the annual meeting before the election, and Wally Su sincerely hoped he would live long enough to fulfill the boy's wish.

He gazed at his daughter and his nod was painful. "Yes, Miyoko. This is something I must do. I must rid myself of this burden. I can no longer bear it, and I refuse to take it with me to my grave."

Miyoko nodded. "As you wish, Father." She paused and then she asked softly, "When?"

"At the annual commission meeting, right before the election."

Miyoko raised an eyebrow.

"He'll be disqualified and he'll lose everything, you know. And it will be all your fault."

Wally coughed painfully and then nodded. "Who cares?

He's enjoyed all the riches of the world for the last thirty years, and that was all my fault too."

Suge Dominion had spent his whole life doing battle in the trenches and navigating the line between the business world and the bing. He was a tried and tested G and he had a reputation for calculated thinking and swift brutality, and he had no problem slaughtering a whole army of enemies if that's what it took to protect his fam.

For as far back as Suge could remember he had been his big brother's keeper. He was a problem solver and a killer, and he had dedicated his entire life to making sure the sharks of the world didn't bloody up Viceroy's waters, and today wasn't gonna be no different.

But the frantic call he'd just gotten from his nephew Barron had caught him by surprise. His brother was running an intense campaign in a real cutthroat political bubble, so it was normal for a foe to toss a couple of grenades in their bunkers to see what they could blow up.

But this shit right here was different. The stuff Bump was talking went way beyond the realm of dirty politics. This shit here cut right into the core of the company. It rattled the foundations of Dominion Oil and sliced through the meat and down to the gristle-bone.

"Yo, we gotta fix this shit!" Lil Bump had been damn near panicking over the phone. "Not only do we have to stop Wally from testifying, we gotta make sure his documents never see the light of day. This is bigger than just Ruddman trying to get at my pops. If this shit gets out then everybody—you, me, and Mama—we could all go down!"

Suge was well-schooled in the runnings of their business, and so was everyone else in the game. There wasn't a politician in the world who hadn't gotten his hands dirty at some point in his career, or who hadn't snuck behind the bushes and gotten his dick sucked by an ugly muthafucka, and his brother Viceroy was no exception.

But shit in this game had a way of coming back to haunt you, and no matter how carefully Suge examined the current situation it was looking like his brother's dick, and the Dominion family fortune, were about to get run through a meat grinder.

Suge had a reputation as a fixer. A closer. The kind of dude you called when help was no place else to be found. Cleaning up shitty messes was what he did for a living, and he was one of the best of his kind in the game. But for the life of him he couldn't find a single way to wipe up his brother's spill this time. None of his normal go-to sources had the kind of power he was looking for, and not a single course of action he had available would lead him to a resolution that would keep his fam's gold in the safe and their necks off the chopping block.

It looked like Suge was straight outta mojo this time and his big brother Viceroy was about to be shit out of luck.

That is, until he remembered a beautiful nightmare from his past by the name of Miyoko Rose Su.

Miyoko Su had been Suge's boo thang back in the day, and if she hadn't been about twenty different kinds of crazy their relationship might've had a real good run. A beautiful slim goody with mad sex appeal, she'd been raised in Okinawa until her parents divorced when she was thirteen, and then she came to the United States to live with her father.

Wally Su, Miyoko's father, was a razor-sharp corporate attorney. Him and Viceroy had done a lot of shady business together in the early days when Viceroy was climbing the ladder and Wally was the county clerk. He had raised his daughter Miyoko in the suburbs of Houston, and when she was fresh out of law school and working for her father's firm, Suge had the good luck of running into her at a state dinner. The spark of attraction between them had been instant and undeniable, and Suge had snuck her into a coatroom and gotten him a piece of them drawers right there at the banquet.

Wally Su had disapproved of their relationship right from the jump. He was one of Viceroy's dirtiest cronies, and they'd gotten down on quite a few highly profitable under-the-table deals together. Suge and Miyoko proceeded to get their swerve on in a hot and very public sexual fling that had her old-school Asian father climbing the walls.

Wally Su tried to stop it. He gave a fuck about all the cash he was raking in from the Dominion fortune or about how greasy Viceroy kept his greedy little palm. Wasn't no nigger from the other side of the tracks ever going to be good enough to put his black paws on his flawless porcelain-skinned baby girl.

But Suge had been wide open on the chick and he didn't give a fuck what her daddy said. It didn't stop Miyoko neither. A part-time model for high-end designer wear, she was brilliant and beautiful and hot in the ass for him. An exotic freak in the sheets, Miyoko took everything Suge had and threw even more right back at him, and for a minute there she had him pretty much whipped too. Suge had never, ever ran into a woman whose swerve game was just as powerful as his, and the sparks they ignited in each other had felt like rockets going off in his drawers.

They had become a couple damn near overnight, and since they were forced to sneak around behind her father's back, Miyoko had to make a choice as to which one of the men in her life rocked her world: Her daddy or her *Big* Daddy.

It wasn't long before Suge's brand of sweet chocolate whip appeal got her strung out on his rhythm. The girl was hooked on him like a base-head. He had her stuttering and feening for that meat. She wanted to bounce on his dick the first thing every morning and the last thing every night. He couldn't shake her ass off even if he wanted to. She stayed hot and thirsty. She was running a fever and Suge was her Tylenol.

All that shit was cute for a couple of minutes, but then the crazies started coming out of Miyoko and Suge got a peep of her true colors. She got clingy and possessive. She had crying jags and jealous fits. Every woman who looked at him became her personal rival, and if the chick was black then she became a federal suspect. Her burning fear was that Suge would leave her for a bangin sister, and she became envious of every black woman who so much as looked his way.

The shit hit the fan one day when they were having lunch on the street at an outdoor café, and it just so happened that a fine, big-booty sister walked past wiggling her hips and looking like a delicious platter of candied yams and barbequed ribs.

Outta nowhere, Miyoko jumped out of a trick bag.

"You're fucking that bitch," she blurted, a dark look of suspicion clouding her eyes as she watched the girl's wide hips and bubble ass sway down the street. "That's the ghetto bitch you've been fucking, isn't it?" she demanded. "Isn't it, Superior? *Isn't it?*"

Ghetto? Suge thought she was bullshitting for a second, but when he saw the rage on her face and the tears in her eyes he knew his girl was out there for real.

But then suddenly a lightbulb went on.

The pretty black girl walking by was just some random sister going about her business, but Suge wasn't one to let a good opportunity fly and he jumped all over that shit.

"Damn," he muttered, shaking his head and looking guilty as fuck. "You got me, Lil Bit. Shit, I'm busted, baby. I'm sorry you had to find out about her this way. I'm a dirty muthafucka and you deserve way more than what I been giving you. I hate that our thing is over, but you need to gone and find yourself a better dude."

Suge had expected the tears and he was ready for them shits, but he wasn't ready for all the rest.

"You cheater!" that nut screamed at the top of her lungs. She jumped up and sloshed a glass of red wine in his face and then proceeded to turn the whole damn restaurant out. "You're a fucking cheater!" she screeched as she snatched their plates and silverware off the table and started hurling them out into the open street. "A no-good fucking cheater!"

Suge had paid off the restaurant and sent her home crying in a taxi. He figured he was finally rid of her psycho ass and that was the end of it, but he couldn't have been more wrong. Miyoko was bent. She started stalking him. Straight up tracking his dick like a bush hunter. That crazy chick busted all the windows outta his brand new whip and cracked a carton of raw eggs all over the plush interior. She broke into his mailbox and set that shit on fire, then showed up at Dominion Oil and told everybody she was strapped with a bomb.

Muthafuckas poured out of that bitch with a quickness!

"Fix this shit," Viceroy had warned him when her bomb turned out to be a bunch of giant peppermint sticks taped together. Miyoko's father was his ace in the hole and Viceroy needed to keep him in pocket. "Get rid of that crazy bitch and keep her ass quiet!"

But it ended up being Wally Su who put the brakes on all his daughter's bullshit. As a conservative Asian it embarrassed him to no end to have his daughter acting such a public fool, so he put his foot down on her neck. He lied and told Miyoko he was taking her back to Okinawa to visit her mother, but once he got her there he stuck her ass in a padded room for six months and threatened to keep her there forever unless she left that black dick alone and got her head right.

It had been more than ten years since Suge had last seen Miyoko, and even though their families still ran in the same ultra-rich social circles, to Suge's relief she had followed her father's orders and left him the hell alone.

But now he needed her, and he needed her bad.

Cancer was eating at Wally Su's guts from the inside out, and after making his millions the good old grimy way, his conscience was eating at him too. He was threatening to expose all

of his crooked business dealings, including the ones he'd fina-
gled with Viceroy, and Suge just couldn't let that shit happen.

So, as much as he hated to, and as bad as his gut was telling
him not to, Suge was gonna have to get with Miyoko again,
and he was gonna have to get with her real quick. As the former county clerk, Wally Su had registered and deposited the
forged set of documents down at the courthouse like he was
supposed to, but the real set of documents—the ones that
matched the set that Zeke Washington had—were floating
somewhere out there in the world. In Wally Su's world.

Suge could only shake his head at that yellow-bellied old
bastard. He would have killed that coward if he wasn't already
dying. Because for the last thirty years Su had racked up ten
percent of every dollar Dominion Oil took in the door, and
he'd gotten rich as fuck in the process. For thirty long years he
had held those documents for ransom and kept his mouth
closed, and now all of a sudden that bastard had loose lips and
snaggly teeth.

Suge shook his head again. Death musta been a real muthafucka because Su was pulling a sucker move if Suge had ever
seen one. The Wally Su he'd known and respected back in the
day was a muh'fuckin' gangsta. An original G. Wouldn't no real
slick-ass Asian mobster voluntarily stuff his own ass into a can.

But regardless, Suge needed those damn documents. He
needed them in his fuckin' hands like pronto. When the commission met and Wally Su got up there and started confessing
like he was on death row, Suge needed to make sure that the
three pieces of paper that could break the Dominion bank and
get his brother put under a jail were nowhere in sight.

And that's where Miyoko was gonna come in.

Many years had passed since he had laid his pump game
down on her but that didn't matter. Suge was every bit the
player today as he had been back then, but with age and experi-
ence he'd grown even smoother with his flow. He was confident
that he could convince Miyoko to slide him those documents.

His tongue game alone used to make her forget her own name and she would sell her daddy to the devil for just the memory of his stroke.

It was gonna be like dangling carrots in front of a cross-eyed horse. Wherever he led was where Miyoko would follow. Suge knew he was about to be playing a real dangerous game, but he didn't see any other way around it. His brother needed him. Dominion Oil needed him. He wasn't about to let his family get ass-fucked into the poor house, and he wasn't about to let some half-dead Asian or some very old memories of some very delicious pussy hold him back neither!

CHAPTER 16

Bunni was just too excited! She had company coming over and she'd spent the entire morning scurrying back and forth around the mansion trying to make sure everything was set and ready to go.

GiGi Molinex had said she would be there by two, and Bunni had told all the maids to make sure they cleaned up extra good and she had asked Mrs. Katie to rustle up a couple of trays of cucumber sandwiches and granola bars and any other nasty shit that white people liked to eat.

It had taken her forever to pick out her gear, and even though Mink kept saying it was only gonna be an interview and wasn't none of it gonna be on TV, Bunni was still stepping lovely in her finest strip club rags from 125th Street.

"Where is she?" Mink busted up in Bunni's bathroom and complained when two thirty rolled around and the chick still hadn't shown up. "You sure this chick is white?" she huffed under her breath. "'Cause her ass is on CP time!"

Cool as a breeze, Bunni glanced at her watch and dabbed a little bit more Secret under her arms.

"She's coming, Mink, damn! Give her a chance. She works in Dallas but she's really from Hollywood and she prolly don't even know her way around here! She mighta got lost or caught a flat tire or something."

"Yeah, whatever." Mink smirked as she headed out the door. "Or maybe her ass is walking all the way from Los Angeles, Bunni! Did you ever think about that?"

"Nope!" Bunni said, twisting her lips behind Mink's back. "The only thing I'm thinking about is getting my ass on TV!"

Los Angeles was the city of angels but there were also a fair number of demons lurking around that town, and little did Bunni know it but GiGi Molinex wasn't flying high on nobody's wings.

In fact, GiGi wasn't from Los Angeles at all and she damn sure wasn't a television producer by any stretch of the imagination. What she was, however, was a swindler, an ex-prostitute, and a seven-days-a-week career criminal. To top it all off, she was also a red-hot liar and a damn good one at that.

After traveling the country living from grift to grift, GiGi had landed in Texas where she became a highly paid sugar baby and the part-time slut muffin of one of the most powerful attorneys in the state, Stewie Baker. As a "personal companion," GiGi traded favors with some of the richest men in politics, swooping in to lay her fiery con game down whenever somebody important needed distracting. With a beautiful face, a fuckable body, and a head full of luscious scarlet-colored hair, the type of distracting GiGi did always required quite a bit of cash.

GiGi's hustle had been in a lull when out of the blue, Larry Dawkins, Stewie's campaign manager, called in a big favor. He needed her to go on a quick mission to dig up as much dirt on a political foe as it would take to keep him from winning the election and snatching the commission chairman's seat out from under Stewie, and that's exactly what GiGi was determined to do.

She scrolled through a folder full of pictures she had loaded up on her iPad. Her target was Viceroy Dominion, and after talking to Bunni Baines on the phone and studying all her stuff on Facebook and Instagram, the plan was to use one of Viceroy's sons to take the powerful oil man down.

GiGi had a choice to make and both of them looked damned delicious. The middle son, Dane, was little more than a college boy, but he was a chocolate hunk of gorgeous goodness that she wouldn't mind giving a nice little go. And according to his LinkedIn profile, Barron, the eldest son, was a big-shot attorney and a senior executive at his father's company. He was tall and just as good looking as his brother so sliding up under either of them would be a pleasant win. GiGi had a feeling Barron might prove to be the tougher nut to crack, but with her flaming red tresses, green eyes, plump tits, and extra-bouncy ass, there wasn't much she couldn't talk her way up on.

GiGi knew she had the sweetest face in creation and a purring, kitteny voice, but her greatest asset, even greater than her irresistible sex appeal, was the talent that had earned her nearly everything her heart desired: her thirst for attention and her vivid imagination. GiGi had been blessed with a wicked little tongue, and ever since she was a little girl she'd had a knack for making up stories and luring people in so convincingly that most people—especially men—fell victim to her lies and believed them to be true.

Of course, most women weren't as susceptible to GiGi's "stories" as men were, but that had never bothered her back then and it damn sure didn't bother her now. All it did was make her work harder to deliver her message much more convincingly, and these days she was a master at her game.

She swiped her finger and scrolled through the last few pictures in the folder. The Dominion mansion was one of the largest and stateliest that GiGi had ever seen but she wasn't about to let that slow her down. She was about to do a job on Viceroy Dominion, and she was scandalous enough to pull every trump card in the deck in order to get what she wanted.

"Are you ready for them?" Frank, GiGi's fellow grifter asked as they climbed into the rented van that bore a fake peel-away logo of a local television station on both sides.

Grinning, GiGi hitched up her short green dress as she slid her long legs and stacked frame into the passenger seat and got ready to go on an adventure that could dictate the fate of the entire oil regulatory body.

"I was born ready for people like them." She threw her head back and laughed, letting the wind toss her long, fire engine–red mane out behind her in all directions. "The real question is," she asked with a devilish glint in her green eyes, "are the Dominions ready for *me*?"

Suge stepped up in the offices of Su International like he owned that bitch. He was walking into enemy territory and he welcomed the fighting urge that surged inside of him. Half-dead or not, he knew Wally Su still hated the guts of the gully nigga who had downstroked his precious daughter straight outta her mind, and he wondered what the old man would think if he knew Suge was about to ask her to pull a deadly sin on his ass and commit the worst kind of treason.

Dressed in casual but expensive clothing and carrying a huge bouquet of five dozen roses, Suge charmed his way past the ground floor receptionist and rode the elevator up to the twelfth floor where the administrative offices were housed.

"Delivery for Miyoko Su," he said cordially. He smiled as the secretary's eyes got big and she exclaimed with glee at the sight of the beautiful blood-red blooms.

"Right this way," she chirped, ushering him down a long, carpeted hall that overflowed with the scent of old money. "Ms. Su's office is the second door on the left."

Suge shook his head as he walked calmly down the hall. Dangling a bunch of pretty flowers in front of a silly broad did the trick every time. There was something about an armful of blooming petals that yanked their common sense string and made them drop their guard faster than they could drop their drawers.

Pausing outside of Miyoko's office, Suge took a second to pull his own shit together. His crazy ex-girlfriend was now a top regulatory attorney in the state of Texas, and whether she knew it or not she held the key to Dominion Oil's future. The last time he'd seen her he had fronted her off and tossed her to the curb when she got all fanatical, but this time the tables were turned and he was at her mercy. As bad as he hated it, Suge needed Miyoko. He needed her to help him get those goddamn documents and to convince her daddy to die with his lips tightly zipped.

She was looking at her computer screen when he stepped into the room, and she glanced up just as he closed the door behind him.

"Superior."

She said his name with all the grace and beauty one woman could possess, and Suge's dick immediately stiffened and all the swag in his mouth dried right up.

He had forgotten just how beautiful she was. How sensual and downright fuckin' sexy. She had a certain scent to her that he had never smelled on another woman. An erotic animal-in-heat aroma that lurked just beyond the surface of her skin. With her long legs, high ass, creamy skin, and gorgeously wide eyes, Miyoko had what it took to knock his most erotic fantasies right out the park.

"Lil Bit." He called out her nickname smoothly, commanding the black snake stretching in his pants to back the hell up and sit down. "Long time no see, baby. How you been?"

"I always knew you'd come back to me," she said quietly. Her special scent leaped across the room and slid up his nostrils, catching him in her vapors. "Yes, sooner or later I knew you would come."

Ahh shit! The hair on the back of Suge's neck stood up and a warning chill ran down his spine.

"Is that right?" he asked coolly, setting the fresh roses down on her wide oak desk. She stood up and came from behind her desk and he eyed her from head to toe. She didn't look a day older than she had the last time he'd laid eyes on her. In fact, her hips had spread a little and she looked even better.

"You were on my mind," he fronted. "So I decided to come by and see how you were doing."

"And why is that?" she asked, fucking with him as she locked her smoky gaze on his.

Suge swallowed hard as she stood there looking at him with that old hot something in her eyes. At one time they'd had some real good shit going on between them in the sheets. Some *real* good shit.

"Okay, I need you," Suge admitted, getting sucked in by the promise in her eyes. A whole lotta years had passed but there wasn't a damn thing stopping them from getting naked and picking up right where they had left off. Him fucking her lights out and listening to her scream out his name . . . yeah, with her father half-dead and out of the way, there was nothing and nobody standing between them getting their shit off nice and righteously except . . . Suge's heart banged hard in his chest . . . Mink.

Nobody except Mink.

"I'm afraid you're too late," Miyoko told him as he spread a mound of softened butter over a slice of warm bread and passed it to her. They were sitting in the back booth of a cozy French restaurant where Suge had taken her so he could get in good and work his mo down on her. Finding her father and killing him would've been easy and Suge had no problem smoking the old bastard, but that paperwork would still be floating around out there somewhere and he couldn't risk having that shit end up in the wrong hands.

"Look, I know your father is planning to run his mouth in

front of the commission," Suge said coldly. "I need those papers your father's sitting on," he told her pointedly. "And I need you to help me get them."

"What's in it for me?" she asked, running her glistening pink tongue over her lips.

Suge stared at her. Feeling her out and sizing up how hard of a push she could take. Miyoko was sitting there looking sexy as hell, but staring deep into her slanted exotic eyes Suge could tell she was still coo-coo as a muthafucka.

"Look, baby. Here's the deal," Suge said, taking her tiny, bird-like hand in his as he broke it down for her. He was gonna have to flex his swag because he could already tell she wasn't gonna roll over and make it easy for him. "My brother is running for office at the railroad commission. The word on the street is that your father is going to try to take him down and knock him outta the box by dropping a dime and hitting him with some papers from an old stock deal."

He squeezed her pale fingers gently. "I need your help getting those papers back before the Railroad Commission meets in two weeks to confirm the ballots. Trust me, your father is making a big mistake, Lil Bit. If he bucks and drops a dime on my brother I swear to God I'm gonna make sure his whole empire goes crumbing down in the dirt. And you know I will."

Miyoko didn't look pressed in the least. "It's too late, Superior. None of that matters to him anymore." She shook her head and tossed her long black hair over her shoulder. "Zeke Washington already beat you to the punch. He had a long visit with my father and he asked him to testify to the truth before the commission. My father agreed because he is dying. He's ashamed of what he's done and he wants his conscience to be clear and his soul to be cleansed. Your threats mean nothing to him at this point."

"Is that right?" Suge said coldly. "So after years of leeching off every warm body he could find, now big bad Wally Su is scared to face the devil? That crook is gonna 'fess up to the world and put his whole hustle on blast?"

Miyoko nodded. "Yes, he is. It's the honorable thing to do."

Suge scoffed deep in his throat, making a sound of blatant disrespect. "Your daddy's been sucking Dominion dick for thirty fuckin' years, baby! I'll tell you this, if Viceroy gets buried, Wally Su's ass is gonna get buried even deeper. Dead or alive. If our company goes down, his shit slides off too!"

"Didn't you hear me?" Miyoko asked, still smiling. "My father is *dying*, Superior! His body will soon return to the earth and his soul will be welcomed by the ancestors. He has nothing left to lose in this life, but everything to gain in the next one."

"Bullshit! So what about you? He's gonna jump his ass in the grave and leave you back here broke as hell to clean up his mess? What about all that shit he talked about protecting you?"

"Oh, he's protecting me," Miyoko said with her eyes dancing with amusement. It was a very rare thing to see the great Superior Dominion squirm and she was enjoying it. "My father has already taken the necessary steps to ensure the firm's assets are protected from any liabilities that might arise due to his past behavior. A fund has been set up to compensate the victims of any legal claims against him, and that's the extent of any recourse that either your family, the Washingtons, or anyone else might have."

Suge sat up straight and swallowed hard. His best chance at saving his family was slipping away right in front of his eyes, and for the first time in a long time he felt desperation creeping up on him. "Look, I need your help, Lil Bit. I need those papers, baby. I know you know where they are, and I know you can make them disappear. For old times' sake, will you hook me up?"

"You're asking me a question, but I've already asked you one too," she reminded him sweetly. "What's in it for me?" she asked, studying him like his dick had soy sauce on it.

Suge knew what time it was. He was gonna have to schmooze her ass. Court her and cater to her. He hated to step off in it, but she had him by the balls and he had no other choice.

"Tell me what you want. Whatever I can do for you, you've got it. What you want, baby?"

Miyoko smiled slyly and dropped her gaze. She kicked off her shoe and extended her bare foot under the table, sliding it up his leg until her slender manicured toes were wiggling all over his dick. When she looked up again her eyes were blazing and her cheeks were flushed red with excitement.

"I want what I've always wanted. I want *you*, Superior Dominion. I want *us*. I want us to go back to being the way we used to be. To doing all the things we used to do."

Suge's whole mouth went dry at the sight of the naked lust in her eyes. He remembered their sheet-soaking marathon fuck-outs and how Miyoko could do that squeeze-pump motion with the back of her throat that used to make him wanna suck his thumb and pass out.

"C'mon, now," he tried to front her off one last time. "You don't wanna fuck with me, baby. Ain't nothing changed over here. I'm still that same old doggish piece of shit who broke your heart ten years ago. You're way outta my league, Miyoko. A beautiful woman like you ain't gotta make no backward moves, baby. Let's just get down on this business together and—"

A cold look flashed across her face and she jammed her toes deeply into his crotch and curled them into his nuts. "Zeke Washington sent me a hundred long-stemmed roses yesterday," she said quietly. "He asked me to meet him for dinner this evening so we could discuss how to—"

"Whoa-whoa-whoooa!" Suge reached into his crotch and gripped her foot in his hand and got ready to backpedal like a mutha. This chick wasn't about to roll over without making him pay her price. Deep inside he had known what it was gonna be like when he walked through her door, but he'd also

known what was at stake. This was about to be some real give-
and-take shit, and hate it or love it, Miyoko was standing on
top. Fuck the dumb shit, they were playing her game now and
she was the Big Mama in charge.

Their eyes locked and they came to a silent agreement. This
wasn't gonna be no simple business transaction. This chick
wanted to be wined and dined and romanced to the max. He
loosened his grip on her foot and gently massaged her toes.
Miyoko closed her eyes and a soft sigh escaped her lips. Suge
kept on rubbing, massaging her right where he knew she liked
it. He was well aware that he was selling his soul to the devil
but there was no way around it. If he wanted to keep his
brother out of jail and keep the Dominion fortune in the family stash, then it was looking more and more like he was gonna
have to roll with Miyoko's program and take one for the team.

The Texas county jail was hot and crowded in the female
section of the unit. General population housed every type of
criminal from petty thieves to accused murderers. Tempers
could flare up at any moment over the smallest of issues. Emotions ran high and patience was short. A small percentage of
the girls were sociable and they did their time with positive at-
titudes, while some of the butch bitches moved like predators
trying to extort, rob, and assault anyone they thought might be
weak. The correction officers didn't give a fuck either way.
They collected a check and stayed the fuck out of the politics
of the jail. It was common knowledge that a pretty young
chick with curves like Dy-Nasty's was a prime target for
dykes, ugly jealous chicks, and corrupt-ass male *and* female officers.

It was almost lunchtime and the inmates were preparing to
go down to the chow hall. Dy-Nasty had just woken up and
quietly made her bed. She hated jail. She kept to herself and she
didn't play Spades or gossip like the rest of the chicks on her
wing. Her time was usually spent sitting in her cell and mulling

over how the hell her plan had backfired. She had been calling her mother, Pat, over and over again trying to get some advice, but all she got was her voice mail. There was nothing she could do except sit chilling on county ice and spend every waking minute of the day plotting on how in the fuck she was gonna get the hell up outta there.

"Ayo hoe," a cute but ghetto bully named Stanka said as she walked up on Dy-Nasty with two gutter-looking inmates. "What you in here for? You stole something?"

"Excuse me, do I know you?" Dy-Nasty curled her lip and shot back. "And who the fuck is you calling a hoe? I suggest you and these dyke-ass broads you with back the hell away from me."

"Bitch don't play like you crazy," Stanka said as she rolled her eyes and grilled Dy-Nasty even harder. "I know who the hell you are, *Stink Mink*, and you know exactly who I be too." She giggled. "I be the champion chick who kicked your ass in that 7-Eleven parking lot, baby, and if you keep talking tough I'ma kick it for you again, Mink."

"Mink?" Dy-Nasty twisted her neck sideways with a disgusted look on her face. "Um, you better get it right, Miss *Stanka!* My name is Dy-Nasty and I don't look shit like that ugly trick Mink! Don't you ever get me confused with that low-level hooker again. Mink's just an amateur and I'm really about this life."

Stanka couldn't help the puzzled look that appeared on her face. The venom in which this "Dy-Nasty" chick just spit made her second-guess herself for a few moments. She sounded real convincing but she looked just like Mink.

Is this lil thot playing mind games with me?

"Yeah, a'ight, bitch," Stanka responded with a smirk. "Who you trying to run game on? Your scary ass just tryna flake out so I don't stomp a puddle in ya tail again."

"Look, ma," Dy-Nasty said, swelling up and ready to fight. She didn't give a damn if she was outnumbered or not 'cause there wasn't no fear in her. The rules of the street applied even more so in jail. You met aggression with aggression. Yeah, she mighta been a lil shook when they first tossed her in the back of the car and brought her up in here, but once the bars clanged over the jail doors the Philly in her took over and all that fear shit had flown out the window. *Sheeiit,* she was just as mad and bad as everybody else up in there, and just like Stanka, she was ready for whatever.

"I'ma say this shit for the last time. My name is Dy-Nasty, I'm from Philadelphia, *Pistol-Vania,* baby, and it ain't a bitch breathing Texas air that puts a drop of fear in my heart. Matter of fact," she said, throwing up her hands, "forget all this talking 'cause I ain't with it. Ga'head, bitch! Pop the fuck off!"

Dy-Nasty squared up and was aiming her fist dead at Stanka's face when a voice boomed out on the wing.

"Stop all that fucking yelling and line ya'll dirty asses up for chow," a big black correctional officer ordered.

Stanka and her crew backed off and grilled Dy-Nasty as they walked away.

"You lucky the CO came, but I got something for that slick mouth of yours, bitch. Just wait and see," Stanka said, balling up her fists as she moved on down the wing.

After lunch when all the inmates' stomachs were full, some of the girls went to watch TV and others went to their cells to catch a quick nap. Dy-Nasty rushed over to the wall to hit the phones up. She needed to find a way to break out of there as soon as possible. Her hood senses were up and she understood the politics of her environment. She had fronted real hard on Stanka, and by jailhouse rules the girl absolutely had to react or she would look like a pussy. Not only that, the predators would try to get at Stanka and her crew and cause them problems that they didn't want or need.

Dy-Nasty was totally without a clique in this hot country jail, and if she wanted to get outta there without getting her face sliced up, then she had to bite the bullet on this one and call the one person who could help her, but would probably tell her to go straight to hell. She was also gonna try to reach her mother Pat again, but she was running out of options and although she hated to do it she was gonna have to cash in her last bargaining chip and be something that damn sure didn't come natural to her: humble.

CHAPTER 17

Viceroy was getting fitted for a fly-ass business suit in the most expensive men's clothing store in Austin. He was there for a preliminary meeting with representatives from the state election, a few industry men, and of course the other candidates on the ballot. Usually he would have had his personal tailor come to his crib and whip him up something fresh to wear, but he had decided to go to an exclusive store in Austin so the people in the capital city could see one of the richest men in Texas in the flesh. Viceroy had risen up from the bottom of barrel and statistically he wasn't supposed to make it out of the Houston ghetto. Most of the cats he'd run the streets with in the hood were either dead or in jail. Those who had survived had ended up being nothing. Just a bunch of barefoot, pork-rind-eatin', baby-making, weed-smoking country boys who were happy to shovel dog shit for a living.

That probably would have been his fate too if Viceroy hadn't been so damn devious and ambitious. Fuck playing the cards he was dealt, he had switched out the entire deck and plucked from the bottom of that shit. He'd always kept his eye on some real cold cash. That cycle of living and dying piss-poor and scrounging for pennies had never appealed to the barracuda in him.

"Mr. Dominion," Jonas, one of Viceroy's advisers, said as he walked over to him. "Your meeting starts in forty-five minutes, sir. I'm just keeping you aware of the time constraints, sir."

"Now, Jonas." Viceroy smiled as he looked in the mirror. He was freshly swagged up and checking himself out. "You know you can't rush perfection. Them muthafuckas gonna wait for a winner like me. The party don't start until I walk in the door anyway."

"Yes sir, you're correct," Jonas said as he waited patiently for his boss.

Viceroy was feeling himself and he wanted to step into the meeting with supreme confidence. It was very important for him to stay on top of his game. This business he was in was cutthroat as hell. Your closest friends would scheme and plot on you backwards and forwards if they thought it would help them rise an inch higher in the ranks of the rich and influential. And who knew that shit better than him, because that's exactly the way that he had done it!

Forty minutes later Viceroy walked through the doors of a large extravagant office. He walked up in the spot with much pep in his step like he owned the joint.

"Hey fellas," Viceroy's voice boomed as he entered the room feeling like a don. "How's everybody doing today? Let's get down to business, gentlemen, shall we?"

A long table was in the middle of the room where state officials, business competitors, campaign managers, and political figures sat waiting. It was a serious meeting of the minds and everybody in that bitch was hiding a pointy shank up under the table. Viceroy was skilled in how to move in a room full of blood-hungry wolves, but when he saw Rodney Ruddman sitting in the mix he almost blew a fuse.

Muthafucka! Wife-fuckin' muthafucka!

That little bastard sat there in his high chair looking like a fuckin' tree stump. He was wearing an expensive shit-brown suit and had a cold smirk on his froggish face.

Viceroy was fuming on the inside, but on the outside his shit looked like it was perfectly together. Regardless of their personal war, the two men made respectful introductory comments and proceeded with the matters at hand.

After an official read a few required statements from the eligibility packet, some fat white boy stood up and started briefing them on the campaigning process. He might as well have been speaking Greek because Viceroy didn't hear a damn thing he said. He was too busy grilling Rodney Ruddman. The very existence of that fat fuck made Viceroy burn on the inside and his mind was totally focused on vengeance. Suddenly Ruddman's phone flashed on the table and he got up to excuse himself.

"Excuse me fellas, this is a very important call that I have to take," Rodney said and then he leaned on the table and looked directly at Viceroy and grinned. "There's a sweet little lady with an itch on my line, and I'm the only one who has the kind of tool that can scratch it."

Viceroy blacked the hell out.

"You little sawed-off muthafucka, you! I'ma kill yo runt ass!" Viceroy roared as he jumped over the table faster than anybody had expected him to move. He lunged straight for Ruddman's pork-round neck and started going to work on his ass.

Quick punches and kicks were being exchanged with Ruddman taking the brunt of the most brutal hits.

"Get this crazy fool off me!" Ruddman yelled as Viceroy wailed off on his ass. He was getting fucked up from one end of the table to the other, and he threw a few haymakers in there too while trying to ball up and cover his fat head.

"Stay the fuck away from her!" Viceroy hollered as he got in one last kick to Ruddman's gut before they were able to pull him off his ass. "I swear to God you better stay the fuck away from her!"

The room was wrecked. Paperwork had been scattered everywhere and chairs were overturned. A state official stood up and announced that the meeting was cancelled, and Viceroy and Ruddman were escorted out of doors at opposite ends of the hall.

Everyone was stunned speechless, but Viceroy and Ruddman were still raging strong.

"That's right you son of a bitch!" Viceroy growled with spit flying from his mouth as they pulled at him and led him away. "There's a lot more ass-whipping where that came from, you fat fucker! Next time you so much as speak her name I'ma knock your coward-ass clean the fuck out!"

"Are you okay, Rodney?" an older white man asked Ruddman on the way out the door. "What was that about? For some reason I thought you two were close friends."

"Just because we're both *black* doesn't mean we're friends!" Ruddman snapped as he tried to fix his disheveled suit and re-cover from that good-old-fashioned beat-down. "One of these days I'm gonna fuck Viceroy Dominion up if it's the last thing I do! If it's the *last* goddamn thing I do!"

The doorbell rang at the Dominion Estate and before the butler could get to it, a blur flew past his eyes and Bunni damn near crashed and burned trying to answer it.

"Well, *hellooo* there, you must be GiGi!" Bunni snatched the door open and posted up with a hand on her hip looking fabulous in all her ghetto glory. "I'm Bunni Baines! Ya'll just come right on in!"

In a flash Bunni's eyes scanned the gorgeous chick from her thick mane of wavy red hair down to her fly Zanotti shoes, and they exchanged pleasantries as she led them toward the Dominion's huge den area where Mink and Peaches were all dressed up and waiting. P was feeling himself because outta nowhere Viceroy had changed his mind about him. He had forgiven them for jumping in the fight when he went after Selah, and he even said Peaches could stay at the mansion for as long as he wanted.

"Mink and Peaches, this is GiGi Moldiness and"—she cocked her hand behind her ear and batted her eyes at the hairy white man carrying a huge camera and dragging in behind them—"what's your name, caveman?"

"Frank," he said, grinning good-naturedly. "My name is Francois but you can call me Frank."

"Frank and GiGi," Bunni said, turning to beam at Mink and Peaches, "this is my best friend Mink Domino and my big brother, Peaches."

Mink took one look into GiGi's emerald green eyes and turned toward Peaches and fake sneezed. "Ha-*ratchet*!" flew outta the side of her mouth and she covered it up with a big ol' sniff and a real quick cough.

Peaches caught her drift, and dressed in a tight, powder-blue sleeveless shift dress that accented every last one of his bulging muscles, he jumped to his feet and held out his hand. "Pleased to meet you," he said to GiGi, grinning real wide and showing his dimples. "My sister was so happy to get your call."

Bunni took over. "Please, sit down, sit down!" She flitted about like a nervous butterfly. "That's what we got all this furniture for. Have a seat right over here." Bunni directed her visitors to a thick black leather couch on the other side of a large coffee table. "Y'all thirsty? You want something to eat? I have some cabbage soup and cucumber sandwiches in the kitchen. I'll be right back."

"What a lovely home you have," GiGi complimented Mink as she sank her curvy hips into the plush leather sofa and crossed her shapely legs. "It must be wonderful to reside in such a beautiful place."

"The house ain't mine, but thank you." Mink smirked, her

bullshit alarm sounding off like a siren as she stuck her nose in the air and sniffed around like she was smelling a rat. She was definitely not feeling this chick but she had to give it to her. Mami was decked out. Hair laid, titties puffed, hips spread, dress clinging, and fine jewels sparkling everywhere.

"Well, it's beautiful," GiGi gushed. She reached up and tossed her flaming hair with her fingers and the monster rock she was sporting damn near poked Mink in the eye. "Simply lovely."

"Yeah, it's a'ight," Mink said and then leaned forward with her elbow on her knee and cupped her chin in her hand. "So how was your flight from LA?" she probed, vowing that if she caught this trick in one damn lie it was gonna be out the door for her! "Not everybody gots what it takes to handle this Texas heat."

"Actually," GiGi responded, "My company is in L.A. but for the past few weeks I've been based right here in Dallas. I'm a regional manager and I travel around the country scouting for new talent." She laughed softly. "And to answer your question, I'm just fine with the heat. Believe me, if I couldn't handle it then I wouldn't be in the kitchen."

Mink cut her eyes at the slick little side snipe. *Strike one!*

Bunni came back with a servant who was pushing a silver cart bearing a tray of cucumber sandwiches on crustless wheat bread and several bowls of piping hot cabbage soup.

"Lunch is served!" she sang out brightly, then winked at Mink and Peaches and side-muttered, "This is for the clear folks, y'all. I got us some chicken wangs in the kitchen!"

GiGi accepted a sandwich and took two nibbles off the tip and then set it back down on her plate. She dotted her the corner of her mouth with a lace napkin and took a sip of lemon water and smiled.

"Well, now that lunch is over let's get down to business, shall we?"

"Oh, fa'sho, baby!" Bunni slapped herself on her round hip.

"That's what I'm talking about! Business is the name of this game!"

GiGi reached into her tote bag and pulled out a small voice recorder. She nodded at Frank and he stood up and began adjusting his camera.

"I hope you don't mind if I turn this thing on while we talk. I'll still take notes but I find this way faster and much more accurate because I would hate to miss anything. Oh, and Frank needs to take a few pictures too. My bosses will need to get a feel for the set if they're going to shoot from here."

Bunni nodded, her eyes big and greedy. "Yeah, girl! Go right ahead. Snap-snap-*snap*! We ain't got no problem with none of that."

GiGi gave her a bright smile. She turned her tape recorder on and Frank stepped away and got to snapping pictures.

"So," she began, flipping open a yellow pad like she was ready to roll. "Tell me what life is like in the house of the Dominions? Which one of you is the funny one, who's the most serious, and who's the most flamboyant?"

Bunni opened her mouth but Peaches jumped in first.

"Well, *I'm* the most flamboyant gal in all of *Texas*," Peaches said as he blinked rapidly, fluttering his fake eyelashes. "I'm the ray of sunshine that gives these two little heffas their glow."

Everybody except Mink bust out laughing as Peaches cracked them up by yapping about how he was a glamorous headlining diva and how Bunni and Mink were just the extras in his movie.

"So, Bunni," GiGi said brightly after the laughter calmed down, "I've read all about Mink and how she was kidnapped as a child. I remember hearing on one of those talk shows that you and Mink grew up together in a New York City slum. Tell me, exactly what type of employment were you ladies engaged in before coming into your fortune?"

"Oh, we was performers," Bunni said proudly as Mink

bucked her eyes at her. "We got up on stage and entertained a bunch of willies every night."

GiGi looked real impressed. "You mean, like thespians? You two performed on stages like on *Broadway*?"

"Hell, naw!" Bunni waved her hand and giggled. "We danced on a stage at a titty joint called Club Wood!"

GiGi nodded like she got it, then pursed her lips together as she scribbled *strippers* down on her notepad.

Bunni started bragging on herself next as she and Peaches battled wickedly with their tongues trying to out-do each other. Mink sat back and eyeballed her friends, but she was totally uninterested in telling GiGi shit about herself. She could smell traces of a very familiar game coming all outta the glammed-up white chick's pores, and she didn't understand why Bunni, and especially grift-master Peaches himself, hadn't already sniffed around and picked up a whiff.

"So, now that us pretty *girls* have chatted and gotten to know each other a little"—GiGi beamed and winked at Peaches—"it's time to find out more about the *men* in the Dominion family. Of course Viceroy Dominion would be a major part of any television show, but I understand there are three sons in the family who might be interesting as well. When can I meet them?"

Bunni poked her lip out and shook her head. "Naw, see here now this is an *us* thang. I mean, yeah the Dominions can get a little play ere' now and then too, but you got the stars sitting right here!"

GiGi's smile wavered and she looked perplexed.

"Oh!" she said brightly. "I thought you knew? Our shows have a clause that states the entire family has to be involved. It's the only way our audience can get an authentic feel for the true nuances of a family. If we exclude anyone from the equation it makes it seem as though the family has something to hide and perhaps isn't being forthright, which of course"—she shook her head and her curls bounced—"just leads viewers to change the channel."

Bunni sat up straight. "Well hold up now. I ain't saying they can't be down, I'm just saying they can't be down *right now*."

"Well, why is that?" GiGi asked, chipper as shit.

"Well, 'cause they not home right now!" Bunni snapped.

GiGi showed her perfect teeth as she flashed Bunni a big bright smile.

"That's not a problem," she said, flipping her notebook closed as she clicked off her tape recorder and dropped it inside her bag. She motioned to Frank, who nodded and switched off his camera then yanked the plug out of the wall. "How about we just reschedule our visit for a more convenient time for everyone?"

"Like when?" Bunni wailed.

"Like when the rest of the family is home," GiGi said sweetly as she rose to her feet and sashayed her sexy round butt toward the door. "Especially the *men.*"

CHAPTER 18

Me and Suge were at his house playing a game called Pin the Tail on the Porn Star. We had gone to the racetrack earlier and he'd won a nice big purse. He took me to the mall and let me spend the whole damn thing, and now I was paying him back.

I had dug into my bag of tricks and given him a hot little show. I felt freaky as hell as I stood on his big bed and posed butt naked and urged him to take all kinds of pictures of me in my porn star glory. My body was built for the camera and I damn sure didn't have nothing to hide. I was the type who could rock the cover of joints like *Towers of Tits* and *Ass Almighty* magazines, and Suge was loving every scrumptious angle I tossed my hips at him from.

I had shown him what I was working with and now I was on my hands and knees licking him like a cat. I started at his neck and I was working my way down to the grand prize.

"Girl, that tongue is sumpthin else," he muttered as I sucked and panted and swirled my pink tongue around his dark nipple. Suge's chest was rocked up with muscle and his arms felt like they were made of iron. All that hardness had me turned the fuck on and my pussy was leaking little puddles all over the place as I shimmied down lower and snaked my tongue in and out of his navel.

His dick was packed full of lead, and only the very top of his mushroom crown was somewhat soft. I concentrated on that part as I squeezed my titties around his shaft like a foot-long hot dog between a nice soft bun. Gripping my tits and pinching my own nipples, I flicked my tongue out and licked at the sweet slippery liquid that was oozing from the slit in his head, and hummed as I rolled it around on the roof of my mouth.

Suge put his big paws on my shoulders and thrust his strong hips back and forth, giving me the erotic titty fuck of a lifetime. I leaned back a little and guided his dick to my stiff nipple and flicked it back and forth, sending sparks of pleasure flying straight to my clit as I squeezed my legs together and turned myself out.

I jacked his dick in my tight fist and gave it a few more long, thorough licks, then I maneuvered my body until the juice from my pussy was dripping right into his mouth. We sixty-nined like a mutha, and Suge ate my tender meat so deliciously that I kept sliding off my suck game and falling off on my gobble.

Suge got impatient and said fuck all that. He flipped me over and jammed his thick dick up in me until I shrieked and hollered, "Ow! Too fuckin' much!" Gripping my ass-cheeks in his palms, he idled right there for a few to let my coochie get loose and adjust, then he slammed them last two inches up in me too!

We went at it like battle cats, trying our damndest to out-fuck each other. It was a gladiator contest up in that bitch and both of us were winning. I lay there with my legs cocked wide open as his dick drilled up in me and sent sparks shooting through the back of my pussy. I was loving the fuck outta his muscular weight riding on top of me. My titties were smushed against his chest, and his bucking hips pounded me damn near through the mattress as he went for his and made sure I got mine too. Dude put some real good lovin' down on me and he didn't stop until my pussy was scuffed and plunged and nice and sore.

When we were finally empty and exhausted and all out of cum, we stumbled to the shower together. Suge had just washed my pussy for me like he usually did, and he was wiping drops of water off my back when outta nowhere he hit me with some bullshit noise about us needing to keep our shit under wraps.

"Check it out, Mink. We're gonna have to slow this down a lil bit, baby girl. It ain't just about us no more, you understand?"

I poked my lip out. "Why? What are you talking about?"

He smoothed my hair off my shoulder and kissed me on the back of my neck.

"I'm talking about me and you, baby girl. And what we do."

I shrugged. "It ain't nobody's business what we do. Everybody in the whole world knows I was adopted, so we ain't even really related, Suge."

"Yeah. I know," Suge said quietly. He turned me around and kissed my forehead, then gently patted the beads of water on my puffed-up breasts. "But that ain't how this type of shit works. My brother is running for state office now. It's gonna be a cut-throat political campaign going on up in here. That adopted shit ain't gonna mean a damn thing to the voters."

I wasn't going for it.

"Look, I know Daddy Viceroy don't want nobody bringing bad light on the Dominion name, but I'm a LaRue so he don't have to worry about me."

"Yes he does. He's gotta worry about everything. Them white liberal fuckers gonna be digging deep up in his ass to see what kinda shit they can pull out. We can give 'em nothing to work with on this end, baby. It's my job to make sure my brother is straight, and me and you can't let 'em pull nothing out on us."

I stood there with my hair frizzing into curls and my lil heart about to melt. "But that ain't what you said before," I sniffed. "When we talked about this before you said you didn't wanna stop."

Suge reached out and took my chin in his big old rough hand and pressed his juicy lips to mine. "I *don't* wanna stop, Mink. I swear to God I don't. And we don't have to. But we *do* have to go way underground with this. At least for right now while I handle my business."

"So you ain't never gonna be my boo-thang no more?" I asked him with big fat tears filling up my eyes.

Suge reached out and pulled me into his huge strong arms.

"Look here, Mink. Let me ask you something, baby girl. When you're running a tight race and your shit is on the line, who you gonna put your money on? The jockey or the horse?"

I looked at him like he was crazy. Dude knew damn well I didn't know shit about betting on no stank behind horses.

I shrugged. "I'ma put my money wherever you put yours."

"Why's that?"

I shrugged again. "Because you always win."

"Think about it," he said, his big hands gripping my shoulders. "If the jockey breaks his leg lining up at the gate, can the horse still get out there and win the race?"

I shrugged. "Yeah. You just gotta get you another jockey."

"But if the horse stumbles going into the gate, can the jockey jump out there on the track and give the race a go?"

I grinned a little bit. "Hell no. It's a horse race, not a jockey race."

A smile lit up in Suge's eyes and he nodded and pat me on the hip. "Damn right. I ain't no light in the ass jockey, Mink. I'm a muthafuckin' racehorse, baby. The fastest stallion on the track, and you can always put your money on me. You got that?"

I nodded and pressed my face into his hard, damp stomach as a tear slid out my eye.

"Do you trust me?" His voice was low and strong, rumbling from his belly.

I nodded and dug my sniffling nose deeper into his rock-hard gut.

"Answer me, Mink. Answer me like a grown-ass woman." He put his finger under my chin and lifted my head until we were staring into each other's eyes.

"*Do you trust me?*"

I trembled. "Yes," I answered tearfully, copping to something that I had never in life said to *any* fuckin' man. "I trust you."

He pulled me close and kissed the top of my head.

"Baby girl, I'm always gonna be your boo-thang. I'm gonna need you to be a big girl and remember that too. No matter what goes down or how fucked up shit might look, can't no other woman get what's yours, and Big Suge is always gonna have love in his heart for you. You hear me, girl? Always."

CHAPTER 19

"GiGi just called! She said she's cancelling our next appointment because her bosses said we need some more drama around here!" Bunni plopped down on my bed the next morning and reported with a frown. "She says we ain't got enough of a groove to boost up the ratings with our own show. She says our shit is stale and dry and we need to get something real hot poppin' if we wanna be stars on national TV."

I sighed and dug my head deeper into my pillow. My ass was miserable. It had been four days since Suge had practically cut me off and I missed him like a knocked-out front tooth. Even though he said we could still see each other from time to time, I was mourning his ass like an old lady whose sailor husband was lost out at sea.

"Did you hear what I just said? GiGi is kicking us to the curb! She said this joint ain't interesting enough for no reality show!"

I waved Bunni off. "That heffa's just mad because we don't have no drive-bys popping off around here. No thots walking the stroll, no strippers riding the poles, and no drug dealers slanging crack neither."

"Well then we need to get us summa that shit real quick!"

I raised my head and glared at Bunni and rolled my eyes. "If you wanted all kindsa drama you shoulda stayed your tail up in Harlem. Be grateful there ain't no Punchies and Guttas and none of them other kinds of fools running around up in this bitch."

"But how are we gonna get on TV when ain't nothing happening with us, Mink?" she wailed. "It's boring as hell around here! We need to get something shaking, mami! You know, the way we used to do back in the good old days! GiGi says the best shows are the ones where people feel like they can relate to all the crazy shit that's happening in your life. She says it's only when you give TV viewers a real juicy bone to chew on that they tune in for episode after episode. Matter fact, GiGi says—"

"Who gives a good goddamn what GiGi says!" I blasted on her. "GiGi just wanna see a bunch of rich niggas act a fool and get in a train wreck up in this camp! She wasn't tryna give us no show from the gate. That trick must get off on seeing black folks cussing each other out and cutting each other up! Hell, ask GiGi if she wanna go hang out in our crib back in Harlem and wait for Gutta to come kick down the fuckin' door! Now that'll be some drama for her ass! We're rich now, Bunni. Ain't nobody got time for that hard-knock type a' life no more!"

My rowdy cut her eyes at me and turned up her lips and I groaned. I knew what that shit meant and it definitely wasn't good.

"You ain't gotta be down with my program, Mink," she huffed with mad 'tude. "After all the ratchet capers me and you done pulled and all of our fifty-million misadventures I woulda thought you'd be down for at least one more ride."

I threw my hands up. "We done rode this bitch all the way to the bank, Bunni! Look around. We got everything we coulda ever dreamed of and then some. We don't need no trashy white chick with fake titties, a booty pad, booger-green eyes, and Chinese-apple color in her hair to tell us what our reality is!

This right here is what *me* and *you* did, Bunni. This is *our* flim-flam! We schemed our asses off for this hustle! Fuck GiGi. I say we kick that trick to the curb. Don't nobody need her around here no way."

Bunni nodded. "Yeah, uh-huh. I see what time it is now. You done let this lil bit of change go to your head, Mink. You all up on your high horse tryna insult GiGi because you jealous of her. Go 'head. Admit it. You's a hater, Mink! You salty 'cause GiGi got a booty and she's damn near cute as you, and that's why you don't wanna get down with my reality show!"

I shook my head. Stunned. "What the hell do I gotta be jealous of GiGi for? Name me one thing that heffah got that I ain't got?"

Bunni gave me the stank face as she raised her eyebrows, twisted her lips, and then hit me right where she knew it would hurt.

"A man."

"That was shitty," I told her. "That was real low and shitty, ma."

Bunni shrugged. "And so is your attitude, Mink! Now c'mon, dammit. I'm about to call her back and beg her ass. I'll invite her to that fancy election luncheon Viceroy is having and tell her she can meet all the men in the family if she promises to come by."

I smirked. "Yeah, well that oughtta bring her mining ass running straight through the door." I turned my back on Bunni and shook my head. My rowdy was getting straight bamboo-zled. Mizz GiGi was a hustla. A real-live working girl, and I sure as hell wasn't talking about on no TV.

It was Sunday afternoon and Suge was pushing the brand-new, triple-white, three-hundred-grand Bentley Mulsanne down the highway as he headed toward the Dominion Estate. He had driven his truck to Miyoko's crib so he could take her to the movie she wanted to see, but she had ditched out on him saying her father had called for her and she needed to go see him.

"I'm sorry, I won't be able to hang out with you," she said with a sad smile. "My father had a pretty bad night," she told him with a worried look in his eyes. "His doctor is with him now but I'm not sure how much longer he'll be able to avoid a hospice."

Suge wasn't the type to wish an enemy good, and he hoped like hell Wally Su would hurry up and kick the damn bucket so he could get away from his crazy-ass daughter!

"Can you do me a small favor, Superior?" Miyoko had asked just as he was leaving. "Would you drive my car today and bring it back a little later?" she asked. "I keep hearing a clicking sound that's making me crazy. The dealer came and looked at it a few times but they claim there's nothing wrong. Could you maybe drive it for a little while and see if you hear anything?"

With the music pumping some smooth jazz cuts, Suge hadn't heard anything out of the showroom-sharp luxury convertible except the sweet purr of the high-powered engine, and as he entered the gates of the Dominion Estate he paused to drop the top as he rolled up to the front door.

"Suge!" Mink screamed as her, Bunni, and Peaches tagged each other with fat jiggly water balloons. They were running around barefoot on the far side of the driveway filling up balloons with cold water from the garden hose and throwing them at anyone in sight.

"Ughh!" Mink hollered as Bunni threw a red balloon that caught her on the nose and exploded.

Mink squeezed her eyes closed and laughed as water dripped down her pretty face. She was dressed in a pair of black cut-off shorts and a pink and white polka-dot bikini top and her navel looked like a deep dimple in the pit of her toned stomach.

Suge leaned back in the whip and laughed right along

with them. There were torn bits of colorful balloons strewn all over the driveway and the three of them were soaking wet from head to toe. Mink gasped and cursed, then jumped up and down as Peaches caught her with another shot dead in the face, and Suge couldn't help appreciating his baby as he bit his bottom lip and checked out her sweet curves.

"I'ma get y'all!" Mink squealed, shaking her hair and wiping water from her eyes. "I'ma get both of y'all shady asses!"

Bunni was dressed in a t-shirt and some spandex, but Peaches was dressed in a pair of tight cut-off jeans just like Mink's. He wore a rainbow striped halter and had his curly wig tied down with a colorful scarf.

"What are you sitting there laughing at?" Mink yelled as she ran toward him brandishing a fat yellow balloon that jiggled with water.

"Hold up, now!" Suge warned, holding his hands out to ward her off. "These are some expensive leather seats right here, baby. You can't be getting these babies wet. They're real, girl. Real."

Mink leaned over the passenger door dripping water and breathing hard. "These babies are real too." She giggled, glancing down at her bulging breasts and erect nipples. "And if you stick out ya tongue I'll let you get 'em nice and wet!"

Suge gazed at her with hot lust in his eyes. Mink was his type of chick. With her sand-colored skin and pretty smile, not to mention those round hips and that bubble ass, she was exactly what a man like him wanted by his side.

"Oooh!" she said and flung the yellow water balloon toward Peaches. "Check out your new whip, playa! White on white on white!" she said, admiring the off-white exterior, the off-white leather seats, and the matching off-white carpet. Why you didn't tell me you was getting you a fly-ass ride!"

Before he could answer she propped her damp booty on the edge of the door and then swung her gorgeous legs over and plopped down into the passenger seat.

"This is *real* nice!" she said, pushing buttons and twirling knobs and checking out all the bells and whistles. "When did you get it, today?"

Suge shook his head. "This lil shit ain't mine. You know I like my rides like I like my bootys," he said, reaching across the seat and pinching her lightly on her thigh. "Big and strong. I'm pushing this around for a friend."

"A *friend*?" Mink said, playing with the buttons like a lil kid and sliding her seat back and forth. "Well it must be a real good friend because this ride is sweet as hell—"

Suddenly she leaned forward and peered closely at something near the stick shift. "What is this . . ."

Suge braced himself as she pinched an extra long strand of jet-black hair between her fingers and pulled it out like it had coochie crabs clinging to it.

"Ewwww, *yuck*!" Mink frowned, balling her lips up in disgust as she flung it in the backseat. "The hell is this? This some old nasty *white chick's* hair!"

"Oh no it's not," Suge protested, but then she pulled another strand from the carpet near her foot and held that one up in the air too.

Her pretty eyes blazed with heat. "Frontin' ass nigga! *Friend* my ass! That's why we had to take our thang underground, huh? So the next bitch you chilling with won't find out? I see your new 'friend' ain't the type of chick who can use my comb, huh?"

She flung the door open and jumped out of the ride glaring at him with New York fire in her eyes. "I see how you living! You must be crazy tryna run that weak-ass okey-doke on Mizz Minaj, boy-o!"

Suge shook his head 'cause he shoulda known better than to even come this way.

"C'mon with all that, Mink. That ain't no white girl hair. I swear to God it ain't. Besides, what did I tell you? There ain't a woman in this world who can take what I got for you, baby."

"Bullshit!"

Her booty jiggled in her shorts as she stomped her way back over to Peaches and Bunni. He saw her crouch down for a second, and then suddenly she whirled around and charged back toward him with her fist cocked high.

"You muthafucka, you!"

She hurled a blue water balloon as hard as she could and Suge barely had time to duck when—

Splat!

That shit busted right on top of his head and Suge sat there feeling like a sucka as cold water dripped down his face and soaked his shirt.

"You's a grimy muthafucka, Suge Dominion!" Mink screamed over her shoulder as she stomped inside the house. "Just a grimy muthafucka!"

Suge nodded as the door slammed behind her. A piece of shredded blue rubber slid down his nose and landed on his bottom lip and he nodded again. A grimy muthafucka. Yep, that's exactly what he was.

While Mink was bitching and whining over her runaway horse, Miyoko was holding the reins firmly in her hands and making her stallion giddy-the-fuck-up. It was obvious that the chick was freaky and looking for a powerful stud to parade around town, and she wasn't gonna stop until her horse was at a full gallop and she was humping on Suge Dominion's dick.

Miyoko wanted to be everywhere Suge was, and she got off on all the attention they sparked when they walked into a room together. "There's a play I've been wanting to see," she gushed as she made a list of all kinds of public shit for them to do, "and you know the opera is in town too. I'm starting a new bikram yoga class for couples, and I have two tickets to the Met Gala in New York. It's a red-carpet affair and a hot new designer wants me to introduce his line of evening gowns. I'd really love for you to be my escort. Please, baby?" She got on her tiptoes and nipped sexily at his ear. "Please?"

Miyoko was a slick manipulator. She had his ass on a tight string and Suge was at her beck and call. Every time he even thought about acting like he wanted to buck, she quickly reminded him that *he* needed *her,* and if she wasn't able to get her father to reveal the location of his precious papers, then his brother and his company would simply be shit out of luck.

Suge knew the deal. When she said jump, he asked how high. He put on a nice tuxedo and took her to the opera, and two days later he was naked from the waist up in her bikram yoga class where Miyoko got jealous and stormed out claiming too many white chicks were in there eyeballing his ten-pack milky way and rocked-up arms and chest.

They hit the spa in her neighborhood together and got couples' massages holding hands, and they drove down highway 67 to South Dallas Café and ate greasy soul food and sock-it-to me cake out the ass. They had swung by the gym late one night to work off some macaroni and cheese and sweet potato casserole, and they were tossing back shots in the Jacuzzi when Miyoko made her move.

The crazy chick had dove down to his crotch and damn near drowned her drunk self trying to give him some head underwater. Suge had never fought off a blow job in his life, but he fought that night. She had wiggled like a wet snake as she rubbed all up against him and tried to yank down his shorts. She came up on her knees and managed to rip his drawstring out, and they both gasped as they looked down at his crotch and saw what was waiting for her.

Nothing. A nice soft dick and a pair of knocked-out sleeping balls!

Suge was done. He did *not* want to fuck Miyoko Su and she couldn't suck his dick neither! Shoving her horny ass back into the water, he cupped his hands around his dick and balls and broke the hell up outta there!

CHAPTER 20

After taking that long-ass bus ride Gutta had just pulled out of the rent-a-car lot in a fly all-white Benz truck with his homey Shy riding shotgun. They were cruising through the streets of Dallas taking in all the unfamiliar sights and sounds.

The Harlem nigga inside of Gutta couldn't help but make him think he was the smoothest and toughest gangsta to ever hit Dallas. The thug-hustla in him wanted to take over the town and show these country niggas how it was done.

First things first, he told himself. He could floss around town later, but first he had to settle up some old debts with one of the slickest, grimiest, sexiest broads he had ever met.

The thought of Mink LaRue sent his blood boiling hot. If that greedy bitch thought she was gonna come down here and live it up happily ever after without fearing his consequences, then she had another fuckin' think coming. Shawty had played the fuck outta him. She had dissed him and tricked up his stash like he was one of them weak nigs she ran through out in the streets. Gutta wasn't the type of beast to let even the slightest transgression slide by. Mink had gotten evicted from his apartment and sold off all his furniture while he was doing his bid in prison, and when he finally got a chance to kill her ass she had slipped out of his grasp.

And now, somehow her thirsty ass turned out to be the long-lost daughter of some fucking ga-zillionaires, and she was all on *Okrah*, flossin' and smiling like shit was all gravy. But he was on her ass now and the time was right to catch her out there. Gutta knew a prime opportunity when he saw one, and this was gonna be the perfect lick to get at her throat and get at some cash, all at the same time.

"It's hot as all hell down here, son," Shy said as he rolled his window down, excited as fuck to be out of New York for the first time in his life. "Yeah, gimme all dis good ol' country air!"

Shy stuck his head halfway out the window and screamed, "Harlem in the muhfuckin' house, ya heard!"

He threw in his Big L CD and turned the speakers on blast. They mighta been in Texas but they still wasn't riding around listening to what nigs in the north called "that country shit."

Gutta leaned back and pushed the whip, but he couldn't front like he wasn't excited to be outta New York too. He trusted that his young cannon Shy would handle his business when it came time to put that work in, so he let him enjoy this moment freely.

Before violating his parole and breaking up outta Harlem, Gutta had Googled the Dominion family and found out that they lived in a high-end part of town called Mayflower Estates. They were gonna have to do a little foot scouting to get up close on the sick-money crib, but nothing in the world was gonna knock them off their grind or deter the two hungry hood niggas from their mission. They were rolling freely in a new state where nobody knew them, and this alone amped up their determination to get at some big dollars. And to get at Mink's grimy ass, too.

When they drove into the extravagant community of mansions that sat tall and majestic behind securely-locked fancy gates, Gutta and Shy were both in awe. This shit right here was for high mothafuckin' rollers only, and it made Gutta redefine his petty-minded definition of ballin'.

"These bitches look like muh'fuckin' castles," he said under his breath. He could see why Mink had brought her ass down here to try to gank these fools outta some yardage. This here was the goddamn jackpot! Chit-ching!

"A'ight, it's time to focus yo," Gutta told Shy as he cruised slowly down the long, winding roads and rolled past golf courses, marinas, and lakes. "We gotta find out which one of these huge fuckin' pads Mink is hiding her ass in. I'm sure it ain't a whole lotta black people living out here so keep ya eyes open."

The Benz they were pushing had a nice tint on the windows so it was hard to look in and see who was inside. Gutta liked that shit because the last thing he wanted to do was get scoped out and spotted by Mink before he got the chance to lay his plan into action and get his hands around her neck.

"Ayo, G. Slow down a little bit and look at that shit," Shy said. Gutta hit the brakes as they peeped a gate that had a huge letter D engraved on it.

"Let's pull up on it, bruh," Shy suggested. "This could be the spot."

Gutta pulled up to the gate and saw that there was a long plush path leading up to the luxurious mansion. *Damn*, he thought to himself as they sat there staring like tourists. He would love to build one of these mothafuckas right in the middle of the projects. He was street dreaming like a mutha though, because that shit would get robbed and looted from day one, right down to the doorknobs.

"Yo, I got a feeling this is it, man. Their joint looked just like this in the pictures I seen on Google. But we can't sit out here like this," Gutta said as he peeped the situation. "We stick out like escaped convicts out in this bitch, and these niggas ain't even got sidewalks so we can walk around and case this shit on foot."

They were turning shit over in their minds trying to figure something out when they saw a sweet Lexus coming down the driveway. Gutta hit the gas and peeled off from the gate and made a U-turn just out of eyesight of the Lexus's driver.

"Dayum," Shy exclaimed, in awe of the fly whip that had just pulled up in front of the big *D* on the fancy gate. "I wonder who that is in the nice little G-ride, Gutta."

"I'ono man."

Gutta waited a few moments as they watched the driver lower the window and push the intercom at the gate and say something they couldn't hear. Moments later the window went back up. The reverse lights lit up and the car backed up a little bit, then turned around and got back on the road and slowly drove away.

"What was that about?" Shy asked.

Gutta shrugged. "Fuck if I know but we 'bout to follow that whip and see where it takes us."

Gutta was a master at stalking victims in the streets. He had honed his hunting skills in the concrete jungles of New York City and he was an expert at tracking down big targets. He kept his eyes on the mark as he followed his unidentified prey up and down the streets of D-town, which was known for sippin' lean and riding mean. About half an hour later they followed their mark to a jam-packed mall called the Galleria.

"Oh shit, son! Somebody going shopping B," Shy said as they pulled into a parking lot a couple of spots away from their target. "That's w'sup 'cause a nigga tryna get fresh. I wanna see what type of style these Texas niggas got."

They watched as the driver's side door on the Lexus swung open and a sexy-ass honey bun emerged carrying two big shopping bags. She was bright-skinned and slim, but with a phat ass and long, shapely legs. She had on a pair of tiny pink shorts and a tight white tee, and Gutta and Shy were both impressed as they watched her balance in her pink high heels and walk sexily toward the entrance of the mall. Jumping outta the whip, they casually followed her inside and proceeded to shadow her every move.

The mysterious woman went from store to store. Gutta figured she was returning clothes because her big-ass bags kept getting smaller and smaller. After a while she made her way to an expensive jewelry store and that's when Gutta decided to make his move.

"Yo Shy, g-mack for a little bit and do some shopping," Gutta said as he glanced at his reflection in a store window to make sure his shit was sharp. "I'm 'bout to go holla at shawty and see w'sup with her. If something comes up I'ma hit ya jack."

Gutta strolled into the jewelry store with a nice hot gwap in his pocket. He walked right past the little light-skinned honey who had her back to him. *She lookin' crazy good, I gotta get at her lil bad ass!*

Gutta acted as if he was paying her no mind as he checked out a few iced-out chains, watches, and bracelets.

"Ayo, jeweler," Gutta said to a short Italian man standing behind the counter as he reached in his pocket and pulled out a fat knot of bills. He'd stolen some loot out of a burning car in Harlem and after washing and drying them shits they smelled like soap powder and were nice and crisp. "I'll take this Hublot Fusion right here with the black diamonds, and whatever this beautiful queen right here wants too. It's all on me. I got it."

The woman turned around, clearly caught off guard as she looked Gutta up and down with her gorgeous face and pretty eyes. She twisted her mug like *nigga who the hell are you?* Gutta laughed inside because he knew how to ease all that shit up. He stared into her eyes and hit her with the gangsta smile that all the ladies loved.

"That's a nice gesture but I have my own money," the sexy thing said with a slight attitude. "I don't come cheap and I know nothing in this world is free, so I'm going to respectfully decline. But thank you anyway."

Gutta nodded. "I expected that," he said truthfully. "To keep it all the way real with you I was just trying to get your attention. Besides, I can tell a woman with style and grace such as yourself is holding her own. You're right though, nothing in this world is free, but the swag you got baby . . . that's priceless." He held out his hand. "My name is Gutta by the way."

She let her face go blank. *Gutta? I know his mama ain't name him no damn Gutta.* She looked him up and down once again. He looked very strong and he came across very confident. Dude had a rough and rugged look about him that was almost kinda criminal, but he was dressed a lot better than any thug she'd ever seen. She stared a little harder. His eyes were intense but his smile was very handsome and it spoke to her. Real loud.

"Nice to meet you," she said finally, giving up her hand. "I can tell by your accent that you're not from around here, Gutta," she said, sounding more relaxed. She caught a whiff of his expensive cologne and it tantalized her senses. "Where are you from?"

"I'm from New York City, sugar. Harlem," Gutta said, maintaining eye contact and stepping closer into her space. "I'm down here with my business partner trying to put a couple of things together. I want to invest in a few companies and see if I can plant my feet down here in D-town. I'm all about handling my business and taking things to another level, you feel me? What about you? What you into pretty lady?"

"I'm a socialite," she told him, feeling his New York lingo and wondering just how deep his pockets were. She usually went for the square, clean-cut type of dude, but something about this guy was sparking her interest. He looked like he could take a big bite and devour her ass . . . and she liked it.

"I host parties at a lot of clubs and special events," she lied with a smile. "But my father is in the oil business also so basically I do whatever I want."

"Well, maybe you could show me around sometime," Gutta said, making sure she saw his eyes roaming all over her body. "Or you could invite me to the next event you host. I mean, that would only be right since you turned down my gift, ya know?"

They laughed and made more small talk as Gutta counted out the cash for his watch and waited for the jeweler to package it up.

"Sure, I might be able to show you a few places," the delicious-looking chick said with a grin. "And maybe I'll let you buy me a drink one day since you like to pay for stuff."

"It's all good baby," Gutta responded smoothly. "Let's exchange digits and see what we can make happen. By the way what's your name shawty?"

"My name is Pilar," the sexy socialite with a daddy in the oil business told him. "Pilar Ducane."

"Why you gotta go outta town?" I asked Suge with my lip poked out. He had just got his butt back in town a couple of days ago and now he was talking about rolling right back out. I looked out the window as we sped down the highway in his humongous silver monster truck. We had gone out to get some ribs and coleslaw and he was driving me back to the mansion.

I crossed my arms over my titties and frowned as I leaned away from him in my seat. "I'm getting real tired of you running all over the place without me, dude."

He had the nerve to laugh. "C'mon now, sugar," he reached out and ran his big old hand down my arm and tried to pull me back toward him. "You knew I was a working man when you met me." He shrugged like it was a small thing. "It ain't nothing major, sugar. I just got some work to put in."

I heard what his mouth said but I wasn't tryna believe that shit. For a lil minute now I had been picking up a real shady vibe from ol'Mister Suge and I didn't like it. Ever since he had rolled up to the crib in his so-called "friend's" whip and I pulled all them white-girl hairs outta the carpet, his ass had been numero uno on my suspect list. I mean, we'd be chilling at the mansion one minute and the next second his ass would be flying out the door, gone. Or we'd be out on the town laughing and eating, and then his cell phone would buzz and he would duck somewhere deep in the cut to answer that shit.

I had mad love in my heart for Suge and I knew he was feeling me for-real, for-real too. I hadn't busted him in no out-right lies and I couldn't put my finger on nothing specific, and yeah, he still treated me like a queen and sexed me like a fiend, but a rat was stanking up a storm somewhere in Texas and my hood instincts were telling me to keep my guns aimed high.

You better NOT be tryna put no mack game down on me! I cut my eyes at him and stayed on my side of the monster whip. This fool must didn't know! Suge was all gorilla and his game was gully from head to toe, but when it came to bustin' slick backdoor moves this here shit was a mismatch! I was a *LaRue*, baby, and Mink Minaj had robbed, lied, and cheated on more niggas than a little bit! Hell, it was in my nature to creep and scheme, so I knew it was in a rich nigga's nature too. I'd *better not* find out Suge was tryna roll over me. I would hate it for his ass. I really would!

I had already told Bunni about my suspicions and she just fronted me off and said I was paranoid.

"For real, Bunni. I got a funny feeling, girl. Something ain't right with his ass. I told you about that white girl hair that was all up in the whip he was pushing. Whoever that trick is she was shedding like a damn sheep dog! For real, girl. That little voice in my head is tryna tell me something!"

"Quit it, Tasha Pierce!" she snapped. "Every dude in the world don't cheat all the time like we do! I know a dick swinger when I see one and Uncle Suge ain't one! Besides, if he was creepin' my titty woulda been itchin' by now. You just been sitting around this mansion too long getting fat and happy so now you making shit up. Look, I know this dude who got a banging new club in Georgia. Let's take the jet and fly to the ATL and crash us a party. That'll give your freaky butt something to do besides worry about where your play-play uncle is pointing his dick!"

I nodded. Partying in the ATL sounded real good to me.

"You think Dane wanna go?" I asked. "He can roll with us if he's bringing the get-high."

Bunni sucked her teeth. "Forget Dane! Don't nobody need his dick-swinging ass," she spit with her eyes flashing. She dug down in her bra and came out with a small bag of loud. "You just call the pilot and tell him to warm up the jet, mami. I got my own damn stash!"

Suge was a hardcore gambling man and he knew when the odds were stacked against him. This situation with Miyoko was coming to a deadly crossroad and if she caught him out there the right way he was either gonna come up snake-eyes or crap the fuck out. She knew how bad he needed to save his brother's ass so she was yanking the little tiny hairs around his nuts trying to corner him in her box.

It was because of Viceroy that everybody in the family ate off lovely plates, and the risk Suge was about to take was necessary and unavoidable. If he played his hand right then the family would be cool. But if he got thrown off his game just a little bit . . . well, from the oldest to the youngest, everybody was gonna take a fall.

Shit had gotten real tight with Miyoko in New York and she'd almost trapped his ass and got her some. The girl was determined to ride his dick by any means necessary and quick thinking was the only thing that had saved him.

"Superior . . ." she had moaned, smelling like a whole magnum of champagne as she pressed up against him in the crowded hotel elevator after the Met Gala. They had been tossing back drinks with celebrities and politicians all night long and every chance she got her hands had been sneaking toward his dick.

"Wait till I get you upstairs! This is going to be so fucking good!" She cornered him in the elevator, panting wetly in his ear. Standing wide-legged in her red Versace gown, Miyoko reached for his nuts and squeezed them through his pants while shamelessly rubbing her hot crotch on his rock-hard thigh at the same time.

"Whoa-whoa-whoa now!" Suge had jumped back and grabbed her wrist, extracting his limp meat from her hand as he hunched his shoulder and dodged her flickering wet tongue. "C'mon, now." He laughed and played her off for the crowd of riders. "Mess around and set off these smoke alarms and we'll be stuck in this elevator all damn night."

The chick was half-drunk and all hands as they walked down the hall toward the suite she had rented for them. "I'm gonna blow your nuts through the roof tonight," Miyoko promised as she stumbled along beside him telling him all about the bomb head she was about to lay in his lap. "I'm gonna suck your toes, tickle your balls, lick your ass—"

Suge sped up, hurrying ahead of her as Miyoko's sweet little lips spouted pornographic reminders of their youthful fuck fests and promised to do all the freaky shit she knew would turn him out. There had been a time when just hearing that shit rolling off her tongue would've been enough to set his rocks off, but his shit was nowhere near hard as he rounded the corner to the suite ahead of her and did the only thing he could do to make sure his dick stayed out of her mouth for the rest of the night. He turned the corner, yanked the fire alarm, and emptied the whole damn building out!

CHAPTER 21

Bunni had picked the wrong damn joint to party at. The Cotton Tail wasn't nothing but a strip club for black dudes who liked white booty, and I wasn't feeling it not one damn bit.

"Get in the groove!" Bunni urged me as she joined a bunch of skanky white scrippers with cotton balls taped to their asses as they bunny-hopped all over the stage.

That cut "Blurred Lines" was playing but there wasn't a damn thing blurry about Bunni as she stuck out like the chocolate bastard child of the rabbit litter screaming, *"I know you want it!"* at every dude in sight.

I had smoked some good gas earlier and now I sat at the bar getting toasted up on some Ciroc and juice as I watched scenes from the Met Gala on the huge overhead television screen.

"Excuse me." A light-skinned older dude with thick glasses touched me on my hand. "Good evening. Can I buy you a drink?"

I glanced down at his shiny Hublot and in a flash my ass reverted right back to my trick-'em-up days and Tasha Pierce was out in full force sniffing on the prowl. The first thing I did was case his ass from head to toe. In two seconds flat I could tell you if the leather on his shoes was imported or domestic, if that sweet lil sucka on his wrist was a Big Bang or a King Power 48 MM, if the platinum blue sapphire on his finger was official or a knock-off, and whether his cologne was China-man up the street slum, or if it was some delicious Black Afgano for three hundred grips an ounce.

I stared at the chain around his neck and my hood-o-meter registered that shit at certified white gold. The frames on his glass were thick as shit but them bad boys were definitely Moss Lipows.

The muthafuckin' game was on! My titties broke out in a sweat and my mouth started watering. A tingly flush rushed over me and my scalp got real hot. But then I remembered. My days of tricking niggas off were over. I had given up the thrill of the dog hunt for the comfort of a velvet-covered porch. No matter what kinda yardage this mark had in his pockets, I probably had *way* more than that in minez.

"No thank you," I said reluctantly, coming down off my lil high. I felt like a lint-picking crack head who had searched the whole damn floor for a phantom piece of dropped rock but had come up empty.

I ordered me some more hen-hen then sat back and watched all the celebrities coming and going on the red carpet. Some of them were looking good as shit, but others looked a hot funky mess out there! They needed somebody like me and Bunni to show them how to adorn themselves in finery and showcase their best assets.

I watched Kim Kardashian walk up looking like a damn space cadet in some ugly blue outfit. Everything she put on looked cheap and ratchet so I wasn't surprised. A little while later I spotted Rihanna sporting this bad-ass white diamond-necked belly shirt with a matching mermaid skirt. The outfit was banging but I wasn't feeling all the tats and the crimped hair. Janelle Monae looked real cute as usual, but that beaver stretched out on her head was fucking me up. Next I saw this

tall Asian chick shaped like a damn banana as she stepped up in
the hottest freakin' Versace I had ever seen. It was red with tiny
sequins and it had a split down the side, and the body-hugging
waist swept royally from side to side. Her jet black hair was
piled up on her head in a real sweet swoopie up-do, and she
was smart enough to stop, strike a pose, smile left, center, and
right, and then she waited while her escort walked into the
frame and smiled for the camera too. He was a big, hunky nigga
dressed in a slammin' tuxedo. Fine as shit, bald and chocolate
with a sexy-ass smile that—

"Oh, shit!" I screamed so loud that dude standing next to
me jumped back and all the titty-shaking bunnies dancing on
the stage froze in place.

"What's wrong?" Bunni slid down off a pole and ran over
to me barefoot with a twenty-dollar bill hanging outta her bra.
"Mink wha—"

"That *muthafucka!*" I jabbed my finger at the television
screen as my nigga Suge posted up and threw his big arm
around the slinky Asian chick and grinned as the paparazzi
snapped, snapped, snapped at least a million goddamn times.
"That *lying* muthafucka!" I picked up my glass of vodka and
flung that shit dead at his shiny bald head. "That *l-l-l-l*," I stuttered with grief, "*lying muthafucka!*"

Suge had made his escape and chartered a private jet back
to Texas. He landed in Dallas happy as fuck to be rid of Miyoko
for a minute, but knowing that he still had an even bigger problem to take care of: Mink.

His cell phone had started vibrating before he could get off
the red carpet, and if security hadn't been so high at the Met she
probably woulda busted up in that joint and turned shit out.

Suge grinned as he jogged up the stairs of his brother's
mansion. He liked Mink's type of jealousy. The girl was like a
skittish lil filly. She knew she had the legs to run a helluva race,

but she was too young in the head to put her faith in the prize that was on the track.

"You busted nigga! I *busted* you!" She jumped on him as soon as he walked into her room. Ignoring that noise Suge pressed her up against the wall and gripped her thick delicious booty happily in his palms.

She shrugged him off. "You went your black ass to New York after you ran me some line about you had to work!" she blasted on him with her pretty eyes flashing with heat.

"I *was* working," he said simply as he pulled her closer and inhaled her sweet scent.

"Uh-uh!" she bitched, pushing him away again. "Ain't nobody stupid! I saw your gaming ass walking down the red carpet in your fly tuxedo with your arm around some stringy-haired chopstick! Who *was* that bitch?"

"I can't tell you," Suge said, grinding against her plump softness, his dick wide awake and nice and hard.

"You can't tell me? Are you serious? You over here tryna get you some drawers but you can't tell me what you was doing all up on TV with some other chick?"

Suge shrugged as he buried his lips in her neck and kept right on feeling her up. "There's a lot of shit that I ain't never gonna tell you, Mink. That's me. But what I *will* tell you is that I missed you. I ain't playing no games and I ain't running you no lines. But I need you to trust me, baby girl. Can you handle that? Are you woman enough to say fuck what that TV told you and really, really trust a man?"

Mink was getting heated too now and she moaned a little as her tongue darted out and she licked his bottom lip.

"But I seen y'all together, Suge! The whole world seen y'all and you was all hugged up on her like . . . shit, what was I supposed to think?"

"You wasn't supposed to *think* nothing. You was supposed to *believe*. I gave you my word that couldn't no other woman get nothing that I have for *you*. And I meant it. You gotta decide where you gonna put your money at, Mink. Who you going for, baby girl? The jockey or the horse?"

"The horse," she said grinning.

"That's right, baby girl. The horse." Suge kissed her on the neck then tapped her twice on the ass as he pulled her shirt over her head and raised her thin cotton skirt in the air. He knew she had the right answer in her. His baby was the best damn horse in the stable, he thought as he got down on his knees so he could get a taste of what his mouth had been watering for. He pulled the crotch of her panties aside and got ready to go to town. Mink was a fine-ass pony, Suge thought as he dove right in with his tongue and lips. He'd put his last dollar on her rump any day.

CHAPTER 22

It was almost noon on a beautiful Saturday when GiGi Molinex drove up to the gates of the Dominion mansion and pressed the intercom button to be admitted. It was the second time she had come to con Bunni and her sidekick Mink out of information that might be useful to Larry and Stewie, and while she was sick of talking in circles, she *had* gotten a few decent nibbles off the foul-mouthed ghetto bunnies, and she was planning to lean on them real heavy today so she could gobble up a whole meal.

She had played a neat little head game with Bunni, scaring the shit out of her by cancelling their appointment, only to agree to give her one more chance when the poor girl called back begging.

It was a clever little psychological ploy designed to make Bunni feel ever so grateful, and now GiGi's mind whirred like a computer as she waited to be buzzed in the gates. She had yet to meet Viceroy or any of his sons, and she promised herself she wasn't leaving that house today until she laid eyes on them. She peeped down at her bulging cleavage and giggled. And until they laid eyes on her too!

The small speaker near the gate crackled and a deep, monotone voice said over the intercom, "This is the Dominion residence. How may I help you?"

"GiGi Molinex!" she sang out with a charming southern accent. "I'm a cable television producer and I'm here to meet with Bunni Baines."

Moments later the tall, majestic gates swung open and GiGi drove her bogus production van onto the grounds of the estate. When she pulled up outside of the front entrance a handsome valet in a red and black uniform greeted her with a smile and opened her door so she could exit.

"No, no, no," she told him as she reached out and closed the van's door firmly. "Just tell me where to put it and I'll park it myself." A look of surprise crossed the young man's face and GiGi flashed him a bright smile. "Sorry. Company policy. Our insurance policy is just restrictive like that."

She parked a few feet away from a sexy red Maserati and a shiny black Bentley. Both cars looked to be brand new, and there wasn't a speck of dust on either of them. GiGi climbed out of her van and tugged down the hem of her slinky thigh-high designer dress. She'd worn a thong to eliminate any panty lines, and the fabric of the crimson red dress felt soft and slippery on her bare ass-cheeks. Her flaming hair hung in thick ringlet curls and she let her curvy hips sway loose and free as she sauntered up to the front door with a look of excitement in her devilish green eyes.

The valet smiled and rang the doorbell for her. The door was opened by a slim white man with dark hair and wire-rimmed glasses.

"Hi there!" She held out her hand and smiled brightly as she struck a pose. She was tanned and toned and her dress was nearly the same color as her hair. It had a plunging neckline and a high-riding belt, and she knew the contrast between her tiny waist and her sexy hips made her look quite stunning. "I'm GiGi Molinex. I have an appointment today with Bunni Baines."

The man was professionally dressed and seemed to be an official of the household, but still, he couldn't help but check GiGi out and flash her a beaming look of approval. "Please, come in, Miss Molinex," he said, extending his arm for her to take. "Right this way."

GiGi might have been sick of talking in circles to Mink and Bunni, but trust and believe they were getting sick of talking to her ass too!

"I don't think that trick is ever gonna give us no reality show," Bunni complained to her posse. "She's frontin'. When she called me this morning all she wanted to do is ask a bunch of questions about Papa Doo and the guys. Especially Barron. What the hell? *We* the ones who gonna be headlining the damn show, and she don't wanna know nothing about how we get down?"

"What kinda questions?" Mink asked.

Bunni shrugged. "Stupid shit like, 'What's the most embarrassing thing that ever happened to the family' and 'What would Viceroy's worst enemy say about him.' That nut even asked me if the Dominions had one secret that would devastate the family if it ever got out, what would it be? Like I fuckin' know!"

"Errm herrm," Peaches sang. He was sitting on the sofa with one of his stallion legs crossed over the other one at the knee as he lazily wagged his dangling foot. "Sumpthin' ain't right with her," he said in Paul's deep voice. "You better keep your eyes and ears open on this one, honey."

"Well *I* sure as hell ain't feeling her fake titty ass with her cement glue–injected booty," Mink piped in. "That bitch ain't got shit on me or Serena Williams, but I told you that shit right from the jump."

"She just don't be hearing nothing I have to say," Bunni bitched, and then leaped to her feet as Albert escorted GiGi into the room.

"Speak of the devil," Peaches muttered under his breath.

"Hey, how you doing, GiGi!" Bunni flashed the white chick a fake, cheesy smile. "I bet your boss is ready for us to make a demo, ain't he? So are we getting us a show or what?"

GiGi smiled and tossed her luscious mane of curls. She looked like a red-hot devil as she stood before them in her slinky mini-dress and floor-stabbing high-heels.

"Sorry, Bunni." She turned to her and made sad, apologetic eyes. "I haven't heard anything yet because they're still deciding. I'm not the only producer they have scouting talent out in the field, you know. There are several other families who are going through this same process and they're all anxious to find out if they made the cut as well."

A few moments later the King Kong of the house strode purposefully into the room and all the chatter ceased.

"Excuse me," Viceroy said, his voice booming with authority. His attire was impeccable as usual, and there was no hiding the fact that everything he had on was pure cream. "Has anyone seen Barron? He's not answering his cell phone."

"I saw him earlier this morning but I think he left a while ago," Mink offered.

Viceroy nodded. "Thanks. Lunch is about to be served, and if anyone cares to join us, they can."

"Naw." Bunni waved her hand. "That's okay, Papa Doo. We'll get us something to snack on later—"

"Mr. Dominion." GiGi stood up quickly and flashed him a smile that was bigger than the whole damn state of Texas. She smoothed her dress over her hips and switched her ass toward him with hungry determination in her eyes.

"Pardon me," she said, grinning hard enough to crack her powdered cheeks as she extended her manicured hand. Her pores leaked pure sexiness as she held his grip in her soft fingers and fawned at him with her kittenish green eyes.

"My name is GiGi Molinex. I'm a producer from a major

cable network and I must say it is truly an absolute honor to finally meet you."

Viceroy looked her up and down like she was crazy at first,
but as his eyes settled deep into her plump, milky cleavage he
smiled as though he was digging her vibes.

"I've interviewed several of your family members," GiGi
said, beaming up at him, "and I've certainly done my research
on you. You're quite the accomplished man, aren't you? It was
amazing to read about your brilliance and perseverance after
your tragic accident. Not to mention that you have such a colorful and hilarious family. You must be so proud of them!"

With Mink and Bunni sitting on one couch, and Peaches
all dolled up with his legs crossed on the other one, Viceroy
looked like he couldn't decide whether that shit was a compli-
ment or some fighting words.

"Uh, yeah," he said, side-eyeing them. "I must be proud of
something. Will you be joining us for lunch, Mrs. Molinex?
Grilled rib eyes and steamed crab legs are on the menu for the
event today."

"Uh-uh, no lunch!" Bunni jumped up and cut in. "We
gotta talk about a demo—"

"*Miss* Molinex," GiGi said with a quickness, turning her
back and igging the shit outta Bunni. "And yes, I certainly will
join you," she gushed. "Thanks for the invite, Mr. Dominion.
Which way is the dining room?" She flashed him a buttery
smile. "I'll follow your lead."

Bunni stood there with her lip poked out as GiGi balanced
on her forty-inch heels and wiggled her meaty ass behind
Viceroy as he held out his arm and escorted her to the dining
room.

"Hold the hell up," Bunni bitched with her hand on her
hip. "Did this chick just ditch us for Daddy Domino?" she
squeaked. "I know she ain't just rise and fly her squiggly ass up
outta here!"

"Errrm herrrm," Peaches nodded with his lips tooted up. "That's exactly what Miss Thang just did."

Bunni stomped her feet and plopped back down on the sofa, pissed. "Soon as a nigga with a little bit a' dough walk in the damn room some people start acting all shady and shit!"

Mink laughed. "What? You think just 'cause a heffa is white and from the 'burbs she don't have no chicken in her?" She waved her hand. "Girl, bye! That cluck-cluck just let loose a pussy fart under Viceroy's nose and blew that sucka wide open. We've done that same shit to plenty of niggas," she said as she chuckled at her home girl.

"Yeah, that heffa is a bird all right," Bunni said. "But she got one more time to flap her wings at me like that and I'ma have to crack her eggs and pluck her wide-ass straight bald!"

Mink laughed again as she stood up and patted her toned tummy. "You do that, girl. But in the meantime I'm about to be on my surf and turf grind so I'll be joining Viceroy for lunch too. Come on, Bunni. Your greedy butt know you don't miss no meals and you sure as hell don't let no crab legs pass you by, so let's bounce."

"Yeah, you right," Bunni said as she hopped up and imitated the way GiGi had sashayed her hips and rolled her booty when she followed behind Viceroy. "Mizz GiGi must don't know! Her vanilla wafer ass betta not be playing no games with my damn reality show or I'ma have to bust her one!"

There was lots of chatter around the dining room table as the staff carried in large roaster pans filled with steamed Alaskan king crab legs and platters stacked high with juicy, succulent cuts of grilled beef. GiGi made sure to push through the crowd and maneuver her way into a seat next to Viceroy, and Bunni was no more than an afterthought as she captivated his attention and talked to him nonstop. Just to keep it looking legit, every now and then GiGi would turn and glance over her shoulder and ask Bunni a question or two, and if Bunni got too long-winded with her answer she would cut her off real quick and jump right back in Viceroy's face.

The food was being served when Dane entered the dining room and gave his greetings to the family.

"Hey Pops." Dane came over and paid his respect to his father and shook his hand. "Sorry I'm late. You've got a good crowd. How's everything going with the campaign?"

"We'll talk about that later," Viceroy said. "This is GiGi Molinex." He nodded, making the introduction. "She's a television producer and she's here to learn more about our family."

Dane took one look at the delicious red-headed bundle of curves perched on a chair next to his father and licked his lips. He had lassoed a couple of cowgirls who looked like her when he was in college, and the look in his eyes told her he wouldn't mind roping her up and taking her to his little fuck pad upstairs over the garage.

"Pleased to meet you, Dane," GiGi gushed pure sugar as she shook his hand and noticed how fast his eyes dropped down to her bulging tits. She could tell he liked what he saw so she allowed their handshake to linger a little bit as she squeezed his fingers and gave him a seductive look. "I've been told that you're Viceroy's second son. I can see you're just as handsome as your father, but tell me. Are you as charming and high-spirited as he is too?"

GiGi made sure to put some extra heat on every word she spoke, and she smiled inside when she saw the burst of excitement light up Dane's handsome brown eyes.

"I do all right," he said, damn near drooling as his eyeballs slid all over her. "In fact, I do just fine."

GiGi had no shame at all as she flirted with the rich young sucker right at his father's table. And Dane didn't either as he stood over her with his eyes digging into the split between her breasts as he caught her bait: hook, line, and sinker.

Dane glanced around the table at the few empty seats left on the other side, and then he looked at Bunni like he wanted to boot her out of her chair and sit down beside GiGi. Instead, he walked away reluctantly and took a seat on the other side of the table.

With the food served and small individual tins of hot drawn butter passed around, Viceroy said a quick prayer and everyone dug in.

"So," Bunni elbowed GiGi and asked. "What do you think about us so far, GiGi?" She was getting sick and tired of all the ass-kissing GiGi was doing with Viceroy, not to mention all the coded convo that was going on back and forth across the table between her and Dane.

"You can go 'head and tell me. I'm strong and I promise I can take it. Do you think our family has what it takes to have a reality show or what?"

"Well, Bunni," GiGi drawled and shifted her booty around in her seat until she was halfway facing Bunni. She took one look at the deadpan set of Bunni's face and she flashed her a fake smile that was supposed to come across as genuine. "I honestly can't answer that yet. I mean, I've only been around you and your wonderful family a couple of times, and there are still so many things that I don't know about you. It's still far too early to tell, but I've been taking great notes and getting a lot of great vibes from everyone since I've been coming here, that's for sure."

"Great vibes my *huh!*" Bunni sucked her teeth and mumbled. She wasn't tryna hear none of that yuck-yuck mealy-mouthed shit! "It's more like you been getting a lotta great looks—ouch!" she squealed as Mink pulled one of her moves and pinched the shit outta her under the table.

"You've been getting a lot of great *film*," Mink said, covering shit up real smoothly. "Your camera dude was way deep in the beeswax the other day, man! I caught dude all up in my panty drawer taking pictures!"

GiGi waved her hand and pooed her. "That's nothing," she said with her voice dripping sweet tea and honey. "If you want to be successful on a reality show you've gotta be willing to show America your clean laundry and your dirty laundry too!"

"Who the hell said I got any dirty—ow!" Mink snapped as Bunni pinched her on the tender skin on the back of her arm. Glaring at her rowdy, Mink dipped her fingers into her water glass and got a big chunk of ice and pressed it to her throbbing skin.

"Oh, by the way, Mr. Dominion," GiGi said loudly, stealing the attention back as she ignored both of them and leaned in close to Viceroy and flattered him with her pretty smile. "I've never had steak quite this delicious before! Is this imported beef? Does your cook use a secret seasoning or something?"

"It's a goddamn cow!" Bunni snapped. "One of them snotty-nosed things they got running around out there in the yard! Y'all crackers grow 'em out there in California too, don'tcha?"

GiGi spun around in her seat until she was fully facing Bunni. The beaming smile never left her face, but her eyes were cooler than the other side of the pillow as she nodded her head and said brightly, "Yes! That's it! That's the kind of real talk it takes to get a reality show, Bunni! Don't hold back. Americans want to be shaken out of their mundane normalcy. Our viewers want to engage with people who say exactly what's on their minds. We need the rest of the family to behave just like you! Shocking! Startling! Salacious! Sensational! Scandalous!"

"Stupid!" Mink leaned over to Bunni and whispered. "That trick means stupid, slow, simple, and silly as hell!"

Somehow GiGi managed to schmooze herself up on a tour of Dane's garage apartment, and all Bunni could do was walk around the den stomping her feet and mumbling under her breath with an attitude while she and Mink waited for them to come back.

"That heffah ain't right," Bunni fumed. "She's supposed to be focusing on me you and Peaches, but all she been doing is tossing that damn red ponytail up in Viceroy and Dane's damn faces!"

Mink shrugged. "That's because them two got something in they drawers that me and you ain't got in ours. I'm telling you, Bunni. You better not sleep on this one. Game is over here sniffing out *game*, baby. GiGi might look like a dumb valley chick but she's a hustler, honey. She's just as slick with her shit as the rest of us. If not more so."

When GiGi finally came back she and Dane were laughing and joking like they were old friends. Bunni's eyes narrowed as she saw GiGi hit Dane with that killer smile of hers then slip him her number on the low. The chick was smooth, Bunni had to admit. Smoother than a baby's ass!

"Hey," she interrupted the little flow they had going on. "What's up, GiGi?" she asked as she barreled across the room and joined her and Dane in the parlor. "I know you not about to leave now, are you? I mean, tell me sumthin, damn! How was our meeting? Are we good? Is your boss gonna send us a full camera crew so we can get this show rolling or what?"

Igging Bunni, Dane glanced at his wristwatch. "I gotta make a quick run so I'll leave you two to talk," he said, cheesing all up in GiGi's grill. "I sure hope to see you again sometime soon, GiGi," he said as he walked off. "You know where I stay now so don't be a stranger."

That cheery-o smile she had been laying on Dane dropped completely off GiGi's face as she turned to look at Bunni. "Thank you for inviting me into your home again, Bunni," GiGi said, her words real flat like she didn't need Bunni no more and was tired of fucking with her. "Y'all have been very interesting and like I said before, I'm going to run my assessment by my supervisors and see what they think your family can do for our ratings and stuff and whatever."

"So that's it?" Bunni blurted. "You been here all day talkin' folks to death and you still don't know if we'll get us a show or not? Well are you at least gonna let them know how much we got it going on and that we're ready to blow up your open slot?"

"As I told you," she said slowly, like she was talking to a tree that just didn't get it. "We still have a few other families to interview. We will get back to you as soon as we have an answer," GiGi lied, "and if it all goes well I will personally give you the good news and broadcast your family to the world. Don't worry, Bunni," she said, a slight grin creeping over her face as her eyes slid across the room and roamed up the staircase where Dane had just disappeared. She had way more planned for this family than Larry or Stewie could ever imagine. Way more. In fact, she didn't really give a damn about Larry or Stewie, or what kind of dirt they needed to derail Viceroy Dominion's campaign. She had stumbled upon a prime opportunity and GiGi was about to look out for *self*. Damn right. She was gonna jump on one of those Dominion men and ride his wave all the way down to the bottom of the sea.

Grinning big time, she pat Bunni on the hand and gushed. "Yes, please don't worry, dear. I *promise* this isn't the last you're going to see of me."

Barron smelled her way before he saw her. Even above the mouthwatering odor of the delicious meal that was drifting in from the kitchen, he picked up on her scent. She was wearing the kind of perfume that black women never wore, and it slid up his nose and tickled his nuts before he even laid his eyes on her.

Damn! he screamed inside as he rounded the corner and saw the ass on the red-headed white chick who was standing in the den talking to Bunni. She had on a hot red form-fitting dress that hugged every last one of her curves, and Barron's eyes went all up and down and underneath that shit as he approached them from behind.

"What's going on here?" he interrupted their conversation and asked with a charming smile. "I wouldn't have missed the luncheon if I'd known we were having such beautiful company today."

Bunni smirked. "You don't hafta know every doggone thing, Barron! This here is my little thingy-thang, okay?"

She leaned in toward GiGi and said, "This is the real stuffy one I told you about. His name is Barron but they call him Bump. Is that hood enough for ya?"

"Barron!" The sweet-smelling beauty held out her hand. "GiGi Molinex. I've heard so much about you. Pleased to finally meet you."

Barron gripped her hand and stared. Her green cat-eyes bounced off the hues in her slinky dress and he couldn't help wondering if her down south hair was anywhere near as flaming hot as the hair on her head.

"Pleased to meet you, Ms. Molinex—"

"Call me GiGi." She flashed him a bright, open smile and held on tightly to his hand. "I insist."

Barron grinned back at her. "Well then, pleased to meet you, GiGi. Welcome to our home," he said. "I saw the television van outside in my parking spot," he said, "but where are the cameras?"

"I already told you this is my thingy-thang, Barron!" Bunni barked. "GiGi is a TV producer and she's gonna put me in a reality show!"

"I said I *might* put you in a reality show," GiGi corrected with a pleasant smile. "Right now we're still in the information-gathering stage. We have to find out as much as we can about your family so we can determine if this is a match for our viewership."

Barron scoffed and shook his head. "Sorry, but everybody around here knows how I feel about reality shows. I think the world has seen enough ratchet chicks get on television and fight with their baby daddies."

"Why they gotta be ratchet just because they keep it real for America, Bump? At least they ain't walking around with paper towel rolls stuck up they ass like some people around here!"

GiGi laughed as she took Barron by the arm and turned on her charm. "Studies have proven that the majority of television viewers are tired of scripted drama. They want spontaneity and people who have the types of problems in their lives that most women can identify with. While you may call it 'ratchet' lots of women call it their reality."

Barron shrugged. "That's cool, but what made you decide to come here? Our family isn't that exciting and we definitely don't have the kind of scandals that are made for television. I mean, Bunni probably has a lot of juicy lockup stories she can tell you about the trashy life she lived in New York City, but the rest of us are just regular southerners." He chuckled. "To be honest, our lives are so boring we'd probably put your viewers to sleep and get you fired. I don't think you wanna bother with us."

"Well." GiGi grinned and her smile was so sexy and gorgeous that Barron's wood jumped up high in his pants. "I beg to differ with you Barron. I think you're plenty interesting," she said, cozying up close on his arm. "And handsome too. Is it possible for us to get together privately at some point so we can sit down and have a little chat?"

Barron nodded as drool damn near slid down his chin.

"I have some wine chilling in my suite right now," he said smoothly.

"Sorry, I was just about to leave, so I'll have to take a rain check. But tell me, what kind of wine do you prefer? Red or white?" she asked with a sexy giggle.

"White, baby," Barron licked his lips and said hoarsely as he stared mesmerized into her smoky eyes. He leaned in close to her and whispered in her ear as his dick throbbed nice and hard, "I like it white all day and all night too, goddammit. Definitely white, baby. White . . . white . . . *white.*"

CHAPTER 23

It was late night inside the Dallas County Jail and the female inmates could be heard talking shit, gambling, and just being loud for no good reason. Dy-Nasty was stretched out on the top bunk reading the obscene messages scribbled on the ceiling and walls by the countless prisoners who had occupied the cell before her. The dim light that stayed on burning all night long reflected the mood of the women in lockup, which was gloomy and depressing. What made matters even worse was that Dy-Nasty's cellie was going through heroin withdrawal. The bitch was moaning, groaning, and farting up the whole damn cell.

The entire bag was grossing Dy-Nasty out, so she pulled the thin blanket over her head and thought hard about getting up outta that hellhole as she fell into a troubled sleep.

She was up again bright and early the next morning.

"Yo, Ceee-Oooh!" Dy-Nasty sang out as she pounded on the door about thirty minutes before breakfast was due to begin. Between her dope-sick cellmate and her graphic nightmares she had barely slept at all. Even in her dreams she had been feening to get to the phone, desperate to make contact with Pat, her mother and one true friend, who she hadn't been able to reach in a minute. On the real, Dy-Nasty was truly worried. It wasn't like Pat to just not answer her phone, and she had a feeling something funky was going on back in Philly.

"Yo, CO!" she hollered again. "Cell two fifty-two needs to use the phone! Hurry up and crack the damn door!"

The male guard on duty had been nicknamed Shaka because of his athlete's build and dark African features, and he had a hot jones for Dy-Nasty. He was a mean son of a bitch but he usually let Dy-Nasty get away with some things that other inmates couldn't.

"You know it's too early to use the phones," Shaka said as he grinned at Dy-Nasty through her cell window. She batted her eyes and licked her luscious lips at him in return. Shaka was used to thirsty inmates tryna get at him, but he liked Dy-Nasty's ghetto Philly ass. "A'ight, check it," he said, submitting. "You looking good so I'ma let you rock today."

Shaka opened the cell door manually and let Dy-Nasty out, and she slowly switched her lovely gangsta booty past him as she gazed up at him seductively. Shaka was her early morning connection to the telephone so she needed to keep his Mandingo ass on a string. She knew there were hella cameras all around, but she also knew how to flirt on the sly and send a nigga a cheap thrill. She had a couple of hating hoes breathing down her neck because they saw how good Shaka treated her, but she wasn't stuttin' that shit. They could have his ass, she just needed him in her pocket for a while so she could make her little moves.

Dy-Nasty hit the phone and anxiously dialed Pat's number again hoping that she picked up this time. To her surprise Pat picked up on the second ring.

"Hello," she snapped after listening to the recording and accepting the call. "Who the hell is it?"

"It's me, Mama," Dy-Nasty said, happy to finally hear her voice. "I'm locked up down in Texas."

"Ahhh shit!" Pat exclaimed. "What in the world happened, baby?" Pat sounded shocked but she was also excited to hear from her baby girl. "Sweetheart, I had a funny feeling something was going on with you!"

"That's why I been trying to call you, Ma," Dy-Nasty said as she looked over her shoulder. It was almost time to line up for breakfast so the cells began to open up and sleepy faces emerged out in the hall. "I was at the airport about to come home and them down-south bitches set me up and got me knocked! I need your help, Mama. Where the hell you been at? I was getting worried."

"Ohhh, girl. I been going through some drama myself," Pat said, sounding shook. "Some big mothafucka walked up on me outta nowhere and tried to kill me. I pulled my knife on him but he fucked me up and threw me in a damn Dumpster. Can you believe it? I hurt my back real bad and got my arm broke and shit, and now I keep having these real bad spasms that keep me running back and forth to the hospital. That nigga's lucky he got the best of me though 'cause if I was a little younger I woulda cut his giant ass to pieces."

"Damn, Mama!" Dy-Nasty said, distressed. "It's some crazy-ass people out there! You gotta be easy walking around there on them streets. And fuck a knife, I want you to get you a burner. I'm glad you a'ight but I need you to help me now. You know it's all Selah's fault that I'm locked up in here. She got all stupid over that ugly engagement ring, and now I don't know what to do!"

"You still got the money, right? That two million they was supposed to put in your account?"

Dy-Nasty sucked her teeth. "Hell, no. It's gone. Them cheapskates closed the account and took all the money back! I don't even have enough change for no soap or deodorant or nothing up in here."

"Damn Indian-givers!" Pat said, sounding pissed. "They coulda let you keep that!"

"I know, Mama. But these rich people is stingy like that. I

don't know what to do! I don't know nobody down here and I need me some help!"

"It sounds like you jammed up, baby," Pat said, feeling real bad for Dy-Nasty. "You should try to call Selah and talk to her."

"I been tryin'. She won't take my calls!"

"Selfish bitch!" Pat sucked her teeth. "I guess you gonna have to bite a bullet then. Maybe eat you a slice of humble pie."

"Huh?"

"You gonna have to go for Selah's soft spot baby, and hit her there."

Dy-Nasty scrunched up her face. "Where? In her eyeball?"

"No, you damn dummy!" Pat spit, "In her *heart*, girl. Hit her in her heart. Try to get in good with her and use whatever you can to break her down. You gonna have to come across like you remorseful and you wanna be useful and do something good for her at the same time."

"Yeah!" Dy-Nasty said getting excited. "You right, Mama. You right! I'ma call her again right now."

"Uh-uh!" Pat said sharply. "No, don't call her just yet," she explained. "You should write her old snobby-ass a couple of letters first. Make them sound real sorry and try to get on her good side. Rich uppity niggas always like their asses kissed in writing so they can read it over and over again. It might take a little while for her to act right, but you gotta be patient in order for this type of thing to work. Now, you do what you gotta do, you hear me?"

"Yes, Mama. I hear you," Dy-Nasty said, her mind turning. "Thank you so much. I knew you would come through for me! I'ma start putting this shit together right now. I'll call you later. I love you, Pat! Stay by the phone and wait for my next call."

"I will, baby," Pat said sweetly. "I love you too, baby. You just make sure you do what I said, okay, Dy-Nasty? Keep me posted."

As soon as Dy-Nasty put the receiver down she turned

around and caught some skinny Spanish chick breathing down her neck. She was standing there looking like she wanted to use the phone, but she could forget that shit.

"Bitch back the fuck up. It's a wrap for this phone, this shit's minez right now," Dy-Nasty barked, blacking out on the girl for invading her space. She didn't even have nobody else to call but she picked up the phone and started punching in random digits anyway. *Sheiiit,* you had to be forceful up in this joint because bitches would try to play you for a punk in a heartbeat. And Dy-Nasty was nobody's punk. She was on a serious mission now and she was gonna have to step her game up to a whole 'nother level if she had any chance of accomplishing it!

Barron had dropped almost half of his workload at Dominion Oil in order to devote some quality time to his father's campaign, and while he still put in a lot of hours working every day, he found time to play a little bit too.

He had a big problem with everything his father was doing to win this election and get a crack at chairing the commission, and all he could think was that the oil rig explosion had not only bumped Viceroy's head, it had rattled his fuckin' brains around too.

For somebody who had always been so concerned about his image, letting some gigantic black nightmare like Peaches stay at the crib and giving Bunni the green light to have a reality show was some of the last shit the family needed to be doing. But Barron had to admit that some good was coming out of it. That stunning female producer that he'd recently met was really something else. She was a bad-ass white chick, a red-headed sight for sore eyes, and Barron couldn't stop thinking about her. He knew exactly what he could do with some of that and he couldn't wait to get his chance.

Just this morning she had pranced up in the joint in a pair of skin-tight white jeggings that put her long curvy legs and sexy booty bump on full display. Her pert features and her beautiful green eyes had sent a lump of wood rising down in his drawers, and if his father wasn't in the room Barron would've gotten his mack on right then and there.

He had jumped in line to be interviewed for her pre-assessment, and after laying that smooth black man's charm down on her he was pretty sure she would be choosing his family for a film date.

And despite all the eye-rolling and teeth-sucking that shade-throwing Bunni had cast on him, GiGi really seemed to take to him too. In fact, she had thrown him a huge hint about hanging out together sometimes and Barron had tossed her one right back. He had told her breakfast was his favorite meal of the day and that he could eat it anytime, morning or night. She'd told him breakfast was her favorite meal too, and that when it came to pancakes her stomach didn't have a clock on it. Barron loved that shit, and he decided that one day he was gonna put her to the test. They had agreed to meet for lunch and Barron couldn't wait. He had spent the morning jacking off furiously in his room, stroking his dick to all kinds of vivid images of the girl of his dreams, and this time when he nutted in his palm it wasn't Mink's sweet pussy and high, round ass that he saw in his erotic fantasy anymore. It was GiGi's.

It was high noon and Bunni was ready to get her munch on. Selah was sitting on a breakfast stool sipping from a cup of herbal tea. Mrs. Katie had fried Bunni and Mink up a batch of jumbo-sized prawns and whipped up some homemade tartar sauce to go with them.

The two of them were heaping mounds of steaming hot shrimp and fries on their plates when the chimes sounded near the front door of the mansion, and they heard voices laughing and talking in the parlor.

"Who dat?" Bunni looked at Mink and raised her eyebrow as she chomped down on a juicy bite of shrimp.

Mink shrugged. "I'on't know. But it sounds just like—"

"GiGi!" Bunni leaped to her feet and hauled ass out of the kitchen hollering, "GiGi's here! Woot-Woot! My gurl GiGi is here!"

A few moments later they rolled back in the kitchen with Bunni practically dragging the chick over to the counter while her mouth flapped a hundred miles a minute. "I thought you said you was gonna call me? If you brought your tail all the way over here then I *know* you got some good news, right! So what did your bosses say, huh? We in, right? Where's the camera crew and when we gonna get to filming? We in, right? We in there, baybee!"

GiGi had a bright smile on her face as she laughed at Bunni's excitement and greeted everyone sweetly. "Good afternoon, Mrs. Dominion. Nice to see you, Mrs. Katie. How's it going, Mink?"

Mink paused with a fry halfway to her mouth, busting the funky groove right off the bat, but Bunni was like an overgrown puppy as she jumped up and down and damn near peed on the floor at the sight of the red-haired beauty.

"Now, Bunni," GiGi finally turned to address her and answer her million questions. "I did tell you that you'd be seeing me soon, but I didn't know it would be as soon as today. The executives at the station still haven't come to a firm decision yet, although they are in the process of narrowing things down. I'm sorry I don't have a better answer for you, but I'm hoping you'll continue to be patient while we work things out."

Bunni's mouth hit the floor.

"You mean you *still* don't have no answer? Well what the hell you come over here getting me all hyped up for?"

"Well, actually"—GiGi turned slightly and wiggled her fingers over her shoulder with a sugary grin—"I'm here to spend some time with Barron today. We just had lunch at the quaintest French restaurant ever, and he invited me over for a little swim."

Bunni whirled around. If looks coulda killed then Barron's white girl–lovin' ass woulda been stretched out on the floor! He stood there in the doorway with a shit-eating grin on his face that all four black women in the kitchen would've loved to slap off.

"Barron?" Bunni snapped. "What the hell do Barron got to do with this? I keep telling you this is *our* thingy-thang! Barron ain't down with none a' this—"

"Er, Bunni, this is a *personal* visit," GiGi said and placed her manicured hand on Bunni's arm soothingly. "It has nothing to do with our business matters," she explained.

"That's right," Barron said as he walked over and took GiGi by the arm and led her toward the back door. He winked at Bunni and shot her a bitch–ass look. "Chill out, Bunni. Ain't nobody trying to get in your damn business. Believe me, this is all pleasure."

Two days later, GiGi and Barron sat inside of a Waffle House diner having breakfast at four in the morning. GiGi hated breakfast food, but when Barron called in the middle of the night and suggested they go get some, she had hopped up and got dressed and met him there.

GiGi ordered cheesey eggs and pancakes while Barron got himself a big plate of chicken and waffles. They had been talking on the phone constantly, and while Barron was jonesing to be up under her, GiGi had him eating out of the palm of her hand as she kept him on a tight string and fed him little bits and pieces of her time.

"Thanks for meeting me here," Barron told her as he poured syrup all over his waffles. "I couldn't sleep and I was hungry. Not too many women would get out of their beds to come have pancakes with a friend they just met."

"Aww, Barron," GiGi responded as she forked down some eggs. "I know it's only been a very short time, but I feel like we're good, *good* friends. And that's what friends do."

Barron stared at her across the table. He would much rather have been about to eat her than those damn pancakes. He had to admit to that he was feeling Miss Molinex. And on a real deep level too. The girl was just perfect. She had everything he wanted in a woman. She was beautiful, she had mad sex appeal, she had charisma, and best of all, she was intellectual and driven toward her own success.

And that's where she had it going on over Pilar. He couldn't stand no greedy, gold-digging chick. While Pilar was thirsty and demanding and borderline desperate to get up in his pockets and be his wife, GiGi didn't need shit from him. She was already doing her thing without his money, and that attracted him. He was feening for her and enjoying her company, and Barron felt their instant attraction was organic.

"Well about this *friends* thing," Barron said as he wiped his mouth with a napkin. "I'm not gonna front, GiGi. I'm feeling you like crazy and I would love to get with you on a deeper level. I think me and you could make something good happen together. And with time and a little patience, I think we could even become a power couple. I'm not trying to force anything on you, I just want you to know how I feel. Besides, since you got up out of your bed to come eat pancakes with me, then I know you must be feeling a brotha a little bit, so why not give me some play?"

Barron closed his little speech out by flashing GiGi that confident Dominion grin. Even though he was adopted, he had Viceroy's charming magnetism down pat. GiGi had long since stopped chewing her rubbery eggs and stomach-bloating pancakes, and all she could do was smile. She waited for a few moments before she spoke, pausing for effect as she stared deeply into Barron's eyes.

"I was wondering when that was coming," GiGi said softly. "I feel like I've been waiting a million years to hear those words come out of your mouth. I really like you too, Barron. I think you're a really handsome, funny, and cool guy. I hope you're asking me to be your girlfriend, because I would love to have a relationship with you. A really close relationship, if you know what I mean."

Barron was amped. "This is unreal, baby. I promise I'll make you happy and you won't regret it." He leaned over the table and pressed his lips to hers gently. GiGi parted her lips and allowed his tongue to snake deeply into her mouth, and they were both enjoying the moment when some old fucker walked by and jammed up their entire groove.

"Yuck!" a big, countrified, greasy-looking white man with a long beard and overalls said loudly. He sneered down at GiGi with fire in his old eyes. "What a fucking disgrace to your race, young lady!"

Barron looked up at the guy with rage written all over his face.

"What the fuck did you just say?" Barron barked as he jumped up and stood face to face with the honky. "It's redneck backward-ass inbred pieces of shit like you that give Texas a bad rap."

"Relax, Barron," GiGi said from her seat like she was used to this type of thing. "It's okay. I'm not offended. Don't start anything with him. Please."

The white man smiled from ear to ear exposing his horrible tobacco-stained teeth. Green, yellow, and black crud was stuck all between the crevices, and that shit was so disgusting it made Barron back up a step.

And as soon as he did the hillbilly took advantage. He drove his meaty fist forward and hit Barron with a gut shot that knocked the wind out of him. The punch bent Barron in half and the man followed up with a right hook to the chin.

Barron dropped to his knees like a sack of potatoes. The crazy redneck then mounted him and started raining blows down on him like he owned his ass. Barron was blocking and weaving most of them but the guy was too heavy for Barron to buck him.

"Get the fuck off of him," GiGi screamed as she slapped and punched the racist in the back of his head. "Get off, you son of a bitch!"

Her feminine blows weren't fazing him at all, and the few patrons that were standing around weren't trying to help her at all. GiGi snatched her plate of food from the table and smashed it over the giant's dome. His head jerked to the side and he froze for a second. He turned around and looked up at GiGi.

"You stupid bitch!" The huge honky spit a nasty glob of chewed tobacco from his inner cheek straight into GiGi's face. "Now take that and sit your nigger-loving ass down!"

As Barron swung wild blows from the floor, the look on GiGi's face was one of horror. It was as if her brain simply couldn't register the disgusting ooze that was clinging to her skin and sliding down her cheek.

Suddenly Barron saw the big man's head snap back. To his surprise, GiGi had put him in a headlock and had a steak knife pressed to his dirty neck.

"Listen to me, you fat ugly fucker," she said calmly with a look in her eyes that even Barron thought was fucking frightening. "I will drive this goddamn knife straight through your grimy Adam's apple and end your miserable fucking life right now."

A trickle of blood slid from his pierced skin and the big man looked like he was scared to breathe. GiGi's hand didn't even tremble as she pressed the knife deeper into his flesh, causing a fresh stream of blood to flow.

"Okay . . . okay," the big man whispered. "Please . . . don't . . . cut me . . . I'm getting up right now."

He rose up off of Barron slowly, and before he could come to a stand GiGi switched the knife's position to the small of his back and pressed it there.

Barron knew what to do. When a Dominion got sucker punched, he sucker punched right back! He rolled from under the man and as soon as he got to his feet he thrust his fist into the redneck's nuts with all his strength. The big fella dropped like a rock and landed face-down on the floor, and Barron followed up with a leaping stomp to the back of his neck.

With his foot pressing down on the back of the big man's head, Barron looked around defiantly. GiGi was still holding the knife, and the other customers looked frightened as they whispered among themselves.

Slowly, Barron reached for the knife and took it away from her. He came up off dude's head and put his arms around her. Then Barron reached in his pocket, grabbed a couple of bills, and threw them on the table. He picked up GiGi's purse then wrapped his arm around her again, and they made their way to the door.

When they got outside the sun was coming up on a new day and Barron had learned something valuable during the night. His new girl Gigi was a bad-ass chick. There was much, much more to her than what met the eye!

CHAPTER 24

Suge was a real smooth playa and laying his hammer down on multiple honeys had always been one of his specialties, but that shit only played out the right way when he was the one calling all the shots. He had promised Mink that he would walk away from her before he violated that special thing they had going between them, but Miyoko was a relentless chick and she had some real scandalous plans for getting up on his down-stroke.

Whatever them Asian monks had done to her when her daddy sent her to the nuthouse in Okinawa, that shit didn't work. She was the same old possessive and manipulative freak that he remembered from way back when, and she was having a damn good time flaunting her power and leading Big Bad Suge Dominion around by his nose like a chump.

She kept her lil cold hands on him at all times. Whether it was riding in the whip, standing in line for a concert, or just sitting down to eat dinner. Every chance she got she would run her fingers up and down his muscular arms or try to slide her hand down his waistband and cop her a little feel on his nuts. Suge now knew how a lotta women felt when dudes pinched their asses and pawed all over their tits. But as fine as she was and as much as he loved pussy, he was not about to fuck Miyoko Su!

"So, when are you going to invite me back to your place again?" she had asked him late one night. He had picked her up for dinner after work and then took her out for hookah and drinks, hoping she would get lit and be too loaded to play with his dick under the table. "Why don't we head over there now so we can be more comfortable?"

Suge shook his head faster than a muthafucka. The last thing in the world he wanted was to get caught in a tight spot with sex freak Miyoko Su again. He had reluctantly swung her by his place one night after she begged and begged and threatened to change her mind about setting up a meeting with her father. Suge had been forced to take her inside the crib and chill with her, but he'd fought that ass off like a champ when she said she had to pee and then pranced outta the bathroom butt-ass naked and masturbating her own pussy.

"Nah, we can't go to my place," he lied. "One of my aunties from Houston is in town and she's staying with me for a couple of weeks. She's an old lady and bringing a chick home over her head would be disrespectful. Hell, she'd probably pull the strap off her purse and whip my ass. You know how old black women do."

Miyoko swallowed that bite of bullshit without a protest, but then she hurled another fast one at him that nailed him right between the eyes. "Election day will be here before you know it. Your brother's closing events should be scheduled by now, already?"

Suge nodded slowly. He knew what time it was. She was playing games with him. Taking him left so she could fake him out right. His mind raced to locate the hidden dagger and knock it outta her sneaky hand before she could stab him with it. "Yeah. He's got a few things lined up on his calendar."

Her eyes probed him as she dug deeper. "What about the event he's planning for his fundraising staff?"

Suge played it cool. He flipped his toothpick around in his mouth and shrugged. "What about it?"

"Nothing," she said innocently, turning slightly away from him as she ran her fingers up the nape of her pale neck and through her silky black hair. "I mean, of course I'd love to attend as your guest, but I'm sure you already have a date. And I'm sure she's the kind of girl who loves barbequed ribs too."

Suge got it. She was being real fuckin' funny. She was still insecure as hell about black chicks and she swore every sister who crossed his path was just dying to jump on his dick and bounce like he was a pogo stick. Miyoko loved riding that "you left me for a black chick" tip that had sent her bat-shit crazy back in the day. Wherever she got around a sister she gave off that *this nigga's mine* vibe that brought out the kick-ass in black women and made them wanna put their foot in her narrow behind and his too.

His eyes were lidded as he grilled her. *One more week.* Just one more muthafuckin' week and he'd meet with Wally, get those papers, and be done with this silly bitch. If this had been strictly about winning some bullshit fuckin' election then Viceroy mighta had to eat the loss. Miyoko was slick and reckless, and ordinarily a gully baller like Suge wouldn't waste a second of his time with an off-balance bitch like her.

But this was about more than just racking up some ballots. It was about the Dominion fortune and their livelihood too. Getting those stock documents from Wally Su could mean the difference between the Dominions maintaining their status, their dynasty, and their standard of wealth, or the entire family rolling up their sleeves and heading out to Mickey D's to flip some burgers.

"Be nice to me, Superior," she cozied up to him sweetly. "I'll keep working on my father and before you know it I'm sure he'll give you everything you want. And what will I have? Nothing. Perhaps not even my dear father's love."

Suge thought about it real quick. He knew what he was about to do was gonna cost him, but when a tough job had to be done it was a tough nigga who got called upon to do it.

"A'ight, then. You wanna go to my brother's barbeque, baby?" He grinned and pulled her slender body into his arms. He squeezed her close then slapped her on her ass when she nodded yes. "Cool. I'll take you. It's next Sunday afternoon at two," he told her, knowing damn well the 'que was going down a day earlier on Saturday. "Wear something real cute, baby. I'll pick you up at one."

"Wait a minute, are you sure we can make that?" Miyoko asked, pressing her hand to his chest and giving him the goo-goo eye. "Remember, I've scheduled our meeting with my father for Sunday at noon, and I wouldn't want to make you late for your brother's event."

"I almost forgot about that," Suge lied. "Don't worry, baby," he shrugged and told her. "The party won't start until we get there. Besides, when black people throw a barbeque we stay at that shit all night long. There'll be plenty of time. First we'll go handle our business with your father and get those papers from him, and then we'll celebrate over a rack of ribs and a couple of cold brews. Maybe I'll take you to check out a movie or something afterwards. A'ight?"

Her eyes lit up as she nodded. "Sounds great! I can't wait until Sunday!"

GiGi was sitting up naked in bed smoking a cigarette and scrolling through pictures on Instagram. Her lower half was covered with the sheet while Barron lay next to her snoring lightly, but her plump pink breasts were totally exposed. They had just had their first sex session that, to her surprise, GiGi had actually enjoyed. Sex wasn't a motivating force or a burning need with her, although she used to be a highly paid call girl and had seen some real good money from it. Of course the men she targeted made it easy for her. Most guys were just suckers for a pretty face, a good rack, and nice long legs. She got with them indiscriminately and told them exactly what they wanted to hear in order to further whatever scheme she had concocted, but she never, *ever* gave a flying fuck about them.

She looked down and grinned. Present company included.

GiGi was a real sex kitten but her real talents were in her trickery. She was a natural conniving slickster, and she had honed her con game by working various hustles. The grind she was working right now was extra-sweet.

Barron stirred around and poked his head up from the pillow. He saw GiGi was awake and staring at her phone, and he dug a couple of boogers out of his eyes and sat up halfway.

"Hey baby." He yawned and squinting at her sleepily. "Are you all right?"

"I had a bad dream and I couldn't go back to sleep," GiGi lied. "I didn't wake you up, did I?"

"Oh you have nightmares too, huh?" Barron asked. "You're not the only one. Mine can get wild and real damn vivid."

"I know what you mean," GiGi said as she tilted her head back and stared at the ceiling. "That's why I don't sleep much, only when I have to."

Barron sat all the way up and pulled her into his warm, naked arms. He pressed his nose into the softness of her hair.

"You wanna talk about it?"

She shook her head quickly. "It's too heavy. I don't want to blow our good mood."

"You won't blow it," he said. "I know we've only been kicking it for a minute, but I'm a good listener, Gi. And I'm here for you. The same way you've been there for me."

"Well, to be honest, my nightmares are always about being abandoned," GiGi started to explain. "You see, my mother was only fourteen when she had me," she said, sniffing back tears as she spun him a bullshit tale. "We lived in a trailer park and she was washing clothes outside in an old tub one day when she went into labor. She gave birth to me on the ground right there by the tub, and then she abandoned me under the back steps."

Barron held her closer and she sniffled and shuddered.

"According to my aunt, my mother was a very large girl so nobody even knew she was pregnant. She left me outside wrapped in a bloody towel and then she went on in the trailer and started washing dirty dishes. Thank God the neighbor heard me crying and called the police. We lived in a small town, so my aunt convinced the officer to let her take care of me."

Barron was speechless. Trailers and washtubs and bloody towels in double-wides . . . He didn't know what the hell to say. Looking into her beautiful eyes it was hard to even imagine that she had gone through that much hardship and still ended up with such a warm spirit.

GiGi cut her eyes at him as she fake-cried softly. She was getting the exact type of response she wanted, but she wasn't done yet.

"So, I lived with my aunt for a long time but her husband was physically abusive to both of us," GiGi said, wiping away fresh tears. "He would beat me and my aunt whenever he got the notion to. He . . . he . . . would also creep into my room late at night." She gasped and shook her head violently. "He would touch me and lick me . . . I couldn't take it."

Barron wrapped his arms around her trembling body and held her even closer. He felt so sorry for her and he wanted to be strong so she could let go of her sorrows and get them out of her soul. GiGi wiped her face with the edge of the sheet and continued to spill her pain.

"When I got old enough I started staying with friends and their families whenever I could. I bounced around from here to there until I finally just stopped going to my aunt's house at all," GiGi said sadly. "I scratched and survived and barely made it through school. But then I happened to meet a few good

people and started interning at a few local television stations."
She glanced over at him and gave him a tiny smile. "And the
rest is history. Somehow, after all my many setbacks, I managed
to scrape together a decent life for myself. And now I've also
managed to find you."

Barron felt his chest swell. "You're a strong woman, GiGi.
Many people don't make it out of those situations the way you
did, and if they do they're often bitter and their souls are very
dim. I'm glad you turned your tragedy into triumph." He
brought her hand up to his lips and kissed her fingers. "I can
still see life in your eyes, GiGi. I can feel your warmth and your
joy. You deserve all the good things this world has to offer."

"But I'm still not perfect, Barron," GiGi said as she pushed
the sheet away and sat on the edge of the bed. "I still don't really
trust anybody. I'm paranoid and I think people are out to hurt
me. I do try to keep a smile on my face, but on the inside I'm
still running from some demons. The way I just did in my sleep."

"I understand," Barron said as he rubbed her back and
tried to console her. "Whatever happened to your mom and
your aunt? If you don't mind me asking."

"My aunt died a couple of years ago," GiGi explained. "I
paid for her funeral. Her husband had run off and left her a few
years earlier, and she was never the same. As for my mother?"
She shook her head sadly. "I really don't care to know what
happened to my mom. She abandoned me once, and I won't
give her a chance to do it again. As far as I'm concerned I
don't have a family. I never have, and I probably never will."

"Well you have me now," Barron said firmly. "You've let
me inside your heart and I swear, I'll never do anything to hurt
you. You can trust me. I got your back, GiGi, I really do."

"Thank you," she whispered softly.

"I'm serious too," he said. "Just the fact that you survived
being born and didn't die out there under a damn step means
you deserve an award. At least in my book you do."

GiGi nodded.

She felt like she deserved an award too. Maybe even an Oscar. She just put on one of her best performances yet, and Barron had gobbled up and swallowed every word of her act. GiGi pressed herself into his chest and sobbed. He couldn't see the smile on her face as he patted her back and rocked her, and nor could he see the golden fish-hook she had just planted in his mouth as she got ready to reel his ass in and set him up for the kill.

Two days later the mansion was quiet and the sun was shining high in the sky. All the working folks had left early in the morning, and Mink was in her suite scribbling all kindsa nonsense in a diary she'd bought. A warm Texas breeze was blowing through the window and Bunni was stretched out on her bed with her eyeballs tearing up a copy of a hot erotic thriller called *G-Spot* when she heard splashing and laughter coming from the swimming pool below her window.

Reluctantly sliding the book aside, she got up and switched her booty across her suite and pulled back the curtains. She peeked outside and immediately her face lit up like sunshine.

"GiGi!" She stuck her head out the window as far as it would go. "GiGi!" she screamed again, then started waving like hell when the television producer, dressed in a deep scarlet bikini, looked up and grinned and blew her a big kiss.

"Are we good or not?" Bunni hollered, sticking one hand out the window with a thumbs up and the other one out with a thumbs down.

GiGi grinned and waved again, then she yelped as Barron dove under water and stuck his head between her legs and lifted her up high on his shoulders.

She shrieked at the top of her lungs as he launched her into the water face-first and she went under flailing her arms and legs in glee.

Bunni's smile dropped off her face and a cold look of anger crept into her eyes as she stomped out of her suite and headed down the hall.

Moments later she was standing beside her roady with evil intentions written all over her face.

"That bitch gots ta go!" Bunni snapped as she and Mink looked over the second-floor balcony at Barron splashing in the pool with GiGi Molinex.

"Fuck is she doing dirtying up our pool again?" Mink snarled looking down at GiGi with the stink face. The shady-ass white chick had all kinds of goodies spilling out of her slinky blood-colored bikini, and Barron's eyes looked like two pinballs rolling around in his horny-ass skull.

"I'on't know, but she gots to get her mackin' ass up outta here."

Mink nodded her agreement. "She sure the hell do. I told you it wasn't no reality show in the works. That grinder's been playing us for fools this whole damn time."

"So how we gonna get rid of her?" Bunni asked with a dark Harlem glint in her eyes. "Should I snatch her by the neck and ding her all up in her mug, or should I just mush that bitch all in her face and drag her down the driveway by her hair?"

Mink smirked and shook her head. "Nah, don't even get ya hands dirty like that boo. If we was back in Harlem I would tell you to put your *foot* up her ass. But on the real, if we ever catch that trashy toy poodle walking around out on the streets we definitely gonna give her a good-old-fashioned Harlem stomp-down!"

CHAPTER 25

Gutta had just come back from taking a swim in the pool at the Hilton Hotel in downtown Dallas. He felt calm and clear-headed as he dried himself off with an extra thick towel, ready to take on his new environment. Shy was in his own room a couple of doors down sexing some freak he had met in the lobby the night before. They had come to Texas to work, but Gutta let Shy do his thing because he had that sexy little chick Pilar on his mind.

They had been texting each other back and forth ever since the day he'd followed her to the mall. Gutta played the half-witty, half-aggressive role with her and kept her laughing. She tried to act tough and was a little stubborn and high-siddity but he could work with that. He knew it was gonna be a challenge to get her to lead him through those Dominion gates so he could get close to Mink, but he was up for it and ready to take control of the situation.

He had just stretched out on the crisp hotel sheets when his phone rang. He grinned his ass off when he saw who the caller was.

"W'sup caramel," Gutta said as he answered the phone.

"Hi Gutta, what are you up to? Did I catch you at a bad time?" Pilar asked. Her voice sounded real sweet, but of course she was thinking he might be laid up with some other bitch.

"Naw ma, not all," Gutta reassured her. "I actually just came from swimming me some laps in the pool and shit, trying to wake my body up. I'm glad you called me though, how is your morning going?"

"I'm straight. I'm about to go get a mani and pedi in a little bit," Pilar said as she admired herself in her bedroom mirror and thought about Gutta's huge arms wrapped around her small waist. She admitted to herself that a thug like Gutta was intriguing, and fucking with borderline lame niggas like Barron had gotten her absolutely nowhere. She'd never been with a street dude before, but after fucking with Bump it was time for her to switch her style up. Out with the old and in with the new.

"So what you got planned for the day? My family's having a little BBQ later on," she told him. "I was wondering if you'd like to join me—I mean if you don't have anything else already planned."

Gutta played it cool. "I got a few business meetings I gotta hit up and see what's shaking," he lied. "But that shouldn't take all day. I should be done kinda early, but don't be taking me to some shit where they don't know how to cook cause a nigga likes to grub and I'ma let 'em know about it."

Pilar laughed. She was digging his aggressiveness and when she thought about it he was just what she needed. Barron was going to be at the BBQ and she wanted him to see her flossing with a strong and thorough nigga by her side. Especially one that was paid. She started scheming on how she could get some money in her pocket, some good dick in her drawers, and some get-back at Barron's ass all at the same time. Gutta seemed like the perfect candidate to make all that shit happen at once.

"I tell you what," Pilar said, grinning her ass off. "If they don't know how to cook and the grub's not slamming, then I'll take you somewhere and let you eat something else, okay?"

"Oh yeah?" Gutta responded smoothly. "Well, I'm the type who likes to eat candy, baby. That real sweet kinda candy."

"You so crazy," Pilar said, giggling like a shy little girl, even though on the low the way he said that shit had her squirming in her drawers. "Get ya mind out of the gutta . . . Gutta."

Gutta laughed with her, hyped as hell that his plan was working out even better than he'd expected. Pilar would be his key into that damn mansion. Instead of doing it Harlem style and bum-rushing up in that bitch, he would ride there in style, straight through the front fuckin' door. That shit was perfect 'cause when he caught up with Mink he needed her to know that she wasn't safe nowhere. Not from a nigga like him. Gutta laughed out loud as he hung up the phone and dug in his bag to get something to wear.

Let the mothafuckin' festivities begin!

It was BBQ time and the tantalizing smell of smoked meat permeated the air. Suge had just lapped and tapped Mink into a frenzy in her suite, then he took a quick shower with her and they smoked some good weed together. That piff had his head nice and buzzed, while the sex his baby had laid on him had his balls humming too. Mink was picking out her outfit when he kissed her good-bye and told her he'd meet her at the 'que, and then headed upstairs to his own suite to get dressed.

Suge entered his cool suite and grabbed a beer outta the fridge and then dressed in a pair of casual slacks and a smooth navy blue shirt. He was a chill, handsome dude and his brawny, muscled-up body was a sight to behold as he headed downstairs and out the back door to join the party that was already in full swing.

Young people were swarming all over the backyard. There was a mix of college graduates and young community organizers who had the spirit of volunteerism in their blood and were passionate about the politics of the day. They had licked stamps, knocked on doors, and made thousands of cold calls trying to strum up as many votes for their favorite candidate as they could. This barbeque was for them, held in their honor as a thank-you from the Dominion family for all the support they had shown Viceroy over the past few weeks.

Mingling in the crowd and greeting the guests was something Suge knew he had to do, and he was damn good at it too. He stopped to shoot the shit with a couple of young bruhs and flirted a lil bit with a few old ladies from the Rotary Club, and after making the rounds one good time he settled down in an extra-long lounge chair to enjoy another beer.

He was kicked back and dozing under the sunshine and getting him a little snore on when a chill washed over him that felt like somebody had thrown a bucket of shade over the sun.

"Hello, Superior."

Goddamn. The voice was slick and cool, but there was no doubt about who had called out his name.

"Lil Bit." He opened his eyes and peered up at her as she loomed directly over him blocking out the sunlight. "I was just about to come pick you up, baby. I must've dozed off for a minute. Damn! I'm probably late. What time is it?"

"Oh, you're not late," Miyoko said, her sly eyes flashing. "But I bet I'm pretty early, huh?"

Suge sat up slowly and looked around. This was gonna be a good one. By now Mink was probably flouncing around out here somewhere getting her barbeque on. No doubt she was gonna act a damn fool if she peeped Miyoko sniffing around anywhere near him.

"You told me the barbeque was on *Sunday*." Miyoko narrowed her eyes and accused him with her hand on her hip.

Suge stood up slowly and scratched his head as his eyes swept over the lively crowd. "Looks like we got us a pretty good crowd going so it must be Sunday then, huh?"

Miyoko pouted. "We had a goddamn deal, Superior! You asked me to do something for you and I asked you to do something for me in return! I'm beginning to think you aren't serious about upholding your end of our agreement." She crossed her arms and glared at him. "I'm not sure I trust you enough to take you to see my father tomorrow. Even if I could figure out where he's keeping those papers, I probably couldn't convince him not to testify in front of that panel next week."

"Don't get hasty," Suge said, reaching out and snaking his hand around her tiny waist. "I made a mistake, sugar," he schmoozed her with a wet kiss on the neck. "C'mon, now, Lil Bit." He slid his hand down her back and pinched her lightly on the ass. "Don't be like that. I told you I was a bad boy, didn't I?"

Miyoko smiled and basked in his affection for a few moments, and Suge knew she'd decided to forgive him when she asked, "Have you eaten yet?"

He tilted his half-empty bottle of beer at her. "Yeah, if you call this liquid shit food."

She took it from him and grinned, then locked her eyes on him as she raised the bottle to her pink mouth and made the amber beverage disappear. Smacking her lips lightly, she stuck her tongue out and ran it around the rim of the bottle, and then smiled and glanced around.

"Everything smells absolutely wonderful. How about we walk around for a little while and then grab a bite to eat?"

Suge reached out and took her hand. He was down for whatever. As long as she wasn't talking about calling off that goddamn meeting with her father tomorrow, then he was her chocolate fuckin' puppet. All she had to do was pull his strings and he'd dance like a muthafucka.

Miyoko stuck right up under him as Suge went around introducing her to the campaigners in the upbeat crowd of young people.

"Oh! I see your brother over there," Miyoko exclaimed, pointing toward a large tent where Viceroy sat at a table surrounded by staffers who were hanging off his every word. A certain somebody was sitting at the table too, and the sight of her gorgeous face made Suge wanna pull up and dig his feet in the dirt right where he stood.

"C'mon." Miyoko tugged at his hand. "Let's go over so I can say hello."

Suge had known this moment was coming and he wasn't shrinking under the pressure and he wasn't about to back away from it neither. There came a time in every man's life where he had to make some tough, life-changing choices, and today Suge was gonna have to make his.

"Sup," he called out to Viceroy as him and Miyoko walked up to the table holding hands. "You remember Miyoko, don't you?" Suge asked his brother as he presented her to the entire table. "Wally Su's daughter?"

Viceroy was born to be a politician because he was smooth as shit. As bad as he wanted that bastard Su dead his face broke apart in a huge smile. "Miyoko! Look at you. All grown up. You were barely more than a teenager the last time I saw you and now you're a beautiful young woman. I bet Wally is damn proud of you. Tell him his old partner said hello."

"Lil Bit, this is my nephew Dane," Suge said, ignoring the heat that was coming at him from the other side of the table and showboating Miyoko like a prize, just the way she wanted him to. "He just got out of college and he's working for the family now."

"How you doing," Dane said quickly and stood up to shake the chick's hand. "Yo, Pops." He turned to Viceroy. "I'm about to take off for a minute and head across town to see about something. I'll be back in a—"

"Ah-hem!"

Bunni stood up from the table and put her hand on her hip. Her cherry-fire–colored dreadlocks spiraled out from her head in a mass of funky waves and her oversized hoop earrings dangled from her ears.

"Dane and Papa Doo ain't the only ones who need attention at this here table!" she said sassily, her eyes shooting daggers as she twisted her lips toward Mink. "Did you forget about somebody?"

"My bad," Suge said, turning Miyoko back toward the table. "Lil Bit, this is my niece Mink and her friend Bunni. They're from—"

"Niece?" Mink shrieked jumping to her feet and spilling her cold beer. "Oh, so now you gonna front me off like I'm just your *niece*?"

"Yep, 'cause that's what you are," Dane said grabbing Mink's arm and spinning her around toward him. "His niece and my sister." He took the beer from her hand and grinned as he walked her away. "My very loud and lovely sister."

"Really, Suge?" Mink snapped over her shoulder, fighting against Dane as he tried to muscle her toward the house. "*Really?*"

"*Uncle* Suge," her boo corrected her loudly, grabbing Miyoko's hand again and intertwining their fingers together in a chocolate and vanilla swirl. "It's *Uncle* Suge to you, baby girl. Get it right. You ain't that grown yet."

If Suge thought us two Harlem heffahs were through with him then he didn't know shit about shit because we were just getting started.

"I'm fuckin' him up!" I bitched as we fell inside the mansion with Dane damn near dragging us through the door. "I *knew* his gaming ass was up to something slick! He's been ducking out and fronting on me for a minute and now I know why!"

"Niggas!" Bunni's voice was full of disgust as she shook her head and twisted her lips. "Did you see how that mofo walked up on us holding that trick's hand? Like we wasn't gonna have shit to say about it? I knew something was up with his ass from the beginning!"

"Y'all chill out with all that," Dane said soothingly as he put his arm around me. "I got some Kush that's so sweet it'll make you forget all about that sexy-ass lil freak on Suge's arm."

"That's the same bitch I saw him with on TV that night! I ignored Dane and kept yappin. That nigga musta been straight up blind because that scrawny-ass heffa was *not* sexy! "Yeah, Bunni, that's the same trick he was cheesing up with on the red carpet at the Met Gala."

"Then we gots to go our asses back out there," Bunni said, pacing the floor and snatching off her earrings. "That nigga puttin you to shame, Mink. He's just disrespectful. We can't let no shit like that slide. We gotta go back out there and clobber his ass!"

"Y'all ain't going no damn where," a deep voice boomed as Suge walked through the back door looking like a muscled-up gunslinger.

Me and Bunni froze for a second. But only for a goddamn second.

"Who the hell was that bitch!"

"Don't be telling us what the hell we can do!"

"I can't believe you brought that bony-ass drink of water up in here!"

"Uh-uh nigga! You got some 'splaining to do!"

We sounded like a room full of cackling hens as we posted up and launched verbal bombs at him from all directions.

Suge didn't give Bunni so much as a glance, but the look he gave me was cold and hard. "Chill out, Mink. I got some business going on and I need you to play your role, lil mama. Be a big girl and let me handle this thang, a'ight?"

"Let you handle *what*?" My whole body felt like a question mark as I stared up in his face. "What the hell is up with that shit? You bring some stray chick up in here—the *same* damn heffa I saw you with on TV, and then you tell *me* to calm down?"

"I told you I had some business to take care of, didn't I? I told you that you could trust me, right?"

"Trust you?" I smirked. "Are you fuckin' kidding me? I wouldn't trust your ass as far as I could throw a—"

"Superior?" The back door opened again and the Asian chick peeked her head inside and called out his name.

"Oh, there you are!" She smiled and stepped in the house, and that's when the wrath of Bunni came down on her and damn near knocked her on her ass.

"Excuse me, Miss Thang! *Excuuuuuse* me! Can't you see black folks is talking?" She pointed toward the door. "This is an A and B conversation so heffah can you kindly C-C-C your damn way out of it?"

"*Excuuuuuse* me!" that bony heffa blasted right back! She had the nerve to pop her neck and imitate Bunni with her booty stuck out and her hand on her hip. "I'm looking for my date, if you don't mind. And yes, black folks *is* tawkin'—" She twisted her lips and stuck out her chin, and then rolled her lil beady eyes real ghettoish and said, "So why don't you try being quiet for once, *okay*?"

"Trick!" Bunni screeched, bopping up on her with her fists balled up. "Who you marking? I'm 'bout to bust you in your grill and snatch you by your extra-silky Remy and wax this whole fuckin' floor up with your ass!"

"Please don't attack me!" the chick shrieked and cowered near the door when she saw Bunni coming at her. Looking scared, she covered her mouth like Bunni was about to knock the taste off her lips.

"Ay!" Suge loomed tall and shot Bunni an evil glance and warned, "Don't even think it, goddammit. That right there is a *lady*, so don't you threaten her and don't you disrespect her either. You better back up and act like you got some sense."

Bunni was on one. "Fugg *her*! Don't nobody give a damn about *her*! You better carry her starving ass back to the greasy little take-out joint where you got her from!"

"I'm sorry." The chick had the nerve to bust a little tear from her eye as she went back to playing her role. "I didn't mean to be nasty, but I won't be insulted in this manner, Superior. Not even by your family members. Perhaps I'd better go."

"Yeah, *go!*" Bunni hollered.

"*Go!*" I screamed.

"Hold up, Miyoko!"

As booming as his voice was Suge sounded like a dick-nipped puppy as he damn near broke his neck rushing over to her, and just seeing another bitch put the hold on him made my heart fall down to the floor.

"I'll drive you home, baby," he said, coddling her ass. "Just let me get my keys and I'll drive you home."

I broke. "*Baby*? Nigga, please! Why in the hell is you calling her scrawny ass *baby*?"

The girl glared at me with the same hater face she had given Bunni. She looked like she wanted to get loose and pop some more yang, but when I raised up toward her she jetted past me and took off toward the front door.

"Lil Bit wait—" Suge reached for her as she went by.

"No," the chick said coldly, staring me down as she held her hand up like a stop sign and then turned her frosty eyes on Suge. "I'll drive myself. And don't bother to pick me up tomorrow either. I'm cancelling our meeting with my father. You were never serious about your promises to me. I'm calling the whole thing off."

Bunni was steady cursing the chick out as she marched her skinny ass toward the front door, but Suge never moved another muscle and neither did I as I stared up into his dark, flashing eyes.

When he finally opened his mouth his voice sounded like ice being scraped off the inside of a deep freezer. "You fucked everything up Mink," he said quietly. "Just like a little kid. I told you, no matter what it looked like I needed you to trust me, and you said you was grown enough to do that."

"I coulda done it!" I protested hotly. "But I ain't *stupid,* Suge—"

"No," he agreed as he walked away. "You ain't stupid, but you jealous as fuck and you're insecure too, and when you fucking with a nigga like me that's even worse."

CHAPTER 26

"That banana-shaped *bitch*!" I fumed as me and Bunni followed Dane outside to his SUV and jumped in with him. This was the last fucking straw! I wasn't fuckin' with Suge Dominion no more in life!

"Did you see that hater-look that snake-faced bitch shot me? That slinky-looking chick was smirking and rolling her eyes like she was a winner for real! Heffah ain't have a bump on her nowhere. That ironing-board ass was straight up and down!"

"Nah, she had a lil bump back there," Bunni admitted, settling into the front seat. "About the same amount of meat that's on a chicken drumette. But she was hatin' all right. Hell yeah, she was hatin'. She's lucky I didn't put my foot in that narrow ass."

I crossed my arms over my titties and fumed in the backseat. I couldn't believe Suge had played me to the left like that, bringing some long-legged Asian chick on the scene when he had just gotten freaky in the sheets with me!

"That nigga Suge is a dick swinger!" Bunni said as Dane pushed the whip down the long driveway. "I told you my left titty been itching, Mink," she said solemnly. "I *knew* something was up with his shady ass—"

"Bunni please! No you didn't—"

"Yo watch out!" Dane hollered. He jerked the steering wheel hard to the right, bouncing the shit outta us as he stomped down on the brakes and left burnt rubber on the road. Pilar's Lexus came barging through the gate. She hit the speed bump hard and sailed in the air, then came down straddling the centerline as she damn-near ran us off into the shrubbery.

Peals of laughter cut into the air as Pilar and her passenger cracked the hell up and kept right on rolling.

"Stupid ass!" Bunni yelled, giving Pilar the finger as I stuck my head out the window and watched the Lexus go weaving down the road toward the mansion.

"That fuckin' girl be buggin'," Dane said, shaking his head as he pulled back onto the road and the laughter faded in the air. "What the hell is wrong with her?"

"She's dizzy as hell, that's what," Bunni snapped, rubbing her neck. "And who was that nigga wildin' out in the whip with her?"

I shrugged in the backseat. "Who knows. Some dark-skinned cat with dreads who had a real big head," I said, and then muttered halfway under my breath, *"and who put me right in the mind of Gutta."*

Miyoko was mad as hell and looking to wreck Suge's world in all directions.

"I'm not helping you get *shit* from my father, Superior Dominion!" she blasted on him as they stood outside the mansion blowing up the spot. People were coming and going and giving them the eye, but Miyoko didn't give a damn. "You let those horrible ugly *things* treat me like dirt just now and you didn't even step in to protect me!"

"C'mon now, Lil Bit." Suge followed her over to her Bentley and posted up in front of her so she couldn't get in. "Forget them chicks. They didn't mean nothing by it."

"Forget them?" she shrieked, her screwed-up face red as hell. "How could I forget them? They were *invited* to the barbeque! They were treated as honored guests while I was snubbed and insulted like a party crasher!"

"Nobody meant to insult you, baby," Suge put his big hand on her shoulder and pulled her close as he leaned back on her luxury ride. "Just relax, girl." The valet was over there giving him a look like, yo, should I call somebody or what, but Suge shook his head and nodded him off. "It was all a mistake, Lil Bit. Just a big mistake."

"A mistake?" she shrieked, pushing away from him and putting her hands on her hips. "Yeah, just like the mistake you made when you told me the barbeque was tomorrow instead of today, right? Tell the truth for once, Superior!" she demanded, shrieking and snotting like she was creeping real close to the edge. "You didn't want me around here today, did you? That's why you told me the wrong day, *isn't it?*"

Suge was weary as fuck and the hysterical chick was making a scene, but he dug deep down into his manhood and gave it one last try.

"Let me take you for a little ride," he said, holding out his hand for her keys. "We can have a couple of drinks down at the marina and talk this thing out, a'ight?"

"Go to hell!" she spit, jerking her keys out of his reach. "You're screwing one of those ugly bitches!" She slammed her tiny fist into his washboard stomach and accused him with narrowing eyes. "Which one is it?" she demanded at the top of her lungs. "Ugly? Or *Uglier?* Which one of those filthy black bitches are you fucking?"

An icy waved washed over Suge and the killer in him peeped out. He didn't give a fuck what it cost whoever. Nobody was gonna disrespect Mink and get away with that shit. No fuckin' body.

"Ay, get gone, Miyoko," he said quietly, keeping himself in check as he got up off her ride and motioned for her to climb in. He wasn't one for disrespecting women but he had been forced to fold a few bitches up in the past.

"It's time for you to go, baby. Get gone."

The chill in his voice stilled the stupidity in Miyoko and immediately the hysteria dried up on her tongue.

"I was willing to do anything for you, Superior." She sniffed and got all weepy on him again. "Anything. Even betray my own father!"

"Gone," he said coldly, pushing his hands down in his pockets as he nodded toward the gate.

"Okay. I'm leaving. But if you still want to meet tomorrow I'm sure noon is still good for my father."

"Fuck your father."

She paused with her hand on the door and a startled expression on her face. "Pardon me?"

"I said, *fuck yo' muthafuckin' daddy!*"

"Superior!"

She pressed her hand to her chest like she was deeply offended. Suge chuckled darkly. The same chick who had just called Mink and Bunni a couple of black ghetto bitches had the nerve to get vexed.

"That's just wrong!" she said. "For someone whose whole family is depending on the Su generosity you don't sound very grateful."

Suge walked up on her slowly. He towered over her and stared coldly down into her eyes, wondering what in the hell he had ever seen in her, even in his youngest, horniest, *freakiest* days.

He pulled his hand out of his pants pocket and reached over and yanked her door open.

"You best get on past those gates before I pick this lil piece of shit up and toss it across the street, ya heard?"

Miyoko sniffed and climbed behind the wheel of her ex-

travagant convertible and slammed the door. She clicked a button and the engine purred to life. Then she pressed another
button and lowered the window and turned to hit Suge with a
murderous glare.

"One day you're going to get exactly what you deserve, Superior! I hope your brother loses this election! I hope my father's
testimony sends him to prison for the rest of his life and leaves
Dominion Oil penniless! I hope the commission takes one look
at those papers and gives every dime of every dollar you've ever
made to Zeke Washington and his family! I hope your lying,
cheating, rotten ass gets—"

Suge took a menacing step toward the car and Miyoko
yelped and stepped on the gas.

"Go to hell, Superior Dominion!" she shrieked as she peeled
down the driveway and zoomed toward the gates. "I hope you
go straight to hell!"

Pilar had scooped Gutta up from his hotel and headed over
to the Dominion mansion late in the afternoon. Gutta was
dipped in designer Gucci from head to toe, but he couldn't
hide his thugged-out swagger even if he wanted to. He looked
over at Pilar, who was dressed to kill and drenched in some old
sex potion perfume that had her smelling sweet enough to eat.
He couldn't hardly keep his eyes off of her tight waist and bubble ass.

"I see you checking me out with the crazy face." Pilar
smiled as she glanced over at him. "What's the matter? You
don't like what you see?"

"Of course I do," Gutta responded as he licked his lips like
LL Cool J. "I'm just kinda nervous 'cause you look good
enough to snatch and I didn't bring my pistol with me. Yo, if one
of these fools tries to get at me are you gonna protect me?"

Both of them played an image in their minds of Pilar's little petite ass trying to protect Gutta's Hercules-looking ass and

they started cracking the fuck up. Pilar had been laughing so hard she took her turn late and swerved real wide into the driveway that led to the Dominion Estate.

"The gate!" she blurted as she hit the gas and zoomed forward. A black SUV was coming out of the gate and Pilar lurched forward and damn near crossed the center-line as she tried to beat the gate and get through before it closed.

"Damn, girl!" Gutta laughed his ass off, grabbing hold of the overhead handle as the SUV veered off into the bushes and blared its horn like the driver was pissed. "Is the food in there that damn bad you gotta kill us before we get to eat it?"

"My bad, but that's your fault," Pilar said as her stomach ached from laughing so hard. "You got me over here dying and shit!"

They pulled up in front of the Dominion house and Gutta saw the joint was packed out. A whole bunch of political folks, old, young, and even small children, were all over the place eating, shooting the shit, and hanging out.

Yessirrr! I'm up in this muthafucka! They done let a gangsta in the house and they ain't even know it! I'm 'bout to turn this shit inside out. I gotta relax and keep my shit sharp, though. The mission is to scope this shit out real tight so I can get inside later on and catch Mink's little lying ass slipping.

Pilar led Gutta through the maze of people and introduced him as her friend named Gutta. She'd wanted to create a little stir up and she got the exact reaction she was looking for. Those uppity tight-asses looked frightened and confused at Gutta, but they shook his hand and tried to act as normal as possible anyway. It was a huge gathering with a lot of people but she was only looking for one person and it didn't take her long to find him. Barron was standing in line by a huge grill where they were serving ribs, and as soon as she spotted him Pilar put her plan in action.

"What you pouting for, ma?" Gutta asked. He had been

searching the crowd for Mink when he noticed that Pilar's mood had changed and she was suddenly looking pissed off. "You a'ight? What's the problem?"

"Nothing." Pilar folded her arms over her titties as she scrunched her face up and put some extra stank all in her attitude. "It's just that this guy I used to talk to is over there and he fucking disgusts me! He used to beat on me and treat me like shit! I can't stand to even look at his ass. I don't want no trouble I just don't like being in the same place with him, that's all."

Pilar had planted the seed and it didn't take long for her to see the fruit sprout from the tree. She could see Gutta zero in on Barron and his posture change very quickly.

"Yo, that nigga over there looks kinda familiar. He the type to put his hands on females? Well I'ma go say w'sup to his punk ass," Gutta said, like he wasn't known for knocking bitches on they ass up in Harlem too. "He look soft as shit anyway."

"No baby. Please don't do that." Pilar gave a half-hearted attempt to hold Gutta back but it was too late. "It's okay, really. I don't want to start anything out here in front of all these people."

Gutta was already making his way through the crowd, and when he got up to Barron he bumped him so hard his plate of ribs fell from his hand and hit the grass.

"Damn bruh!" Barron said as he looked up at the menacing Gutta and immediately froze in place.

"Whattup? You look like you seen a ghost or somethin'," Gutta barked as he narrowed his eyes. "Do you know me or somethin', nigga? You grillin' me with the screw face and shit. Nigga, do you know me?"

What Barron wanted to say was, *Hell yeah, I know you goddammit! I paid you good fucking money to get rid of Mink, my nigga, and you fucked it all up!*

But of course he couldn't say that shit. How the hell was he gonna admit to knowing somebody that he had paid to kill his long-lost sister and dump her scandalous ass in the East River?

"Naw man, I don't know you," Barron said, but the look of shock and alarm never left his face. "It's all good, homey." Barron held up his hand and waved Gutta off. "It's just food, man. I'll make another plate."

"Yeah, nigga," Gutta growled. "And while you at it fix me one too, pussy," Gutta said as he glared down at Barron and challenged him with the killa grill. "But if you feelin' some type of way nigga make a move!"

Barron was stunned. *What the hell is this nut doing at my house and how the fuck did he get here?*

"Yo, who you talking to? Man, *you* bumped into *me*," he said, pushing back with the disrespect. He hoped like fuck Gutta wasn't strapped and about to pop off, but he wasn't about to get played out in his own backyard. "This is Texas, not Harlem. I suggest you watch your mouth."

"Aye, you lil *bitch*—"

Before Gutta could start barking off again Pilar stepped in to defuse the situation. She loved the panicked look she saw lurking in Barron's eyes. It was a look of fear and turmoil. The same look that had been on her face when he walked up in her house and told her he was leaving her.

Gutta was swelling up mighty big, and Pilar decided to jump in before he slammed Barron through the ground in front of all of their guests.

"Chill baby, it's all right," Pilar said as she crammed herself in between the two men. "He's with me, Barron, so step the fuck off. I saw you bump into him and start talking shit. You're such a fucking troublemaker!"

"Yo, Pilar," Barron said, looking even more confused that his prissy-ass cousin was actually flouncing around with this cut-throat Harlem killer. "You need to watch yourself, a'ight? You don't even know who this fuckin' dude is . . ."

"He's none of your damn business, that's who he is," Pilar said as she grilled Barron with hateful eyes. "Just be lucky I saved your life," she said, smirking as she grabbed Gutta by his arm and walked away leaving Barron standing there looking worried as fuck.

Gutta turned back around and grinned at Barron over Pilar's head and then winked. He knew Barron wasn't in a position to say shit because a coward like him would never expose himself by telling the truth about his own dirty deeds.

Barron walked off and Gutta kept right on grinning. So far this was a dope-ass barbeque. He moseyed around and drank free beer and ate free ribs, and entertained the hell outta Pilar, while at the same time he kept his radar up and bleeping as he stayed on the lookout for Mink.

After awhile he ditched Pilar and struck up some casual convo with some loose-lipped white folks and found out that the Big Daddy of the clan was running for some dumb shit and they were counting down the days to election night. Yeah, election night, Gutta stroked his chin and plotted on that ass. He didn't know where the fuck Mink was hiding at, but come election night he was gonna make his move.

Pilar saw him grinning to himself and thought it was all about her. She ran over and grabbed his hand and swung their arms like she was loving life. Gutta's thoughts mighta moved on, but Pilar was still high off that little dust-up she had caused with Barron, and as she laughed and joked with her strong, muscular hood nigga, her mind started thinking of all the ways Gutta could be useful to her. In the streets and in the sheets.

"Nope, I ain't fuckin' with her crazy ass no more," Suge barked into his cell phone and told Selah. Miyoko had been waiting outside his house when he came out that morning, and when he tried to leave she had scampered like a crab up on the front of his truck and stretched her arms and legs out crying and screeching all over the hood. Without a word, Suge had reached up and snatched her by the ankle and dragged her off his shit. She wiggled like a muthafucka as he clamped her down in his strong arms and carried her kicking and screaming across the street. Suge had dumped her frail ass on top of some real prickly bushes, and then walked back to his truck and got in, fuming. He had revved up the engine and was pushing that baby damn near thirty miles over the speed limit as he drew the line for his sister-in-law.

"Look, if you want her father smoked, I'll take his ass out. If you want me to bust up in that county office and set it on fire, I'll burn that bitch down to the ground. I love my brother and I'll do whatever he needs me to do. But Miyoko?" He shook his head and grunted. "No more of her ass. I don't give a fuck what it costs us. I'm not dealing with that crazy chick no more. Not for love and not for money neither."

Selah sighed, then cleared her throat. Suge had given up his entire life in the service of his family, and if he was done with the matter then she knew better than to push him.

"Don't worry," she said. "Nobody could have handled this any better than you did. We'll just have to hit this from another angle. Maybe I'll pay Wally a visit and see if I can reason with him. We were pretty good friends at one time. I helped him a lot when his wife was dying. Perhaps I can talk some sense into him. If not we'll just have to find anoth—"

"Fuck all that talking," Suge cut her off. "You can go see him if you want to, but if that fool don't wanna act right before next Tuesday then I'ma have to roll up on him and choke his ass out."

GiGi was lounging in the hot tub on the roof of a penthouse looking up at the Texas stars. She had on nothing but a bikini bottom as she tilted her head back and exhaled some Purple Haze through her nostrils. She was a wild girl at heart and loved working under the table. When she zoomed in on a mark she named her own price, picked her own jobs, and moved to the beat of her own damn drum. Her beauty and her brains were a lethal combination for anybody who was unlucky enough to get caught in her crosshairs, and right now

she was watching her latest target as he stood near the edge of
the roof drinking Hennessey and looking down at the city.

"Are you going to get in the hot tub with me?" GiGi
asked as she stood up inside the hot tub. "Or are you thinking
about jumping?" she giggled sexily. "I know you're fly and all,
but I don't wanna find out if you can actually *fly*."

Barron laughed as he made his way over to the tub swig-
ging Hen-dog straight from the bottle.

"Naw, I'm not that fly," he said. "I was just looking out
there and thinking about how cool it must be for those who
live a simple life. People tend to think that just because you
have a lot of money life is sweet. They don't understand the
pressures of having to live up to a family name."

"That's very true," GiGi said as she detected the stress in
his voice. She passed him her weed nonchalantly, unsure if he
would hit it, but happy when he did. "You're the son of
Viceroy Dominion and whether you like it or not, you're
going to have to carry the kind of weight that most people
don't understand. But that's okay," she said, her cool hands
finding the tight muscles in his neck and pressing into them
deeply. "I believe your shoulders are strong enough to endure
it."

GiGi stroked Barron's neck, shoulders, and his ego as they
drank and smoked together. And when she thought he was
nice and loose she reached a little bit lower and let her fingers
play all over his rock hard chocolate chest.

"Tell me a little bit more about your father, Barron," she
urged him in a sweet voice that sounded like warm vanilla
syrup. "I mean, I'm so intrigued because you can't help but ad-
mire a man as accomplished as he is, but for some reason I
sense you have some issues with him."

Barron took a big hit of the good weed and then let his
head fall back into her lap as he exhaled the hot smoke. "I'm
not that close to my father right now. Yeah, I love him and
everything, but that dude's got some real shifty ways about

him." He shrugged. "I know it's the accident that has him acting so damn ill these days, but some of the stuff he says . . . I
just can't get past that shit. To be honest, I don't even wanna
work on this political campaign with him. I'm not sure he's fit
for office."

Behind him, GiGi grinned as she gobbled that info up.
"Yes, I read about his accident. It was just horrible. But in what
way has it made him act differently? What is he doing that
bothers you so much?" she asked lightly. "I don't mean to
probe," she bullshitted, because probing was exactly what she
was trying to do, "I just really want to understand where
you're coming from."

Barron took a deep breath and shrugged. "It's not one or
two specific things. It's damn-near everything. His ass was real
ungrateful when he woke up. Disrepectful too. He started treating me like I was his bitch-ass flunky instead of his favorite
son," Barron confessed as he downed another shot of cognac.
"Actually, for the first time ever he started treating me like I
was actually adopted. As if I wasn't good enough to handle the
tasks that he had been grooming me for my whole fuckin' life.
I used to wanna be just like him, but now I don't. I wanna be
better than he is. In every fuckin' way. I'm ready to blow this
bitch be my own man."

GiGi listened intently as Barron passed her back the roach
of the weed. She took one last pull then flicked the burning
ember into the pool and looked up into the night sky, pleased
with where the conversation was going.

"He's still your father, Barron." She exhaled and tried to
keep him going. "I know he loves you and cares for you, but
with everything going on I'm sure things are confusing for him
too right now."

"Confused my ass," Barron said as he glanced over his
shoulder at GiGi. "He's crazy, and I'm not gonna be used anymore by him or anybody else. One minute he wants me to be
down on his team, and the next minute he's talking to me like

I'm some two-bit dick-boy instead of the son he raised and sent to college and law school. Like I said, I still love him and there was a time I would've walked through fire for him. But I think it's time for me to do my own thing. And that's gotta be separate from his thing."

Barron tossed back the rest of the Henny in one gulp. He had drained the bottle and he was good and fucked up.

"Well," GiGi said, stretching as she stood up in the hot tub, "I'm pretty sure whatever you decide to do baby, you will be the *man* at it!" She leaned forward and kissed his bare chest. "You're an amazing person and I believe in you."

"Yeah, thanks for hearing me out," Barron said as he eyed her sexy-ass body. "But I'm done talking about Viceroy. Fuck him. Let's go inside and see what we can fall into. I'm ready to make a splash, but not in that pool."

GiGi giggled, knowing exactly what he meant. She snatched up her things and wiggled her ass seductively toward the entrance of the condo. Before she walked through the sliding glass door she turned around and looked at Barron.

"Are you coming?" she asked in a sexy tone.

"Oh, I'm definitely cumming." Barron grinned and stumbled to the door to get him a hot slice of GiGi Molinex.

"Yeah, this right here is the real thing," Ruddman declared with satisfaction as he studied the three sheets of paper that Zeke had slid out of his back pocket. "I had an expert check it out, and the stock transfer that's on file with the county clerk, that one is a forgery."

"I *knew* that shit!" Zeke exploded as he jumped to his feet. "My pops tried to tell everybody that shit and they called him crazy! He knew what he was talking about and I *always* believed he got cheated!"

"He got more than cheated," Ruddman agreed as he sat with his arms crossed over his stomach. He had just confirmed what young Zeke had grown up raging about his entire life.

That his father's former business partner, Viceroy Dominion, had forged a set of documents and cheated his father out of a shitload of stock options that over time would have made the Washington family filthy rich.

"Your father got *dicked*, Zeke." Ruddman jumped to his feet and yeasted him up. "He got ripped! He got ass-fucked out of a fortune!"

Zeke nodded, wild-eyed and furious. "I grew up my whole fuckin' life seeing them muthafuckin' Dominion kids *flossin!* That bitch-ass son of his is some kinda high-price lawyer riding around in a Maserati, and the other one ain't nothing but a weed-head tricking off his old man's money! I sold packs to that dude before! Even that lil skinny light-skinned one! Them niggas been living *my* muthafuckin' life! The life my father worked hard so that *I* could live!"

"And don't forget that Dominion's wife has been living your mother's life too," Ruddman added solemnly. "While your mother works her fingers to the bone cleaning public toilets in Houston for a living, Viceroy Dominion's wife lives a life of luxury. That woman has never worked a job or gotten her hands dirty in her entire life. It just doesn't seem right that she profited from her husband's trickery and greed, yet your dear mother never got to profit from anything at all."

"Ya damn right it ain't fair, and trust me, that Dominion bastard is gonna pay for that! Word to the mutha, that dirty-ass cheat is gonna get his. He's gonna give up some of that cash or get his wig twisted back! For real. You can bel'ee that!"

"Some of it?" Ruddman questioned. "He's going to give up *some* of it? Why not *all* of it! Look, I called you here so I could help you, Zeke. Viceroy Dominion is a thief. He's a liar and a fraud. But there's a way to go after men like him and take them down. Believe me, I've fought against bigger and richer opponents than him and you don't take them down in the streets, son. You take them down in the *courthouse!* You take your fight to the media. You fall back on the press. You file a lawsuit that exposes all of their slimy, underhanded business deals to the whole damn world. You file an injunction to freeze their assets and make a judge tell them bastards to hand you the keys to their multi-million-dollar mansions!"

"Damn right!" the boy shrieked.

"All you have to do," Ruddman said smoothly, "is get with my lawyers and let them serve Viceroy with a lawsuit. Remember, the man who actually helped him rob your father has agreed to testify in front of the commission that your father was cheated out of what he was rightfully due. Once that happens, Viceroy definitely won't make it to election day."

Zeke gave him a side look. "I know, but I still don't understand why the fuck would ya dude do something like that, though? His ass could go to jail too."

Ruddman shook his head quickly. "Remember, he's dying. He's far more concerned about going to heaven than he is about going to jail. Listen, if you do what I tell you to do, Viceroy Dominion could take an immediate hit. If the commission moves quickly to disqualify him he'll never even see election day. In fact, I guarantee you that once you take the steps I tell you to take, he'll show his guilt by inviting you over to talk. He'll offer you a settlement and try to get you to keep your mouth closed until after the election."

"Oh yeah, and if he offers to tear me off some cream then what am I supposed to do?"

Ruddman looked at the dumb thug like he had a titty for a nose and shit for brains. "You *take it,* lil nigga," he said. "If he offers you some money then you take that shit!"

"Hello Dy-Nasty," Selah spoke into the phone after reluctantly accepting the charges from the Dallas County Jail. The girl had been calling her forever, and after receiving a bunch of letters from the facility she had finally decided to take her call. "What do you want?"

"Mama Selah," Dy-Nasty blurted out to the woman that

she had worked like a dog to double-cross. "Did you get all my letters?"

Selah frowned. Those letters, if you could even call them that, had been a hot mess. Dy-Nasty wrote like a first-grader, and Selah had been appalled at the childish drawings of a family of stick figures with big round heads and sad faces. The one that was supposed to depict Dy-Nasty always had a turned-down mouth, no nose, and tears pouring out of her eyes, and the scribbled caption beneath it would read something crazy like, "Are you still made at me?" or "Will you be my fren? Check the bocks Yes our No."

Selah smirked. "Yes, I got them."

"Okay, then. Since you didn't write me back I'm not gonna run you no bullshit or beat around no bushes. I need to get outta here, Mama. I wanna come home."

Home?

A look of indignation crossed Selah's face.

"What in the world makes you think I would help you?" Heat rose in her as she remembered how she had tied her hair back and slicked her face down with Vaseline to get after the little ghetto troll. "In my opinion, Dy-Nasty, you're a criminal and you belong exactly where you are. Behind bars."

"Please, Mama Selah. Please listen! Didn't you read all them letters I sent you? I said I was sorry, dang! I know I was wrong for the way everything went down and I ain't tryna re-hash no beef with you. But these females is real gutter up in here and I need your help. For some reason these people think I'm Mink! Damn near everybody on this block is itching for a piece of her and it's gonna get real nasty for me unless I get ghost."

"I still don't see how that's my problem."

"I know it's not your problem, Mama Selah, but if you help me get outta here I promise I'll act right! I'll give you your ring back *and* help you get back at fat-boy Ruddman! I swear I will!"

Selah went silent on the other end for a few moments as she contemplated the offer at hand. As much as she wanted Dy-Nasty to rot inside the deepest reaches of a jail cell, Selah also saw the value in having the sly little monster working on her behalf on the outside. And not to mention she wanted her goddamn ring back! Hell, if she was ever going to get back with Viceroy and sleep in her own bed then she *needed* that ring back!

"Okay," she said finally. "I'll think about it, and maybe I'll pull some strings and see what I can do." Then she warned, "But I promise you one thing, Dy-Nasty. If I decide to help you and you cross me again, I will have your ass buried in a graveyard instead of in a jail cell, do you hear me?"

"Yea, yea, yea! I hear you, Mama Selah," Dy-Nasty said with a hint of an attitude. "I'm already in jail so you don't gotta be so nasty!" she sniffed, sounding like she was about to cry.

"I'll be more than nasty if you fuck with me again," Selah said coldly. "I'll be *deadly*. Now, try me if you think it's a game," she spit, then clicked off the phone and slammed it down hard on the table.

Standing in her wing on the other end of the line, Dy-Nasty giggled. She didn't even care that the boojie heffa had hung the phone up in her face. All she felt was relief at the thought that she was about to get a second chance to make some dastardly moves. But this time was gonna be different. She would be slicker and even more cunning. She would make better moves and deal from a slicker deck of cards. And this time she was gonna mark all of her trump cards and play them suckers *just right*.

CHAPTER 27

Viceroy was sitting at his desk in his huge office burying himself in his work. With his campaign winding down he was trying to keep his business in order by handling contracts, looking over emails, and going behind his accountants to make sure his money was right. Viceroy hadn't made it to the top of the mountain by trusting other people to do what needed to be done. True, he had schemed his way into power, but he was also willing to hustle and grind harder than the next man to keep himself at the top.

He was shuffling through some files when his door flew open and he looked up to see his son Barron barging into his office.

"Don't you know how to knock," Viceroy said as an acknowledgment. "Yeah, I'm pretty sure I taught your ass how to knock."

"Dominion Oil is being sued," Barron said as he slapped the paperwork down in the middle of his father's desk.

"By who?" Viceroy asked. Barron had his attention, but he wasn't overly concerned. "Which blood-sucking leech is coming after me this time?"

"Zeke Washington," Barron said as he shook his head. He

knew the potential danger there. "Earl Washington's son. He's claiming that you stole his father's empire and he's seeking restitution, damages, and an injunction against all Dominion Oil assets. And oh yeah"—Barron swept his hand over his face and rubbed the slight stubble of his beard—"if you remember, he also claims to have an original set of documents signed by you and his father that he says will prove his father was cheated out of a fortune."

Viceroy never even blinked.

"I'm not worried about none of that," Viceroy said. "So what, he filed a suit and has a couple of fake documents that won't prove a damn thing? This isn't the first time that old lie has been told. I'm much more concerned about what rock he crawled from under. What made him bring all this up now?"

"Honestly." Barron shrugged. He hated to give his uncle Digger any props, but there was no other way to tell it. "I'm thinking Ruddman put him up to this. I didn't tell you about it right away because I wanted to check it out first, but Uncle Digger claims he got the documents and the info from a source inside Ruddman Energy. And I believe him, too. This feels just like a slimy move orchestrated by that cat. Especially when you look at the timing with Wally Su and all. Yes, if I had to bet on it I would bet it was Ruddman."

"Uh-huh," Viceroy said as he spun around in his chair and thought about that dirty son of a bitch. He wanted to get at that bastard so bad it made his skin itch. Ruddman had some grimy tricks up his sleeve and Viceroy knew it was time to get in his ass and get his hands dirty.

"Contact young Zeke. Bring him here and let me talk to him. Maybe I can make Ruddman's little lawsuit plan backfire on his ass. Maybe I can make him an offer he can't refuse."

A couple of hours later Barron pulled up in a stretch limo with Zeke Washington, just like his father had asked him to do. Zeke walked into the office with a scowl on his face, obvi-

ously wary about being snatched up and brought to the company he was suing in court.

"How are you doing, Zeke?" Viceroy greeted him in a
booming voice. "I haven't seen you in a long time, son. Please
have a seat and make yourself comfortable."

"Nah, I'm cool," Zeke said as he stood in the corner and
folded his arms. "So what the hell do you want with me? My
lawyer is gonna serve you the papers, so all me and you need to
do is square off in court."

Viceroy shook his head as he leaned back in his big dog
chair and lit a Cuban cigar.

"Okay, cool. Let's cut to the chase then, shall we? As you
can probably see, I don't want or need shit from you, Zeke. I've
already got it all. And you don't have shit."

Viceroy looked right into the boy's empty skull and watched
the wheels turning in his head. This fool was just as dumb as his
daddy. In his young mind he'd thought he had the upper-hand
by listening to Ruddman and filing some funky-ass lawsuit.
Did this lil nigga think he was gonna catch him sitting up at
his desk holding his dick and shaking in his drawers?

"Listen Zeke, let me tell you something," Viceroy said in
all seriousness. "I didn't get in this position by bending over
every time somebody wanted to fuck me, okay? What do you
really think you're gonna accomplish with this lawsuit? I have
a whole building full of lawyers who will eat this lil shit up. In
fact, I can have this petty shit tied up in court for the next
thirty years."

Zeke was looking mad as fuck because he wasn't feeling
the way Viceroy was talking at him and Ruddman damn sure
hadn't prepared him for this part.

"From the looks of you I'd say you know the streets pretty
well," Viceroy continued his verbal thrashing. "How about I
just keep it hood for you, then? You see, it's like this young'un,"
Viceroy broke it down. "I'm from the same streets you're from,

and I've had this shit mapped out way before you were born. It don't take much for a muthafucka to come up missing in Dallas, even though I'm not trying to go that route. Listen, I have a son your age and I'm willing to help you out the same way I just helped him. In fact, I offered your father the same position right before he died." Viceroy leaned forward and put his elbows on his desk. "I run a tight ship around here, but I'm willing to bring you on my staff without asking for a drug test or even an application. How's that?"

Zeke was absorbing everything Viceroy said and he could tell he wasn't bullshitting. He wasn't stupid and he knew how to play the game. Who had thirty fuckin' years to spend in court when he could be a hotshot executive at a billion-dollar company tomorrow? Fuck Ruddman. That nigga wasn't offering up no cheese. It was time to make big boy choices and he didn't wanna fuck around and wind up on the losing end of the game.

"So what position are you talking about?" Zeke asked. "And how soon can we make this happen?"

Viceroy smiled, happy the kid was smart enough to see things his way.

"Don't even worry about it, I got you," Viceroy said. "Just report to my Human Resources department on your way out. It's located on the third floor. Tell them your name and my people will take good care of you, and that's a promise."

"Hey Connie." Viceroy pressed an interoffice button the moment Barron had escorted Zeke out of his office. "I've got a new hire for you. Set Zeke Washington up in our system and have him put on the payroll immediately."

"No problem, sir," Viceroy's chief of human resources responded. "What position will he be placed in?"

Viceroy smiled, looking just like a shark.

"The mail room, Connie. Put him in the muthafuckin' mail room!"

★ ★ ★

I had always been the type of chick who walked through life with my eyes wide open. Couldn't nothing ever sneak up on me because I stayed plugged into every scene and I knew where I stood at every turn.

I had never once been true to a man in my whole damn life before, and that's why when I busted Suge and his so-called Asian "friend" at the BBQ it hit me in the gut and I started doubting myself just a little bit. Okay, hell. For the first time in my life I went into surrender mode. Yeah, with my banging body and LaRue good looks, I knew I had it going on in that come-bang-me hood-chick kinda way. Men swarmed at my feet and begged for just a whiff of what I was hiding in that triangle between my thighs, and I had been slamming my sex appeal down on dudes from the time I was twelve years old.

But this was different. Every chick that had ever tried her hand at competing with me had failed. I could slay a bitch and steal her man by just batting my eyes and shifting my hips, but when it came to this new chick on Suge's arm I couldn't help but feel like I was outta my league, out-classed, and out-matched.

"Heffa what you talking about?" Bunni demanded the next morning when I 'fessed up that I had no wins over the beautiful Asian chick who had my boo's nose wide open. "You way cuter than that girl, Mink! You got more titties and you definitely got way more ass!"

I shook my head. Bunni just didn't understand. Everything wasn't about a golden fuck-pole contest. This match-up wasn't about who had the slickest tongue or the bangingest body. I took the prize in that department, no doubt about it. But this shit went way deeper than that. For the first time in my life I felt inadequate because that Lil Bit chick musta been something that I could never be.

I had Googled Miyoko Su and found out that she had

graduated from one of the best law schools in the whole damn country. If that didn't shut me up and sit me down, then nothing would.

"So? Just 'cause she's one of them hot-shot lawyers it don't make her no better than you!" Bunni spit. "You're smart too, Mink! You's one of the best con-mamis in the game, girl!"

"I'm smart, Bunni, but she's *intelligent*. She went to college."

"So what? We know plenty of people who went to college! Some of them are still out there dancing and grinding and making it rain on a stage!"

"But she even graduated too!"

"So *what?*" my BFF bucked. "That don't mean shit! She might be university trained, but can a bitch pick a pocket? Can she bust a slick move? Can she polish up a pole? Is her twerk game on target? Can she gank a mofo for his racks and get away with all her teeth still in her mouth?"

"I don't know if she can do all that," I admitted. "But I do know one thing she did damn well."

"What's that?"

"She took my fuckin' man!"

I felt so hopeless. Life was meaningless and nothing seemed to be poppin' for me anymore. After putting every ounce of conniving energy I had in me into getting my hands on that Dominion loot, I had it. I *had* that shit!

And I didn't know what in the hell to do with it.

Oh, for true, for true, me and Bunni had shopped like two crackheads in a freebasing contest. We'd bought every pair of shoes that we could cram our corns in, snatched up expensive jewelry out the yang, ordered the entire premium line of Glama Glo wigs in every color under the rainbow, and dropped mega dollars for more designer-label clothes than would probably ever touch our backs. I mean, we had *turnt up*, baby. Harlem-style! Our hair stayed did, our nails stayed slick, we got facials and massages every other day, and we ate shrimp, crab, and lobster till we were shitting out seaweed.

Trust and believe, we had washed those Dominion dollars down the drain like they were city water, and just when I was exhausted and we thought our greedy asses were gonna overdose on finery and gloss, I had checked my bank account and that baby was still overflowing!

But right now reality was slapping me right upside my forehead. Me and Bunni were both forced to look in the mirror and face the cold hard facts of the matter, and what we saw staring back at us wasn't hardly cute at all.

We saw me and Bunni!

Two scheming-ass hood chicks who had pulled every racket in the book, gotten hold of more loot than we could ever spend, bought every piece of jewelry, every designer purse, drank more alky, and hit more get-high than a little bit, yet didn't have a damn thing else going on in our empty little lives.

I had smoked loud and got lifted up to the stars every night, and then woke up at noon and put on a brand new wig and got flyer than a mutha. I had pranced outta my suite looking lacy and tasty and spritzed my body in a thousand-dollar-an-ounce stormcloud of good smells, and for what? To groove in what action? To walk around this big old mansion being envied and adored by who? *No damn body!*

The truth was, being rich wasn't cracking up to be what I thought it would be. Without Suge to fuck with I was bored outta my mind. I missed my old life. The life where I woke up to a new misadventure, a new hustle, and brand-new grind every single day. What good was sipping top-shelf liquor and toking the best piff in the country if there wasn't no horny niggas to slick-talk with afterward? Hell, the mansion was way back in the woods with nothing and nobody around, when I was used to project living where I could always get fly and step out my door then switch my ass up on the avenue where the slangas, hustlers, and thugstas were sure to have some drama poppin'.

I had hung out and got high with Dane and stuffed my face with Bunni and Peaches a lot, but I was used to living in the eye of the storm 'ere single day, and no amount of steak and lobster could take the place of the excitement and the happenings on 125th Street. My mood was swinging real low behind that shit and my lip was starting to poke out. I wanted me a hero from the deli up on Eighth Avenue. I was having fantasies about a piping hot slice from the pizzeria up the block from my old crib. I craved some dirty Chinese food and a monster-sized chicken wing from Wing Luck Su.

Believe it or not, I missed my ghetto Granny, and I even missed Aunt Bibby's bald-headed behind too. So with all that on my heart I made up my mind. Mizz Mink was going home! The first chance I got I was taking my ass right back to New York!

CHAPTER 28

Selah had deliberately dressed down and dabbed just a tiny bit of makeup on her face. The last thing she wanted to do today was flaunt her wealth, and standing in her mirror dressed in a regular old pair of blue jeans and a plain white t-shirt, she still looked cute, but she was definitely understated.

She had the doorman bring Fallon's old Toyota around to the front of the house. It had been a present for her fifteenth birthday and Viceroy had bought it specifically for her to use as she learned how to drive. By the time she was old enough to get her license, the Toyota had more dents and dings than a little bit, and Viceroy had surprised his baby girl with a brand new Porsche to celebrate her new driving privileges.

Selah had a flashback to her old Brooklyn days when her father drove a whooptie and struggled to keep the lights on and his children fed. It had been a special treat to get a ride in his old raggedy car because most kids in New York caught the train or the bus everywhere they went.

She drove down the highway handling the Toyota carefully. After years of having her ass touch the seats of only premium cars like Bentleys, BMWs, Maseratis, Porsches, and every now and then a Lexus or a Mercedes, the little Toyota felt hard as a rock. It was way too close to the ground for her comfort, and the windows rattled in their frames every time she hit a bump.

Thoughts of the old times flowed through Selah's mind as she drove. Her and Viceroy went way, way back with Wally Su, and he had once been considered one of their closest allies. He and Viceroy had been bright-eyed and ambitious young men together, eager to claim a stake in the upper crust of the world. They had made a solemn pact and one hand had loyally washed the other, and today Selah was going to sit beside Wally's deathbed and remind him about that shit.

According to Suge, Wally had been moved to a hospice to live out his final days, and Selah was prepared to beg for his mercy and cooperation on behalf of her family. Although Viceroy had been the brains behind a lot of their business dealings, he would've never become as powerful and successful without Wally's help. But Wally would have never become as rich without Viceroy's burning drive and determination either. She had called ahead to the hospice and was told that only those on a pre-approved visitors list were allowed to have access to the patients, but Selah was led in her spirit to show up in person and try to see him anyway.

The hospice was situated on a quiet stretch of greenery that looked colorful and serene on the outside. A spray of bright flowers lined both sides of the walkway, innocent reminders of new life in a place where the primary business was death.

It was a warm day outside, but the stifling heat that hit her when she stepped into the building was at least ten degrees hotter.

"Finally!" A young white man sitting behind the front counter looked up at her with frustration in his eyes. The sleeves on his white dress shirt were rolled up to the elbows, and the sweated-through fabric clung to his pale skin.

"Er, hello," Selah said hesitantly. "I'm here to—"

"Where are the other two?" he demanded, pushing a damp

shock of black hair off his sweating forehead. "I asked them to send three."

Selah shook her head. "Well, I er—"

"Never mind," he snapped. "It doesn't matter. One, three, five . . . the way the stomach bug has run through my staff it's going to take at least ten temps to get us through the madness today. Over there—" He pointed toward a doorway on the right. "You can put your things in a locker and grab yourself a pair of scrubs. Most of our patients are pretty stable for the moment but we've got at least three who could check out at any time."

Beads of sweat had formed on Selah's top lip and she swept her hair back and shook her head. "But I—"

"I know, I know," the young man said impatiently. "It's hot as hell in here. The central air pump went out late last night and I've been trying to get someone in here to fix it all morn—"

The jarring ring of the telephone interrupted him.

"Good," he said, snatching it off the hook. "This is the repairman now." He covered the mouthpiece with his hand and glared at her. "Move it!" he snapped, angling his head toward the locker room. "Get in there and get changed, and when you're done check on our three sickest patients first before they die on us—Baker, Duncan, and the other one I think his name is um—" He glanced at a clipboard that hung from a hook near the desk. "Su. Wally Su."

Dressed in a pair of loose-fitting nurse's scrubs with tiny Minnie Mouse emblems on the shirt, Selah stood over Wally Su's bed and stared down into the face of her former friend.

"Wally," she whispered softly as the gaunt face with the gaping mouth and fluttering eyes stared up at her.

He had never been what you would call handsome, but right now he looked a mess. Selah could see why he'd been so eager to get on Skype and confess to the commission. Wally was almost dead. His flesh had been ravaged by disease and there was a horrible rotting smell oozing out of his open mouth, as though his insides were already racked with decay. And with his body already as good as in the grave, Wally was trying to save his soul.

"Wally!" she said a little bit louder. His eyelids fluttered weakly and he struggled to close his mouth, only to have it fall open again.

Selah studied him. A large sign was taped to the wall above his headboard that had the letters *DNR* in bold magic marker. He was connected to several machines, and one of them emitted a beep every few seconds. Nearly every hole on his body had something running either into or out of it.

Selah raked her hair back with her fingers. She had to talk some sense into Wally. To convince him to honor the pact he'd made with Viceroy all those years ago. It would have been so easy to put her hand over his mouth and pinch his damn nose closed, Selah thought. But did she have it in her to do it?

Selah knew she could do whatever it took to protect her husband and her children, because even if Wally died before he could confess, there was still the matter of those documents he was holding that, no matter what, must *never* see the light of day.

"Wally," she called out again, leaning closer to him. "It's your old friend, Selah," she said. "Selah Dominion. Can you hear me, Wally? Please, open your eyes. Open your eyes if you can hear me, Wally."

She watched as his eyelids fluttered again and then opened wide. For a brief moment they stared at each other and recognition and remembrance flowed freely between them.

And then the look in Wally's eyes changed. Recognition became concern, and concern turned first into fright and then into terror.

"No, no, no . . ." Selah put her hand on his chest and tried to reassure him. "You're safe, Wally. I just came to talk to you. To find out where in the world you put those papers and to ask you to give them to me and spare my family and yours too, any further trouble and embarrassment."

Wally started tossing his head from side to side and Selah was shocked by what had crept into his eyes. Yes, it was fear! Even with one foot already in the grave and his fist raised to knock on death's door, Wally wanted to live! He was afraid of her. Afraid she would shorten his time on earth by a few measly hours, at the most a couple of days.

"Where are those papers?" Selah demanded. His lips moved frantically and she had to practically press her ear to his mouth to make out what he was trying to say.

"Where are they, Wally? I can't understand you. Tell me. Where are they?" she cried.

She lowered her ear down to his moving lips again and then she heard him.

"Help!" he whispered weakly. "Help!"

"Shut up!" Selah snapped. "You weren't crying for help when you were taking our goddamn money and living high on the hog! All those years we thought you were our friend, and now when you have nothing left to lose except your old soft, moldy bones you turn around and betray us! Where's that goddamn paperwork? Where is it?"

"Look un-un-un . . ." he struggled to whisper, "under my . . . nuts!"

Selah hauled off and slapped him. Slapped the holy shit outta him!

"You old *bastard*! I was there for you when your daughter was born! I held your hand while your wife took her last breath! You're a hypocrite, Wally!" She slapped the shit outta him again. "A goddamn hypo—"

Wally's head jerked back and Selah heard his breath catch in his throat.

"Wally?" she said, her eyes searching his face. "Are you okay? Oh my God. I'm so sorry for hitting you. I didn't mean to hurt you, I just lost my temper and—Wally?"

Selah jumped back as Wally's eyes rolled to the back of his head and a trickle of white foam ran from his mouth.

"Wally!" she shrieked as his eyeballs fell back into place and the machine beside his bed began emitting a series of blaring beeps.

Two nurses rushed into the room and began examining him and checking his vital signs. Trembling, Selah stepped away and began anxiously running her hands up and down her arms, suddenly chilled in the midst of the suffocating heat.

"He's gone," one of the nurses finally said. She was an older, heavyset white woman with turned-over shoes and massive sweat stains under her armpits. She glanced down at her watch. "I'm pronouncing him. I'll notify his family and you two get him prepped for the freezer before he melts right into that bed."

Selah stood there in shock as the other nurse, a pretty young Latina who couldn't have been more than twenty-five, motioned for her to come closer and help.

"Yank some of these tubes out, mami, why don'tcha," she said, chewing on a big wad of gum.

"But I-I-I'm not a—"

"You're not an LPN? What, you're an RN?" She glanced up at Selah giving her a dirty look. "Well, none of that crap matters around here," she said, yanking back the sheet and stripping the adult diaper from Wally's still body. She lifted his shriveled penis between two fingers and pulled out his catheter, then tossed the sheet back over him. "We've got so many dropping like flies around here that everybody pitches in to tag 'em and bag 'em. Come on, mamacita. Take his IV out while I call somebody to bring the meat wagon. Hurry up, too. This old boy is about to get nice and stiff."

CHAPTER 29

When Bunni got a wild hair up her ass there was no pulling that shit out. She had finally accepted the fact that GiGi had played her for a sucker, and now she had it set in her mind that she was gonna get her some backsies.

"That bitch is a red hot liar," she told me as she sat cross-legged at the foot of my bed staring at her laptop. A yellow notepad sat beside her and a stubby pencil was stuck behind her ear.

"Which bitch is a liar?" I looked up as a thousand names flew through my mind in a flash. Me, her, Peaches, Selah, Jude . . . "Which bitch you talking about, B?"

"GiGi!" she spit. "She's a damn liar. I don't believe shit she said. Matter fact, I don't think that heffah even works on TV!"

"Why you say that? I mean I don't think we was ever in the runnings for no damn show, but damn. Why would she come up in here from the jump if she's not on a job?"

"Oh, she's on a job," Bunni smirked. "The same type'a job we was on when we first came down here."

I bucked my eyes. "A flimflam? That bitch is tryna catch us in a flimflam?"

"Hell yeah." Bunni nodded. "Check this out." She crawled

up to the head of my bed with her laptop and thrust the screen under my nose.

"Look at this shit!"

My eyes ran down the page as I saw mug shot after mug shot and read charge after criminal charge. "What the hell!"

"Yeah, I been investigating that ass! Mizz GiGi is in the game, Mink. That heffa is runnin' a racket!"

I couldn't believe all the shit I was seeing, but it was her for sure. Mami had aliases out the ass and at least a trillion different mug shots, and they were all different too. In some pictures she was a blonde, in others she was sporting the brunette look. Sometimes her hair was short and sometimes it was real long, she had gone for the jet-black goth style in a few, and in a couple she even had a stud-chick buzz cut that didn't look cute on her *at all*.

"Girl, where'd you find this website?" I said, impressed like a mutha. "Put my name in the box and see what comes up."

Bunni smirked and waved me off. "I already did. You in there, girl. All up in that shit. Me and P, too. But look at all these charges they got on GiGi!"

"Yep," I said, still reading. "And GiGi ain't even her real name."

"Nope," Bunni said. "That shit is Georgia! Georgia Mullins."

"Damn!" I cursed and then whistled as my finger swept down the screen. "That heffa been knocked for all types of shit," I said and read out loud. "Shoplifting, embezzlement, forgery, extortion—"

"Pickpocketing!" Bunni cut in as she scrolled to a new page. "Prostitution, burglary, blackmail—"

"Identity theft! Insurance fraud! Larceny! Wire fraud!"

I shook my head. "This chick is a professional," I said with mad admiration. "She got all kinds of levels to her game and she still managed to stay outta the joint most of the time."

"Yeah, and it looks like she mighta took shit to the ultimate level too," Bunni said with a chill in her voice.

"What's that?" I asked.

"Murder!" she said, stabbing her finger at the screen.

"Stop playing!" I snapped. "We been in the life for years jacking mad niggas too, but that don't make us no murderers!"

"I'm serious," Bunni insisted. "It says right here that three men she was known to date came up missing. The last person them rich cats were seen with was her, and now all three of them are gone!"

I looked at Bunni and she looked at me. Her eyes got all big and mine did too.

"*Ooooh,*" Bunni made the *somebody's in trouble* sound. "Is you thinking what I'm thinking?" my day one girl asked me.

I nodded like a mutha and then both of us bust outta our mouths with the same damn word at the same damn time.

"*Barron!*"

CHAPTER 30

Selah's hands shook like crazy as she put on a pair of rubber gloves and peeled the tape away from Wally's cooling skin. She squeezed her eyes closed and yanked the IV needle from his arm, then wiped her hands on her pants and turned toward the Hispanic nurse.

"Uh-uh," the young thang said. "Don't be looking at me. You're the RN so you should know how this goes." She waved Selah on. "Let's go now. Get him naked and let's do the last offices and then we can wrap him on up."

By the time they were finished preparing Su's body for the morgue Selah's nerves were completely wrecked. She was dripping sweat from head to toe and she needed a drink like nobody's business. At every stage of the process she had opened her mouth multiple times to confess to the young girl that she wasn't a goddamn nurse, but the thought of getting arrested at Wally's deathbed, and how that would *really* fuck Viceroy's campaign completely up, just kept making her shut her mouth again and again.

She stood by quietly as an elderly black man came into the room pushing a metal trolley, and him and the Hispanic nurse loaded Wally's washed and wrapped body on it and strapped him down.

"That's that," the nurse said as the gray-haired man pushed the trolley out of the room and she followed him toward the door. She looked over her shoulder at Selah and said, "We've got another one who's about to go in room one oh five. Hurry up and strip those sheets off the bed and spray it down with Lysol, and make sure you flip the mattress over and clean the other side too. You got it?"

Selah nodded mutely as the young woman walked away shaking her head. "Dumb-ass temps," Selah heard her huff under her breath. "She don't act like nobody's RN to me!"

Moments after the young nurse walked out of the room Selah attempted to make her escape. She crept over to the door and stuck her head out, only to have the chick holler loudly from down the hall, "Hey! Get back in there! There's no way you scrubbed that bed that fast!"

Selah was too damn through. Biting her lip, she rushed back into the room and grabbed the cleanser from the bathroom and yanked the sheets off the bed. She squirted some lemon-scented disinfectant all over the plastic-covered mattress and wiped it down and dried it with a bunch of disposable chux pads.

Grabbing the edge to flip it over, Selah braced her feet and heaved until she held it high in the air, and when she looked down underneath it she damn near screamed at what she saw.

DOMINION OIL, INC.

Well I'll be motherfucking damned!

It was a brown envelope. A big one. The words *Dominion Oil, Inc.* were printed on the outside in bold capital letters.

Selah snatched it with one hand and let the mattress fall back on the frame with the other. She ran into the bathroom and fought her way out of her rubber gloves, then with sweat-dampened hands she tore at the seal on the envelope and pulled out the white sheets of paper that were inside.

Her eyes roamed over the documents and a big smile of relief and satisfaction broke out on her face. She had it! She had the original document that Viceroy had signed over thirty years ago! All these weeks they had been searching high and low and ol' Wally had been sitting on this shit the whole time!

Despite the specter of death that permeated the room Selah was floating on cloud nine. She couldn't wait to show Viceroy. She couldn't wait for him to see that she had pulled some weight and done her part to help the family out. If this didn't convince him that she was down for him and steady in his corner then nothing would. She could see it now: Viceroy would win the election and get the chairmanship position, and as a reward for all her hard work he'd take her on a vacation to Acapulco or maybe to Belize . . . They'd swim in the ocean every morning and sip Petrus Pomeral at three grand a pop under the bright moonlight every night, and then they'd shower together and slide into a nice plush bed and she'd slurp his big black dick in her mouth and lick all up under his balls and . . .

A banging sound rattled the bathroom door and yanked her straight out of her fantasy.

"I'm using it!" she snapped and flushed the toilet with the toe of her shoe. She didn't give a damn what Lil Mama was yakking about out there! The only thing on her mind was getting back to that locker room and getting her clothes and her purse, then climbing in Fallon's raggedy putt-putt and hauling ass over to Dominion Oil so she could slap some very precious paperwork down on Viceroy's desk!

CHAPTER 31

Gigi was decked out in designer traveling clothes as she stood in her stripped-down apartment with the last of her personal items strewn over the bed. It was giddy-up time again, and she was ready to climb on her big black stallion and ride off into the sunset. The state of Texas was no longer wide enough to hold her and all the rip-offs she had perpetrated within its lovely borders, and instinct told her that it was time to make a quick move. Larry Dawkins was furious with her and was threatening to wring her neck, but like all the other men she had swindled over the years, he'd have to catch her first, and even then he'd have to take a number and stand in line.

She glanced around the ritzy furnished condo that she'd lived in scot-free, courtesy of Stewie Baker's dime. Three designer suitcases stood open nearby; one was empty while the other two were packed nice and full. She'd accumulated way more than she could carry this time, and her hands moved quickly and methodically as she sorted through the mounds of expensive gifts, trinkets, and jewels, deciding in a flash what to take and what to toss. As usual her decisions were based on leverage and liquidity. Anything that could be bartered, traded, or ditched off and sold for a quick dollar made the cut, and everything else got left behind.

She felt a brief twinge of something and she realized it was satisfaction. She had racked up royally during her stay in Dallas, and she had to admit she'd had a blast stepping on backs, tripping folks down steps, taking candy from babies, and swindling old ladies for their church shoes during this super-lucrative misadventure. But of all the wicked tools of the trade she had employed, it was her uncanny ability to spot a willing victim that had really paid off for her this time.

GiGi glanced out the window. She'd kept her car running and it wouldn't be long now. She'd snuck out of countless cities and towns under the dark of night before, but this time instead of traveling light she was taking a hostage with her. An ace-in-the-hole, a captive audience, and best of all . . . a human ATM. Yes, for the first time ever Georgia Mullins aka GiGi Molinex, was running from something and to something at the same time. Because this time instead of riding solo, when she hit the highway and watched the city of Dallas fade in her rearview mirror, her latest victim, her delicious chocolate sugar daddy, would be riding shotgun right beside her.

CHAPTER 32

It was election night and everybody was off somewhere doing some last minute shit before heading to the hotel to watch the results come in with Daddy Viceroy. Me and Bunni had been steady blowing up Barron's phone tryna contact him so we could give him the heads up about GiGi's mining ass. That chick was a grifter to her heart, and both of us had a feeling she was scheming to get at Barron's throat, so we had been calling him and leaving messages left and right.

While we waited for Bump to call us back I told Bunni I was going to my room to pick out something tight to wear, but instead I snuck into my walk-in closet and started tossing a few things in a travel bag on the sly.

I didn't have much of a plan in my lil down and out head, but I didn't need one neither. I had plenty of dough and I could park my ass at one of the ritziest hotels in New York for as long as I needed to until I figured out my next step. The streets of Harlem were where I was from, and my hometown was gonna be a real welcome sight. I was actually looking forward to seeing my scandalous Granny and the rest of them old lying-ass LaRues, but other than that, whatever I did next was gonna have to come off the cuff because Mizz Mink was all out of slick moves.

I thought about Bunni and I felt kinda bad. I hated just sneaking out and leaving like this but I didn't have it in me to do no whole lotta explaining. I knew her and Peaches would try real hard to talk me out of going back to New York since they knew Punchie and Gutta were still out there gunning for me and the streets were still hot, but fuck it. After messing up the good thing I had with Suge I just didn't wanna be around here no more and maybe I deserved whatever I had coming.

Every time I closed my eyes I could hear the cold disappointment in Suge's voice when he told me I was too damn childish and insecure to be his woman. That shit had hurt me real bad when he said it, but once I came down off my high horse and wasn't mad no more, it hurt me even more.

I waited until I heard Bunni singing her ass off in the shower and then I called downstairs and asked Albert to have one of the drivers bring me a car around. I scribbled a lil note for Bunni and Peaches telling them I was going home and not to worry about me, then I slipped it under Bunni's door and crept downstairs. It had been hot as hell earlier in the day but it was raining cats and dogs when I got outside, and I jumped my booty in the backseat of the limo and told the young driver named Pedro to put my bag on the floor beside me.

"Hey, P, do you know where Uncle Suge lives?" I asked him when he climbed back in the front. He was dressed in his little black monkey suit with the starched white shirt and all that. He nodded yes. "Cool, I need a ride to his house real quick and then you can take me to the airport. 'Kay?"

I sat back and closed my eyes while Pedro whipped through the gate and hit the highway. Listening to the sound of the rain beating a drum on the limo's roof kept me from thinking about how I was gonna act and what I was gonna say once I got to Suge's crib.

Even with the wet roads it didn't take us long to get there, but by the time we pulled up the clouds had gotten darker and heavier and the rain was making mud outta the hard Texas dirt.

Pedro rolled to a stop and I cracked my window open a little bit and stared at the front door. The dogs were in the kennel out back just a-barking their asses off, and I sat there looking stupid and staring at the door for a real long time as I tried to decide whether or not I was brave enough to get out and ring his bell.

But then the door creaked open and I saw him standing there. His muscled-up chocolate body was covered in a white designer bathrobe that used to feel like warm marshmallows against my skin when he draped it over my shoulders after drying me off in the shower. He stood in that doorway staring me down and I sat in the backseat of the whip eyeing him right back. I don't know if he blinked but I sure as hell didn't, and the look in his eyes was like nothing I had ever seen before.

For the longest time my ass just sat there feeling a mess. I was a con-mami. A hustler. A two-bit thief. I had wiggled these hips around the block more times than a lil bit, and if there was one thing I knew how to do it was play a nigga to the left.

But on the real, to the *right* was where I really wanted to be as I gazed at my big ol' gut buster, the gorgeous killer who had rocked my world, the only dude on the face of the earth who had ever gotten through to my tough, ghetto heart.

And as our eyes locked together across all that space and through all that falling rain, I watched him take a step backwards and slowly . . . close the door.

A big old sniff came outta me as I dropped my face into the palms of my hands. It was over. Our shit was a wrap. He was done with my ass. He had said his goodbyes with his eyes, and now there wasn't a damn thing left for my mouth to say.

"Ga'head," I told Pedro as mad tears fell from my eyes. I wiped them shits away furiously. Mizz Mink didn't cry over *no* nigga! "Ga'head, Pedro," I repeated. "Fuck this shit! Let's bounce!"

"You sure?" Pedro looked over his shoulder. He had mad pity in his eyes as he dug into his pocket and pulled out a clean hankie and passed it back to me.

"Yeah," I told him and nodded. "I'm sure."

Pedro stepped lightly on the gas and the whip was slowly creeping off as I turned to catch one last peep of what I was leaving behind and that's when I saw it.

"Stop!" I shouted and Pedro hit the brakes on that baby real quick. "Wait!" the word tore from my throat in a hoarse, desperate cry.

I watched as Suge's front door began to swing open again.

He was there again. In that swanky white robe looking big and buff like the heavyweight champion of the world. But this time he was holding something in his hand, and as he stepped across the threshold and started coming down the steps I saw what it was.

The rain had started coming down even harder but Suge was one of them gully gangsters. He took his cool-ass time walking toward the whip, putting one foot steadily in front of the other and getting soaking wet with that blizzard of blowing water just'a bouncing off'a his huge frame.

And through it all, his dark eyes stayed locked on mine, and the closer he got the harder my heart banged in my chest. I was shaking by the time he opened my door and I grabbed at his big ol' hand as he reached inside and practically lifted me up outta my seat.

"Suge," I cried as he flipped open the big black umbrella he was carrying and held it over my head to protect me. He snatched me up in one arm and squeezed me up against his huge, rocked up chest.

"I'm ready to be a big girl now," I sniveled through an ocean of tears, but he shushed me and crushed his juicy lips against mine as his tongue tore into my mouth.

I melted completely into him as he tossed that damn umbrella to the side and both of us stood there getting soaked together, our bodies pressed up against each other as we kissed like crazy in all that warm, blowing rain.

Finally, Suge picked me up in his strong arms and started carrying me toward his front door. We were still tonguing each other down when Pedro hit the horn wit'a a lil *beep-beep,* tryna figure out if I still needed that ride to the airport. Airport? *Sheeit,* that flight was a wrap, honey! New York, who? I didn't give a damn about that grimy-ass city because home for me was wherever the hell Suge Dominion was!

I sighed as I snuggled deep into my boo's strong arms. I couldn't wait to get my booty up in his crib. Miss Mink was gonna show and prove that I was a grown-ass woman now, and that home for him could be wherever I was too.

AND THEN . . .

For such a short election campaign it had been a real damn intense one, and everybody in the joint was happy it was about to be over. The precincts would be closing soon and the polls would shut down at that time, but due to statistics and demographics, the election winner would be projected before then.

Viceroy was feeling good and stepping lively as his entire campaign crew gathered in the presidential suite at the Ritz Hotel in Dallas. The buzz of excitement in the air was bigger than anything he had ever felt and staffers, volunteers, and campaign officials were skitting around like a bunch of nervous nellies as the clocked ticked down and the votes began getting tallied.

If there was one person in the midst of the firestorm who was walking around with flame-proof drawers on, it was Viceroy himself. Being the center of this type of attention was right up his alley and he knew how to stay cool and calm under pressure. He almost felt like President Obama on the night before he ordered that hit on Saddam Hussein. Cooler than shit. He walked around cracking jokes, shooting the shit, and putting everybody else at ease with his unruffled chill-under-fire charm.

The fact that he was even still good with the Governor and his name was still on the ballot was sweet as hell. After all that slick shit Ruddman had pulled to get him disqualified he was still standing tall and black. Of course, having that dime-dropping Wally Su clock out before he could testify in front of the commission had done a whole lot to help, and with Selah coming through with the only other copy of the stock option agreement between him and Earl Washington, it had taken all the teeth outta the bear trap that Ruddman had set for him.

In fact, everything he touched had turned to gold. Bob Easton's advice to shoot the undocumented workers ad spot and to reveal Peaches to the world had been a real ratings booster. The reality show hadn't been shot yet, but just the news that his family was gonna expose their throats like that had voters jumping on his tip.

All that left Viceroy feeling pretty fuckin' cock-strong as he strode through the enormous presidential suite dapping folks out and reveling in his own glow. He didn't know which way the election was gonna swing, but with all the odds evened out he felt he had more than a fighting chance to get the win in his column.

He walked into the main sitting area and looked around. The room was packed with people and all of them were there to support and encourage him. He saw Selah and Dane talking to Bob Easton and the four other members of the Gang of Five, and there were a bunch of college kids sitting cross-legged on the floor chatting into their cell phones as they made a few last-minute cold calls to voters who were still straddling the fence.

"It's a freaking dog race!" Fred Stein beamed happily, gesturing toward the large-screened television set where the names of the three candidates and their current standing in the race was displayed. "You're barely trailing Stewie Baker, but you're edging Rodney Ruddman out by a nose."

Viceroy felt a surge of competitive excitement flow through

his legs, like a punch-drunk boxer who was tied on the cards with less than minute to go in the last round.

He parked his ass in a plush chair in the midst of his supporters and glued his eyes to the television screen. The atmosphere was lively and energized and several beautiful waitresses were walking around the suite bearing trays filled with drinks and snacks. He had just tossed back a double-shot of Courvoisier when Selah came over and sat down beside him.

"Where's Barron?" she asked.

Viceroy shrugged and looked around. "I don't know. He should have been here a long time ago."

"Well, I hope he gets here before it's all over," she said, smelling delicious and looking beautifully put together in her navy blue dress and white pearls.

Viceroy grinned and reached out and hugged her tightly. "I've got a good feeling about it, baby. I think we just might pull it off." A waitress walked past and he signaled for another drink. "I know I owe a whole lot of this to you, Selah," he said truthfully. "Getting those papers from Wally Su was some real good shit. But you can tell me, baby," he said, leaning in close to her. "Did you kill him, sugar? Did you choke his ass?"

Selah bust out laughing. It felt so good to be back in her man's good graces. Ever since she had busted up in his office and shoved those precious papers under his nose Viceroy had been acting more and more like his old self.

"You play too much," she told him, flirting with her eyes. Viceroy had been behaving better but she was still stuck out in that damn pool house and she was ready to be inside and in his bed. He had one more night to play games with her. One more night and she was gonna have to rip off his pants and take his ass to the mat.

"Nah." He leaned against her laughing. "I'm serious. Did you do that mothafucka, baby? Did you off his ass?"

The smile dropped straight from Selah's face. Her mug was

brick-wall serious and she stared right into her husband's eyes as she nodded her head and said, "Yep."

It was getting close to crunch time and the final projections were almost in. The race was so tight that the TV announcers covering the local events were reluctant to make any predictions and everyone agreed this thing could go either way.

Viceroy was getting worried. Suge had texted and said him and Mink were both running late, but Barron still hadn't been heard from and was nowhere to be found.

"Where the hell is my boy?" Viceroy stood up and demanded loudly. Heads got to shaking and Selah caught his eye from across the room and shrugged her shoulders as if to say she was just as puzzled as he was.

Viceroy's earlier cool was just about all gone. The liquor was making him tight and the fact that Barron wasn't there for one of the most important events in his career was pissing him off. The boy had been walking around with a real fucked-up chip on his shoulder for weeks now, and as soon as this election was over and things settled down Viceroy was gonna have to get with his ass and tighten him up.

Suddenly folks jumped up and started clapping and screaming with glee. "You just passed Stewart Baker!" one of his staffers shouted. "You're in first place with over fifty percent of the precincts reporting!"

"Yeah!" Viceroy hollered in victory. His heart thudded in his chest as he glanced up at the screen. This shit was between him and Rodney Ruddman now, and Rodney was behind. Poetic fuckin' justice. No matter how cool he tried to act, he *wanted* this shit. He wanted it badder than bad. The joint was really jumping now. There were about fifty people crowded around the television set with their eyes wide and their mouths running a million miles a minute. His posse was chanting now. Loud as hell. Counting down the percentages of precincts that had reported their results, knowing that soon the margin of victory would be impossible to beat.

"Fifty-eight! Fifty-nine! Sixty! Sixty-one! Sixty-two . . ."

Viceroy was just about to open his mouth to join them when his phone vibrated on his waist and he snatched it off his clip.

"Yeah?" he spoke loudly over the roar of his staff.

"What was that?" He stuck his finger in his ear. "Speak up, I can't hear you. Huh? What did you say? Hold on a quick second . . ."

With the eyes of his entire team glued to the television screen and their chants rising in the air, Viceroy slipped out of the room and strode over to the small kitchen in the main foyer of the suite and then stepped inside.

"Stay with Channel Two for more election night coverage! It was looking like a one-man race there for a minute, but suddenly Stewart Baker and Rodney Ruddman both have had a sudden surge in votes. And now, with ninety-seven percent of the precincts reporting, local stations are calling the race for chairman of the railroad commission . . . a three-way tie!"

A deafening roar went up in the presidential suite as Team Dominion reacted to the news. Some were disappointed that Viceroy hadn't gotten the outright win, but others were excited at the chance to keep this thing going with a run-off election.

"Viceroy! Viceroy! Viceroy!" Everybody was jumping up and down and chanting, and then a male voice rose over the noise.

"Mr. Dominion? Where's Mr. Dominion?"

People started looking around and a low buzz of have you seen hims filled the air.

"Has anyone seen Mr. Dominion?"

"Check the bedroom."

"Maybe he went to the bathroom."

"Well, he's gotta be around here somewhere," a young college student offered, and that's when they heard it.

"Eeeeeeeeeeek!" a high-pitched shriek rang out in the main foyer and the sound of a dropped tray and shattering wineglasses rose in the air. "Oh my *Goddddd*! He's been shot! My God, Mr. Dominion has been *shot!*"

To Be Continued. . . .

RED HOT LIAR

Noire

About This Guide

The discussion questions that follow are included to
enhance your group's reading of the book.

Discussion Questions

1. Viceroy has put Selah out in the poolhouse. Was his affair with her sister worse than Selah's affair with Rodney Ruddman?

2. GiGi Molinex has been hired to throw shit up in Viceroy's election game. Will she twist Barron up against his family? Will Lil Bump become her next victim?

3. Bunni was so hyped on her reality show drama that she failed to see the flimflam when it was being laid down on her. Now that she's peeped GiGi Molinex's game, how is she going to pay the red hot liar back and get her hood revenge?

4. Miyoko Su has Suge by the balls. Does his loyalty to Mink outweigh his loyalty to the family? Should he have risked his sex thang with Mink to ensure the preservation of the Dominion dynasty?

5. Rodney Ruddman is a crafty old bastard. Will his scheme against Viceroy end up backfiring against him in the long run? Has he underestimated his longtime arch-enemy?

6. Suge promised Mink that no other woman could take the love he had for her. Her jealousy over his ex-flame could have meant disaster for the family fortune. Is she woman enough for a man like Big Suge?

7. Pilar thinks she's hit the jackpot with her new friend Gutta. Did the scheming country diva bite off more than she can chew?

8. Dy-Nasty called Selah from jail asking for help. In ex-change for being bailed out, she promises to return Selah's engagement ring, which will get Selah off the hook with Viceroy. Should Selah trust her? Does Dy-Nasty have another trick up her sleeve?

9. Mink is slowly changing. Her love for her dude Suge seems to be correcting some of her illicit tendencies. Did finding out the truth about her real mother and all the drama that went down between Jude and her father help her become more mature about her outlook on love?

10. GiGi Molinex just pulled the con game of a lifetime. Is she a better schemer than Mink and Bunni combined? Or will the two Harlem scrippers come out on top in the end?

11. Who shot Viceroy?

What can go wrong when con-mami Mink LaRue
joins forces with her slick-tongued look-alike Dy-Nasty
Jenkins to run a three-hundred-grand hustle on the
super-rich Dominion oil family?

Dirty Rotten Liar

Available wherever books and ebooks are sold

Turn the page for an excerpt from *Dirty Rotten Liar* . . .

CHAPTER 1

Watching your mama take her last breath was a hurtin'-ass thang.

Especially when you had a mannish hater flappin' her gums in your ear and talking trash right over her dead body!

It had all happened so fast. One minute I was chillin' down in Texas tryna pull off the flimflam of a lifetime with Uncle Suge, Bunni, and a skanky chickenhead from Philly named Dy-Nasty, and the next thing I knew, Bunni's brother Peaches was on the phone telling me my mama was about to die!

"The nursing home called and said your mama had a stroke," Peaches had said. "I'm sorry, sweetie, but they don't think she's gonna make it."

With those words swirling around in my head I busted straight up in the Dominion mansion and lied my ass off! I told them rich fools that my boss had just caught a stray bullet in a kick-door robbery, and then I hopped my ass on the first thing smoking back to New York City to see about my sick mama!

I made it up to the hospital just in time to catch the last few minutes of Jude Jackson's life, and I almost blacked out from grief as I stood beside her bed feeling helpless as hell as Mama pursed her twisted lips and reached out to me with her crooked hands like she was tryna tell me her deepest, darkest secret. "*Shhhlll . . . Shhhlll . . . Shhhlll . . .*" she had squinted up at me and gasped. "*Shhhlll . . . Shhhlll . . . Shhhlll . . .*"

I tried my best to make out what she was tryna say, but Mama died before she could spit it out. And now, as I stood next to her body shaking with grief, my bald-headed aunt Bibby clocked me with some wild shit that dropped me right down to my knees!

"There was two of y'all, you know. Somewhere out there in the world you got yourself a sister, Mink, 'cause you was a twin."

My head jerked up in surprise as I squatted down with my ass touching the floor.

"C-c-come again?"

"You heard me," Aunt Bibby snapped. "Ain't nobody stutter! Your mama shoulda been woman enough to tell you the truth straight from the jump!"

"You dirty bitch!" I spit real softly as tears ran from my eyes. Mama's spirit hadn't even left the room yet and this box-shaped bitch was already hatin'! "How the hell you sound talking bad about my mama?"

"How the hell I said it?"

My aunt put her hands on her stud hips and stared me down. She was grilling me with a killer look, but I could tell she wasn't really tryna cut me with no slick talk the way she was known for doing bitches out on the street.

"You're a twin, Mink. You can believe it baby, because it's true."

I wiped my eyes and then smirked at her real shitty-like. Uh-huh. I knew what time it was. Aunt Bibby used to fuck with duji real bad back in the day, and her ass musta been playing with the needle again.

"See there," I told her. "You need to stop shootin' that dog food in ya veins, cause with all that bullshit you talking you *must* be high."

"Ain't nobody getting high and ain't nobody bullshittin' neither, Mink! My brother Moe had *two* daughters, baby. And like I said, you got you a twin!"

I stared down at my mother's still body.

Me? A *twin*?

That shit was impossible!

But then . . .

Dy-Nasty!

That guttersnipe's name exploded in my brain and my heart skipped about five beats! I looked at Aunt Bibby again and all of a sudden the room got real hot and my head started buzzing. I couldn't hardly get no air in my lungs. I tried to say something but it felt like glass splinters were sticking me all in my throat.

All I could think was, *What if that Philly heffa was my god-damn sister?*

I could feel the possibility of it all down in my bones, but I damn sure didn't wanna believe it. *That trifling trick could actually be my fuckin' sister!*

"Uh-uh." I shook my head and slung snot everywhere. "You's a liar, Aunt Bibby!" I moaned as I keeled forward and hit my knees, ready to deny that shit with my last breath. "You ain't nothing but a big-ass bald-headed *liar!*"

"Mink!" Aunt Bibby barked in her jailhouse voice. "Why don't you stand up and face the truth for once in ya life! Everybody in this *room* is a goddamn liar! But the biggest liar of us all"—Aunt Bibby pointed down at the body in the bed— "was your *mama!* Jude Jackson wasn't nothin' but a *lying sack a' shit!*"

Her eyes flashed and Aunt Bibby crossed her muscled-up sailor-looking arms over her tatted-up titties and grilled me. "Now, there! I done said what the fuck I had to say, and I ain't taking none of it back neither!"

I stared at her mannish ass with my nostrils flaring like a racehorse. I wanted to *bite* that bitch! I wanted to shove my fist down her throat and make her choke on her lying-ass tongue!

But instead I stayed right there crouched down on my knees as my aunt continued to lay the cold, naked truth on me.

"Now, don't get me wrong," Aunt Bibby said quietly. "I loved me some Jude, but that heffa didn't have a truth-bone in her whole damn body! Why you think she drove her car into that goddamn river with you sitting right there in the front seat next to her, Mink? Huh? Why you *think*, stupid girl? Not even the lowest, raggediest, black-hearted *trash-ass* mama does no crazy shit like that!"

I grilled Aunt Bibby through a watery haze of tears. Oh for true, for true, I was 'bout to clock this big beefy bitch! Just wear her ass *out* for calling my dead mama outta her name! But before I could come up off my knees Aunt Bibby nailed me with another gut shot when she opened her big mouth and said, "And while ya bullshittin', Jude didn't even give birth to y'all right there in Harlem Hospital like she said, neither."

"What?" I squeaked. "How you know? How the hell you know something like that?"

" 'Cause Jude *told* me!" Aunt Bibby barked. And then she glanced over at my scandalous-ass, welfare-queen grandmother, who sat in the corner styling her stolen Gucci gear with her long pretty legs crossed all proper.

"Tell her, Mama. Tell Mink the goddamn truth!"

My grandmother wagged her leg and nodded. She twisted up her lips like she was still twenty-five and fine and said, "Bibby's tellin' it right, Mink. You got a twin sister, baby. You was about three years old when Jude first brought you around here. She told everybody she went down south and had twins and put one up for adoption. So I guess you do got yourself a sister out there somewhere in the world, baby. I just wish Jude woulda told you how to find her before she drove off in all that cold water and fucked herself up!"

★ ★ ★

Cold water. Cold water. Cold water.

I was freezing inside. All the way down to my trembling bones. All I wanted to do was go somewhere where I could get warm and block out the pain and the noise, but no matter how hard I igged her, my best friend Bunni Baines just wouldn't leave me the hell alone.

Instead of flossin' fly and fancy in a big mansion down in Dallas, Texas, me and Bunni were right back home in the gritty town of Harlem. I was laying on my little cot in her bedroom with my face turned toward the wall and my eyelids squeezed tight. I was sniffling into a boogered-up snot rag I had pressed up against my stuffy nose, and the top of my head was banging like a drum. My breath felt hot and stank as I breathed through my mouth, and my bottom lip trembled as I slobbered and cried into my pillow.

"C'mon now, Mink," Bunni begged me for the two millionth time. "You gots to get up outta this bed, boo! You gotta get your ass *up.*"

I shrugged her off, wishing she would just leave me the hell alone. Bunni was barking about how I needed to get my shit together and get back on my game, but I kept tryna tell her I didn't have no fight left in me. It was gone. All the grime, all the hustle, and every drop of my love for the con game. *Poof.* It was all gone.

"Madame Mink," Peaches jumped in with his deep, baritone voice. "Me and Bunni know what you going through right now, baby. But the funeral is gonna be starting in an hour, darling! Now, I'ma need you to get up out that bed and get yourself dressed, sugar, and ready to roll!"

I laid there and igged the hell outta Peaches too.

Shoot, I wasn't thinkin' about him, and I wasn't thinkin' about Bunni, and I damn sure wasn't thinkin' about going to Mama's funeral neither!

Bunni sighed real loud, then crawled underneath my blanket and snuggled up behind me like she used to do when we was kids. She wrapped her arms around me and spooned me, rocking me back and forth as she tried her best to convince me that I needed to stand up on my feet and face what was left of my shitty little life.

And it was definitely shitty too. Just when I thought I was at the top of my game and everything flowing through my hood was damn good, I'd been blasted with a major shot to the gut that took my feet out from under me and sat me right down on my plump apple ass.

"It's been a whole damn week, Mink," Bunni said from behind me, "and, girlfriend, you ain't put enough food in your stomach to feed a fly! Hmph. You ain't combed your hair or brushed your teef." She backed off of me a lil bit. "And you ain't took a damn bath neither!"

I still didn't say shit. I just laid there in igg mode.

"I don't know why you be listening to that old crazy-ass Bibby *anyway*." Peaches jumped back in with a whole lotta bass in his voice this time. "Jude was your *mama*. And no matter *what* the hell she did, or how she did it, she was still your *mama*!"

"Jude was a *liar*!" I screamed into my pillow. My whole chest ached from Mama's lies and her low-down betrayal. "She was a goddamn *liar*!"

"Ermmm herrrm," Peaches said agreeably, and even without looking at him I could tell his lips was twisted.

"Yeah, that's right. She was a liar. But so are *you*, Madame Mink! Lying is what schemers like us *do*! So get your ass up outta that bed so we can get down to that funeral home and make sure they send your lying-ass mama off right!"

Deep in my heart I knew I had to go pay my last respects to the woman who had given birth to me but I still didn't wanna move.

So I laid there on my shaky lil cot in Bunni's junky room and thought about the next moves I was gonna make in my life. I had always been the type of slick, carefree diva who flounced around flossin' like everything in my life was all Hennessy and weed, but for the first time in a real long time I was forced to take a real good look down the gutter road that I had traveled. I *made* myself remember all the shit I had tried to erase from my mind. All the shit that I had been running from for so many years. The kind of shit that had been way too painful for a thirteen-year-old girl to live with, so she had fought like hell to forget it.